# What Mother Never Told Me

# DONNA HILL

## What Mother Never Told Me

Recycling programs
for this product may
not exist in your area.

WHAT MOTHER NEVER TOLD ME

ISBN-13: 978-0-373-83143-2

www.kimanipress.com

**Printed in U.S.A.**

# Acknowledgments

I must begin by thanking my incredible editor Glenda Howard, whose confidence in me allowed me to bring this story to you. Thanks to so many of my fellow authors who are not only contemporaries but friends willing, without question, to listen, support and encourage. Thank you, Gwynne Forster, for sticking with me for more years than I can count; Francis Ray for your warmth and encouraging words; Rochelle Alers for your friendship and insight; Victoria Christopher Murray for always being willing to share; Bernice McFadden, a hidden gem and my idol; Leslie Esdaile (aka L. A. Banks) for doing the damn thing!; my big brother Victor McGlothin for your friendship and all those good hugs (I'm still thinking of something we can work on together); and Eric Jerome Dickey for always keeping it real.

Of course, without the love and support of "My Girlz" my life would be less full. Big hugs to Debra Owsley—I can't thank you enough for your friendship and for all that you do for me; Michelle Henley, my road buddy, for being there and for caring about me; Nichole Anderson for your friendship and all that you do behind the scenes; Christine Ellington for the sweetness of your spirit and embracing me in it; Donna Knight—girl, you can make me laugh in the middle of the Apocalypse; Valarie Brown and Antoinette Howell, my sisters— even though distance separates us, our hearts keep us close.

To all the book clubs! Wow, there are so many: United Sisters, Sisters on the Reading Edge, Sweet Soul Sisters, Divas Divine, SWER, Sistahfriend Bookclub, APOOO, RawSistaz, Sistagirl Bookclub, Turning Pages, Escapade, Sexy Ebony BBW African American Bookclub… the list goes on. I can't thank you all enough for your love and support, both online and off.

My incredible family; my beautiful daughters, Nichole and Dawne, my amazing son, Matthew—you guys make me so proud each and every day; my wonderful grandsons, Mahlik and Caylib, and my darling granddaughter, Mikayla. I love you all more than you will ever know. My sister Lisa, who loves me unconditionally, my best friend and cheerleader, the real rock of the family; and my brother David for always being in my corner. My mom, Dorothy, without whom I would not be. Your resilience under circumstances that would break many is my inspiration. When I think of you I know that I can do anything. I can fly. Daddy, I still miss you so much. Derek, for giving me the gift of our children and for your support throughout the years. And Ronald, my heart, my history, the soul that inspires the words I write, my comfort, my joy.

Most of all, I thank God for bestowing on me this incredible gift of words and for allowing me to share it with the world.

This novel is dedicated with love to all the wonderful readers who embraced its predecessor, *Rhythms*. It was because of each of you that *What Mother Never Told Me* came into being. I thank you all for the love and continued support. And I hope that this novel of love, betrayal, forgiveness and healing will capture your imagination and your heart, strengthen your friendships and allow you to accept yourself for the incredible person that you are.

Until next time,

Donna

*Every goodbye ain't gone...every shut-eye ain't sleep*

# Chapter One

Her dead mother was alive.

Yet, days after learning the unthinkable, Parris McKay was still unable to reconcile the truth with the lie she'd been nursed and nurtured on for three decades. The enormity of it echoed throughout the cool stillness of the one-room church.

Her emotions shifted between disbelief and anger, anguish and shock, to despair and back again. So she'd come here to the one place where she'd always found answers, balance and a quieting of her spirit.

But even here, the solace she sought was unattainable, a vapor that could be seen but not touched. The letter she held between her slender fingers was yellowed with age and had been freed with the others from their hiding place behind her Nana's stove, its wizened face crisscrossed by the fine lines of an unfamiliar hand, cracked under the onslaught of air and light.

Parris held the letter like one unfamiliar with a newborn—cautious, fearful, yet in awe of its mysteries. There were answers here, etched between the lines that she struggled to see. She knew it, could feel it. She knew if she just looked hard enough she would know *why*.

The words, though not addressed to her, connected her to the woman she'd only imagined. The woman that was buried on European shores after giving birth to her—or so she'd been told. Told so many times that she believed it, became part of the lie. She believed her Nana when she sat her down on her knee, looked her deep in the eyes and said, "Your mama loved you so much, gal, wanted you to have a little piece of somethin' so bad that she begged those fancy doctors to save her baby no matter what. Yessir, that's what she done for ya, 'cause she loved ya. Even fo' you got here."

Imagine being loved like that, so hard and so strong even before you took your first breath. The thought of it filled all the empty spaces that the void of not having her mother left in her life.

And that's the lie she told her friends when they asked where her mother was and why she lived with her grandmother. She told *her* truth. The only one she knew. Now what she knew was no more. The ache of it settled in her bones, squeezed her heart and stripped her throat raw.

What was she to do?

She bowed her head as the long shadow of the cross fell across her lap, deepened as the sun shifted and prepared to settle down for the night. She'd lost track of how long she'd sat on the worn wooden pew, its hardness softened and curved by hips and thighs that heaved, sighed and caressed it throughout the years.

Her green eyes, butterfly quick, flitted from one space to the next as a montage of images gathered around her. How many times had she walked the aisle as a child, a teen, a woman? How many sermons had she heard, christenings and marriages had she attended? How many songs had she sung in the choir? How many times had she looked out on the congregation to see her Nana Cora and Grandpa David watching her with pride? So many.

But how could any of this—all the things that she knew— be concrete when she was no more than an illusion? And if she was no longer real then nothing in her life could be, either. With familiarity now a stranger, she had no choice but to create a new reality. And if not here, then where?

She'd come back, back to her home of Rudell, Mississippi, to be witness to her grandmother Cora's transition. The woman who raised her, loved her, taught her right from wrong, gave her the gift of music…lied to her. Lied. The word burned in her throat, stirring and simmering into something bigger than herself, erupting into an emotion that was so unfamiliar—rage. Parris raged at Cora, raged at her for keeping the secret and nearly taking it with her to her grave.

Cora confessed on her waning breath that Emma, her mother, was alive, was living in Europe, that she'd turned her infant daughter over to Cora only days after her birth and never returned. The only connection Cora had with her daughter through the years was the intermittent letters that filled the tin box behind the stove.

Cora turned the letters over to Parris in the final hours before her passing. They revealed so much and nothing at all. Handwriting style, frequency, location, inquiries about the child she'd abandoned. Yet none of the letters collected for almost thirty years explained *why*.

Why was Parris unworthy of her mother's love? Why did Emma give her away and never come back? Why was Parris told that her mother was dead? And why did the woman whom she'd idolized all her life keep the answers and take them with her?

Parris jerked around, startled by the noise behind her. Her gaze settled—along with her heartbeat—when she saw her grandfather crossing the threshold. She brushed the tears from her eyes only for them to be followed by more.

David swept his hat from his head and walked reverently down the aisle. She made room for him next to her.

"Been wondering where you been for so long," he said in that cottony comfort voice that had cocooned her to sleep on many an occasion.

Parris sighed and rested her head on his shoulder of welcome. Her granddad had been the only doctor in Rudell for decades. It wasn't until about five years ago that another doctor set out her shingle. But it had taken many a dinner conversation, trips to the Left Hand River and loud debates in front of the general store for the townspeople of Rudell to come to terms with a new doctor—especially a woman. Things may have changed in the rest of the world but Rudell, Mississippi, was no different than it had been in the early 1900s, when her great grandfather Joshua Harvey was the preacher at this very church.

"Nana wanted me to go find my mother."

She could feel David's head bob up and down. "And what do you plan to do?"

"It's what I've been sitting here thinking about." She angled her head to take in his strong profile. "I don't want to leave you, Granddad. What are you going to do out here...alone?"

He lifted his square chin just a notch. Not enough for someone who didn't know him to even notice. But Parris knew her grandfather. That tiny tic meant he'd made up his mind and no amount of persuasion was going to change it.

"I'll be just fine. This is my home. I stay here…and I can stay close to Cora." His full lips pinched. "That young man of yours is up at the house, packin' looks like."

The dry muscles of her throat that were struggling for moisture tightened even more.

"Can't sit here crying forever. Not what Cora would have wanted. She'd want you to get on with your life."

"What life!" Her voice splintered the quiet of the church, cracking under the pressure of a question she couldn't answer. She turned swollen, tear-filled eyes on him.

"The life you had, the life you gonna make. You have everything you need. It's up to you to decide what you gon' do with it." He paused a beat. "I been listenin' to you since you been back, humming a little, singing a bit. God and your grandma gave you a gift—the voice of an angel. Now you kin head on back to New York. Ain't nobody gonna fault you none. But when you stand up and sing in front of folks, those notes won't ring true. Every one of them is gonna have an empty hole in it." He rubbed his jaw with a large, dark hand that had the power to heal. "Or you can go find your mama. Hear her tell you what you need to hear. When you do that the hole in those notes and that space in your heart will be filled."

He kissed the top of her head. "Up to you. Whatever you decide you best hurry 'fore that boy leaves without a goodbye." He pushed up from his seat, wincing a little from the nag in his right hip. He made a mental note to ask Cora to rub some liniment on it. He squeezed his hat. The tiniest groan of pain pushed up from his gut, sputtered across his lips. He remembered. His Cora was gone. He blinked away the burn in his eyes with each step he took toward the door. Nearly half a century of loving one woman. He had no idea how he was going to make it. No idea at all.

Parris heard the church door squeak shut. Her slender body shuddered as a wave of sorrow rolled through her. Granddad was right. She couldn't sit there forever. She needed to talk with Nick. Figure something out—about everything, including them.

She gathered the lightweight baby blue shawl that she'd brought along with her, gently folded the letter and put it in her shirt pocket. She took one last look around and walked out.

The sun was easing down behind the hilltops, playing hide-and-seek between the branches and leaves of the towering coves of trees that led to the Left Hand River and separated them from the white part of town. The air was filled with the fresh scents of rich earth, ripe grass, farm animals and simplicity.

That's what she drew into her lungs—simplicity. The slow, easy pace of country living. She'd been home for just about a month and she had yet to see one person hurrying anywhere. There wasn't an abundance of cars. The town was so small, folks walked mostly everywhere. And if they did have a ways to go they hitched a ride.

Gentrification hadn't touched Rudell. Somehow the townspeople were able to maintain their way of life without the onslaught of yuppies, buppies, condos, superstores and coffee giants squeezing the spirit out of them.

She walked up the path that led to her grandparents' home, a neat two-story structure, one of only a half dozen like it in town. Today was the first day that the front door wasn't swinging open and closed from the trainload of grievers that had click-clacked through the house for three days. She'd swear that all five hundred residents of Rudell must have come to pay their respects to her grandmother, and they dropped off a bounty of food, including whole fried chickens, seasoned collards, peas and rice, mac and cheese, fruit salads and peanuts. Granddad would have enough food for the next two months. And from the gleam in some of the widows' eyes and the extra smiles on their red lips, he'd have company, too.

A light went on in the window of the second floor, catching her eye. She watched the silhouette of her grandfather as he slowly sat down on the side of the bed and buried his head in his hands.

Parris shut her eyes for a moment and sent up a silent prayer to ease his heart. When she opened the front door, Nick was at the kitchen table. His suitcase, like a faithful pup, sat at his feet. A medley of mouthwatering aromas harmonized in a "come sit down" tune and her stomach called back in response.

"Hi." The faint greeting hung in the food-scented air.

"Thought I was going to miss you." He pushed back from the table, the old wooden legs of the chair tap-dancing across the highs and lows of the aging linoleum.

"I couldn't let you leave without saying goodbye."

His jaw tightened as he nodded.

"What time is your bus?"

"Six. David…your grandfather said he would drive me to the station."

Uncertainty made them sudden strangers. Instead of reaching for each other they sought the support of chair backs and table edges.

Parris squeezed and twisted the shawl between her fingers. "I can take you."

"Are you sure?"

"I want to."

Nick pushed his hands deep into his pockets to keep from reaching for her, to appear as casual and unaffected as she. He shrugged his left shoulder. "Cool. Ready when you are."

She tried to meet his eyes but the questions that hung there turned her away. "I'll let Granddad know." She hurried toward the stairs and went up.

The door at the end of the hall was closed, but couldn't contain the light within—a sliver snuck out from the bottom and bathed the floor with a path of illumination that beckoned her. She knocked lightly on the door, listened to the rustle of movement and the creek of the four-poster bed.

A half smile greeted her. "Was just resting a bit before I took your young man to the bus depot."

"That's what I came to tell you. I'm going to take him."

The smile came full. He dug in his pocket and took out the car keys. "Drive slow." He handed her the keys.

Parris grinned. "Is there any other way to drive in Rudell?" She leaned up and kissed his gray-stubbled cheek. "See you soon."

"I'll leave a plate out for you."

"Thanks," she said over her shoulder. When she returned to the kitchen, Nick had already taken his bag and was sitting on the steps outside. She pressed her fingertips to her stomach to settle the butterflies that had broken loose. "Ready?"

He angled his head toward her then stood, the long lean lines of his body unfolding like the break of dawn—it was pure majesty.

"Sure." He trotted down the four steps ahead of her and strolled toward the old Ford parked at the end of the path.

As Parris descended the stairs she couldn't believe that she was actually letting him go back to New York without her. Initially, before the full ramifications of her discovery hit her, she'd told Nick that she wanted him to meet her mother. The raw excitement of finding out that her mother was indeed alive overshadowed the questions that began as a light summer shower before intensifying to an unstoppable hurricane, ruining everything in its path. She was battered by the unrelenting winds and rains of confusion, weakened and shocked by the power of deceit, leaving her with only remnants of what she'd been able to salvage. She wasn't the woman he'd met so many months ago when she shyly approached him for a singing gig at his nightclub. She wasn't the woman who captured an audience and held them in her palm like the last strains of a Billie Holiday ballad. She wasn't the woman who walked out on her boss/lover, lost her job and her apartment.

She was someone else now and until she discovered who that someone was, she couldn't be part of anyone's life.

Parris followed Nick to the car. She opened his door first and his hand brushed her wrist. The jolt rocked them both. She stepped back, hurried around to the other side and slid behind the wheel. Nick tossed his bag into the backseat and got in next to her. This was the closest they'd been in days. She could feel the heat rise off his skin and settle around her. If she listened really close she could hear the steady rhythm of his heart. The air in her lungs balled up in her throat. She rolled down the window so that she could breathe and in the blink of an eye, tension crawled into the backseat and hunkered down for the ride, keeping them company.

Forcing herself to concentrate, Parris put the car in gear and slowly headed off toward the end of town and the bus stop.

En route down the main road, they passed the hopscotch of houses, built more for comfort and protection from the elements than design. Some were squat like overripe squashes, others were long and lean like the fields of cornstalks. And some…well, they were just there. She waved at the familiar faces of porch sitters who'd come out to catch a bit of the cool evening air.

"I can only imagine how hard things have been for you," Nick said, breaking the wall of silence.

Parris sucked in a breath.

"I want you to know that whatever decision you make about your mother, your life…your career, I'm here for you."

"I know that." She stole a look at him. "And I never told you thank you for coming here."

"You don't have to. I came because I wanted to. I thought you needed me."

"I did. I still do." Her sigh filled up the space between them. "There's so much happening inside me. I…I can't explain it. But I have to work it out on my own."

He reached for her, rested his hand on her thigh. "Don't shut me out, Parris. Please."

His fingertips were hot coals searing her skin, the heat winding its way to that place in her heart that had turned bitter cold. It would be so easy to let the warmth envelop her, wrap her in the comfort of it, until she drifted off to a dreamless slumber where the yesterdays had never been and there was only now and tomorrow.

What had happened between them in such a short space of time? he thought, frustration and sadness jockeying for position. He'd turned his life around so that he could be the man that she deserved. He'd cut off his ties with Percy back in New

York, paid off his debt. He didn't owe anyone. He could start fresh with a new club that was his and not controlled by mob money. She knew that. He'd told her everything. He'd worked quietly behind the scenes for months to get her a recording contract—the one thing she'd dreamed of, had worked for—and even that didn't put the light back in her eyes. He'd been so sure that coming here, being with her during this dark time in her life, would show her how much he cared, what she meant to him. He'd envisioned them returning to New York together, taking the city and the world by storm. Something beyond finding out about her mother had changed her and in turn it had changed them.

The bus depot came into view. Parris's heart beat a little faster. *Tell him before it's too late.* She pulled the car onto the shoulder of the road and shut it off.

She turned halfway in her seat. "Bus should be here any minute," she said, instead of the words that really mattered.

"Yeah," he murmured, then opened the door and got out. He took his suitcase from the backseat and shut the door.

She stepped out and came around to where he stood. "I don't even have a place to stay if I come back now," she said, the words and the fear tumbling out. "I have no job…."

Nick's hopes awakened. He gripped her shoulders. "Look at me."

Slowly she raised her head and her gaze danced with the dark intensity of his. "We can work it out. *We.* Isn't that what you want?"

"I don't know what I want right now."

"Then let's figure it out together. Do what you need to do here and when you're ready to come back we'll make it work."

"I don't know how long it's going to be."

"It doesn't matter." The urgency in his voice competed with the sound of the arriving bus.

Parris's eyes darted toward the bus and the line of passengers ready to board.

"Just come back to me." He moved up to her, so close that he could feel the vibrations of her body.

The driver blew the horn. "All aboard for Jackson."

Nick snapped his head toward the bus then back at Parris. "Promise me."

Her lips parted to the blare of the horn.

Nick drew her tight against him, so that every dip and curve bent to his will. He kissed her like a Mississippi summer; hot, wet and long, stealing their breath.

"I promise," she said as air rushed back into her lungs and she found herself standing alone on the curb as the bus pulled off. Tentatively she touched her fingers to her lips while she watched the bus kick up dirt and turn the bend. "I promise."

She returned to the car and headed back home, and for the first time in days she didn't feel so terribly alone.

"So you let him go," David said, coming into the kitchen. He moved to the refrigerator and took out the pitcher of sweet tea, placed it on the table between them.

Parris used her fork to move the collards around on her plate, framing the yams and fried chicken breast. "He couldn't stay and I wasn't ready to go."

"Nothing for you to do here. Seems to me that's the reason why you left in the first place—to pursue your dream. This town is too small for you. No dreams here." He eased down into the hard-backed chair and refilled her glass.

"Thank you." She cupped the glass but didn't drink. "I'm

angry at Nana," she blurted out. "So angry." She bit out each word. "I know I shouldn't be, but I can't help it and the anger is eating me up inside."

"Your grandmother did what she needed to do." He glanced away. "What she had to do for everyone concerned. You have no idea the weight she carried all those years." His voice shook with the passion of his convictions, rumbling right down the center of Parris's chest. "So you can go on being mad, faulting other folk, being miserable, or you can do something about it." He stood, drew in a long breath. "All I got to say about it. Be sure to put the food up and turn on the porch light. I'm going to bed."

She watched him walk away, his always ramrod-straight back was suddenly stooped by more than he could carry. And she realized she'd done that, throwing one more boulder on his shoulders—her own weight of uncertainty.

She pushed up from the table. "I'm sorry, Granddad," she called out.

He waved it off with a swipe of his hand and took each step as if he were scaling the mountaintop.

The bedroom door opened and swung shut. She flinched.

She couldn't be another weight. Granddad didn't deserve that. And as much as she tried to convince him and herself that she was staying because she didn't want him to be alone, it was all smoke and mirrors, a parlor trick. She was adrift and she was desperately trying to hold on to the preserver of a life that was familiar. But he was right. Her life was no longer hers and hadn't been for much too long.

She glanced at the clock above the sink. Nick's bus should be arriving at the Jackson airport station in another half hour at best. Possibility jumped inside her. She picked up her plate of uneaten food and scraped it into the trash. If she hurried...

She bit down on her lip. She had her ticket. Her resources were limited. This wasn't a big city. There were no all–night car services. Her gaze rose toward the stairs, and she listened to the heavy footsteps that crossed the floor.

If she hurried… She sprinted upstairs, raised her hand to knock just as the door opened.

"I know all the back roads," David said.

Her luminous green eyes widened, followed by an awe-filled smile. She leapt into his broad chest and he enveloped her in understanding.

"We better get going before we miss him," he said into her cottony soft spirals. He kissed her smooth forehead and stepped back.

She gazed at him and saw the familiar love brimming in his tender brown eyes. She nodded, spun away and ran down to the opposite end of the hallway to her room. Without thinking of anything except getting to Nick before he took off, she tossed her few belongings in her suitcase, snatched up her purse and ran out to meet her grandfather, who had already started up the old Ford.

With Granddad behind the wheel, Parris tried to relax and put her impulsive actions into perspective. She was on her way to catch a man whom she'd let go with no more than a whispered promise of "perhaps," and now she needed to take him up on his offer to house and employ her until she regained some semblance of her life.

She hadn't even offered to drive him to the airport, she thought, flinching inside. Her momentarily buoyant spirits began to sink. What if he'd reconsidered his offer?

"No use fretting about it," David said, reading the frown

lines in her forehead. "He'll either be glad to see you or he won't. And judging from the way he looks at you, I can't imagine him being anything but a happy man."

"From your lips to God's ears." She patted his thigh. "Thanks for this, Granddad."

"Back home is where you need to be."

They bumped along the back roads before suddenly emerging on the main highway. The road was empty. Their only company was the intermittent lights that illuminated the pitch-black roads.

"What are you going to do, Granddad, really?"

He sighed heavily. "Take one day at a time, sugah. I been thinking maybe I'll turn one of those rooms into an office. Start seeing some of my patients right at the house. Cora always took issue with that. Said she didn't want a whole lotta sick folk traipsing in and out of her house." He chuckled at the memory and shook his head. "Yeah, she was something."

Parris heard the wistful note in his voice. She could only imagine how difficult it would be for him. But hopefully his medical practice would fill some of the space that Cora had left.

Her granddad was the definition of country doctor. He still made house calls, had delivered half the babies in town and had treated generations of families. As much as she wanted him to come back to New York where she could look after him, she understood that he would never be happy there. The frenetic pace and the noise would drive him right back to the Delta.

"We should get to the airport in about twenty minutes," he said.

Parris glanced at her watch. Nick's plane was due to take off in an hour. Her heart thumped. She should probably call, let him know that she was coming. Maybe now she'd get a signal on her cell phone, which she'd been unable to do since she'd arrived in Rudell.

She dug her phone out of her purse, studied it as if she'd never seen it before. David stole a glance at her.

"Let him know we're only ten minutes away."

Parris smiled at her grandfather's intuitiveness. She pressed in Nick's numbers and held her breath as the phone rang on the other end.

Just before the call went to voice mail, Nick came on the line. "Parris?"

"Hi, uh, we're…I'm about ten minutes away. Don't let the plane take off without me," she said on a breath of excitement.

"They wouldn't dare."

She heard the laughter and relief in his voice and she began to think that just maybe everything would turn out all right.


Parris faced her granddad as they stood in front of his pickup. So many emotions swirled inside her: sadness, hope, uncertainty, guilt, anticipation.

"I'll write…often," she promised as he held her close, stroking her back. "And I'll come to see you as soon as I can." She looked up into his eyes that held a hundred stories.

He kissed her forehead. "You keep your promise to your grandma, that's all you got to promise me." He squeezed her one last time before letting her go. "It's up to you to make things right, for all of us."

She frowned in a moment of confusion. "What do you mean?"

"You'll know." His smile was tender. "Go on now, before you miss your plane and your man."

Her throat clenched. "I love you, Granddad."

"Love you, too, sugah. Now go 'head."

She reached down for her bag, gave him one last kiss on the cheek and hurried off into the small terminal to find Nick. Once inside the glass doors she took a parting look over her shoulder but David was gone. She drew in a long breath of resolve and hurried through the travelers in search of her future.

Nick spotted Parris before she saw him and he was once again moved by her simple beauty. Her long, slender body covered in satiny soft skin reminded him of warm honey and her curly brown hair which she'd taken to wearing wild and carefree, was the texture of spun cotton. But it was her eyes that had always captivated him—they were green like the color of jade and had the intensity to look beyond the surface and right into your soul. And a voice that could charm the angels out of heaven.

Yet the internal package held so much more. It was the purity of her spirit, her sense of right and wrong and fairness. She'd been willing to sacrifice her own happiness because of her beliefs, which had forced him to face his own demons, freeing himself from the financial hold that Percy had over him and his daughter Tara had.

He knew Tara had never been the woman for him. Their relationship was an outgrowth of his dealings with her father, Percy. She'd always been a "daddy's girl," and what Tara wanted, Tara got. Percy made sure of it. Initially Nick thought it might work, but as time went on and Tara grew more demanding and controlling and began to remind him at every opportunity that her daddy owned him, he knew they were doomed. Finally severing all ties with both of them was the best thing he'd done, no matter the cost. In doing so, he knew he was a better man for it and a better man for Parris—the one she deserved.

He waved over the heads of the stream of travelers until he got her attention.

Parris sidestepped suitcases and bodies until she stood in front of him. "I guess you have this whole thing figured out," she said.

He offered a crooked smile. "Not really. But I guess you know by now that I'm a gambling man."

"This is a big gamble, Nick. I don't know what I may find out. My whole life has been rearranged and I don't know where all the pieces are."

"That's why you have me." He stroked her arm as he spoke. "Wherever the pieces may fall we'll pick them up and put them together."

"You make it sound easy."

"The hard part was getting you here. The rest will be a breeze." He kissed the tip of her nose then took her bag with one hand and her hand with his other. "Come on, we have a plane to catch."

# Chapter Two

Parris and Nick arrived at JFK airport and bumped along with the surging crowd to the exit and joined the long line of tired passengers waiting for cabs into the city.

During the two-and-a-half-hour flight they'd talked and slept, but mostly talked, feeling each other out on this new direction their relationship was taking.

"Are you sure about this?" Parris asked. "I can always find a hotel until I can get a permanent place to stay."

Nick angled himself in the seat to face her. A look of quiet dignity mixed with uncertainty floated in her green eyes, and tightened the corners of her mouth. "When you left New York to come to Mississippi I thought I'd lost you for good. I knew I couldn't deal with that. I couldn't deal with the idea that we hadn't given each other a real chance. And I knew that most of the reason for that was my fault. I had to get my stuff together. And I did. I want us to have a chance. I know this isn't the perfect scenario. But I'm willing if you are."

Parris studied his expression, listened for any hint of doubt in his voice. "The only man I've ever lived with was my grand-father. I've been on my own since I came to New York."

"I definitely can't live up to your granddad but I ain't half-bad." He took her hand. "Look at it this way. My place is a temporary stop, somewhere to lay your head and hang your clothes. Whatever happens while you're laying and hanging will be up to you. Fair enough?"

She nodded. "My Nana used to always say that everything happens for a reason even if we don't know what the reason is."

"You came into my club all those months ago with no idea that it would lead you to this moment. When I saw you that first time I had no idea it would lead me to feel about you the way that I do."

Her heart thumped.

"I thought at first you were just another pretty face with a voice to float to heaven on. But it was more than that. Some-where along the way I fell for you, hard."

She didn't dare breathe or move, sure that if she did this moment would vanish for good.

Nick glanced away then looked back at her. "There, I've confessed." He chuckled to hide his embarrassment. He reclined his seat and closed his eyes.

She shook his arm. His eyes popped open. "How dare you say something like that and then pretend to go to sleep?"

His brows formed two half-moons. "What did I say?"

"You know what you said. How can you tell me something like that?" she asked, her tone part accusation, part trepidation.

"Tell you what? That I'm crazy about you and have been

for months but couldn't tell you until the time was right. Is that what you mean?"

Her heart was racing so hard and fast that she could barely catch her breath. "Yes. Now with everything going on in my life…" She frowned. "Feeling so disconnected and unsure about who I am…"

He cupped her chin, forcing her to look at him. "That's exactly why I told you. So that you'll know that no matter what happens with your mother that I'm here for you."

Her throat clenched. How could she explain the sick sensation that had taken up residence in her gut? The feeling that she was somehow unworthy. When your own mother can't love you it made you question everything about who you are. That's the space she was in right now. The feeling of walking on a window ledge a hundred stories up off the ground.

Nick opened the door to his two-bedroom apartment on the south side of Harlem. He'd lucked out when he found it eight years earlier—before the neighborhood had gone condo, prices soared and the complexion had changed. It was one of the last rent-stabilized buildings in the immediate area. All the others had been gobbled up by the Ivy League university, Columbia.

He stepped aside to let Parris in and she was instantly taken aback at the treasure trove of art, books and music that lined the walls. She was sure she'd stepped into a Black arts museum and not a bachelor pad.

The off-white walls were lined with black framed photographs of legendary jazz and blues musicians and singers, and art from Basquiat, Gordon Parks, Romare Bearden and Jacob Lawrence. Parris strolled along the hall of fame, enthralled by the beauty of Black history—American history—that continued to live and breathe in his space.

She could almost hear the blistering blues of Bessie Smith, the angst of Billie Holiday, the cries of Miles and the pull of Coltrane's "A Love Supreme." Reverently she fingered the framed photo of her idol, Sarah Vaughan, right next to Nick's best friend, pianist Quinten Parker, captured accepting his first Grammy.

Parris turned. Nick was behind her with a smile of "yeah, I know what you're feeling" on his face.

"Every time I walk down this hallway it inspires me." He adjusted the sepia-toned picture of Ella Fitzgerald. "Reminds me of how great we are and all that I need to do to live up to and carry on the legacy."

It was one of the reasons she'd come to New York, to pursue the musical legacy handed down to her by her grandmother Cora, who sought her own moment in Chicago and had the unforgettable experience of meeting Bessie Smith. Music and its purity was what drew her and Nick together, bound them in a way that was inexplicable. They understood the underlying messages, learned how to convey the most abstract emotions through his sax and her voice. The combination, it was said by those who witnessed them onstage together, was to experience an anointing.

"Come on. Let me show you where you can put your things."

He led her down the hall that opened onto a large living room, which was in sharp contrast to "the time gone by" feel of the corridor. This space was a testament to high tech. One entire wall was equipped with state-of-the-art recording and stereo equipment and enough bells and whistles to baffle the guys at NASA. In the corner near the window, perched majestically on a gold-toned stand, was his prized Selwyn saxophone. Goose bumps rose on her bare arms. A flash of the first time she'd seen him silhouetted onstage, his lips wrapping around the mouthpiece, his tongue playing with the reed, the baleful cry of the notes caressing her skin, played before her, shortening the air in her lungs.

The sound of the door opening in the hallway drew her back to the present. She rubbed her hands along her arms and followed Nick to the room. The trapped heat—thankful for release and as happy as kids on the last day of school—rushed out, skipped past them and filled the house.

"Whew. Let me turn on the fan." He flipped a switch on the wall. "Sorry, no air-conditioning in here but it should cool off pretty quick." He set her suitcase down by the closet.

"I'll be fine."

She stepped around him and took in the room. It was definitely a guest room, she surmised. Very simple and utilitarian. The full-sized bed was covered in a beige-and-brown print comforter. A throw rug in the same muted shades of wood sat at the foot of the bed. The only other furnishing was a six-dresser drawer and a nightstand.

"There're clean sheets and towels in the hall closet next to the bathroom."

Parris nodded. "Thanks."

"Look…" He hesitated, wanting this to come out right. "I know this is awkward for you. Before you left to go to Mississippi, things were strained between us. But we were moving in the right direction. At least I thought we were." He stroked his chin with his thumb. "All those things," he said, his hand flicking the past away, "that were obstacles are gone. The only thing that will keep us from being an us, is me and you." He moved. She held her breath. His fingertip touched her cheek. "We're going to make this work. All of it."

"You sound so sure."

"I'm just that kind of guy." He leaned down. So feather-light was his kiss that the only way she was certain of it was the heat that warmed her mouth.

Reflexively she ran her tongue along her lips and let her eyes traverse languidly over him. For months they'd tangoed around the possibility of being together, but Tara and Frank kept cutting in. The music had stopped. The dance floor was clear. It was just the two of them.

They'd come so close on those late nights that they'd worked together, perfecting and practicing arrangements long after everyone in the club was gone.

She'd seen the look of desire in his eyes. She felt her own need in the pit of her stomach. But as much as she wanted Nick, she'd never disappoint her grandmother, who raised her to believe she was worthy of being the "only one," not the "other one." And as long as Nick stayed with Tara, Parris would stay out of his bed.

"Hungry?" he asked, his low timbre penetrating her day-dream.

Parris blinked. Her stomach answered before she could. She laughed, embarrassed.

"I'll take that as a yes," he teased. "Come on. I'm starved. That bird food we had on the plane didn't do a thing for me but make me mad." He took her hand and led her to the kitchen.

They went into his small but efficient kitchen, which from the looks of it was well-used. A spice rack attached to the far right wall was filled. The stainless steel fridge and matching freezer took up the other side, with a two-seat table in the center. Copper and cast-iron pots and pans dotted the countertop in an odd pairing of old and new.

"How about one of my world famous omelets?"

"Sounds great. Can I help?"

"Sure. The bowls are in the cabinet above the fridge and there's a cutting board hanging over the sink."

Parris began her assignment and before giving it much thought she felt as if she'd been in this place and at this time on countless occasions. Their banter was easy. Their movements in perfect sync, as if they'd always worked in harmony.

It was the same feeling she had when they performed together onstage. He knew exactly when to allow her voice to float just above his notes and when to carry them along. They made magic on stage. There was no doubt in her mind about that. What she was uncertain of was if they could make magic offstage, behind the scenes. What you can't have is always so much more enticing. The allure of the unknown.

"What do you like in your omelet?"

She dried off the mixing bowl with a paper towel. "Surprise me."

"Me, I like a bit of everything in mine," he said. "I like the surprise mixture of tastes and textures."

His words, like the score of a movie, were filled with meaning. But that was Nick, Parris admitted as she watched him take mushrooms, green peppers and tomatoes out of the crisper. He rarely came directly at you, but rather around you, beneath you, wrapping you in a lullaby. Before you knew it, you were moving to his beat. She didn't care for tomatoes, but suddenly it didn't matter.

Soon the cozy kitchen became filled with the ting of pots and pans against the iron eyes of the stove top and the splash of water in the sink, while the opening and closing of drawers and cabinets kept time.

"This is really good," she said as the fluffy concoction nestled in her stomach.

"Glad you like it. Omelets are about the only thing I can cook, so I figured I better give it my best shot."

"No complaints from me."

"Could be that's because you were starving."

"Could be," she teased.

He tossed a paper napkin at her and she ducked, laughing at his aim.

Nick raised his arms over his head, stretched and yawned. "Sorry," he mumbled. "Day's finally catching up with me."

The reality of spending the night right across the hall from Nick crept up on her and stole her breath. "I'll clean up since you cooked." She rose from her seat.

"They'll keep until morning. You have to be as tired as I am."

"I wouldn't be able to sleep knowing there were dishes and pots to be washed," she said, lifting plates from the table and looking for the time that had been snatched away.

"Good home training."

She caught the wistful note in his voice, full of almosts, and could-have-beens. Nick's growing-up years had been a far cry from the protective nest she was nurtured in. Where her days would almost always be remembered as endless summers, his would be a desert of desolation.

"Something like that. Nana was a real stickler for keeping up a house," she said, her Southern roots curling around the turn of phrase.

Nick took the forks and glasses from the table to the sink. He moved next to her. The knotted muscle of his arm brushed her, sizzling her skin. Reflexively she jerked on the faucets full-blast, startling them both with the force and tempering the air.

"I should have warned you," he said, chuckling while grabbing a paper towel from the roll. He wiped off the spray of water from his face. "When you turn on the water, the first gush is pretty hard. Have to stand back a bit to keep from getting splashed." He pressed the towel to her forehead then her cheek.

She sputtered a nervous laugh. "I'll know for next time."

"You can have first dibs on the bathroom."

She put her hands beneath the water and scrubbed the frying pan. That meant getting naked and being totally vulnerable with Nick only feet away. She scrubbed until the pan gleamed. She didn't consider herself a prude. She'd had relationships before, been with a man, but this was different. Their boundaries were tenuous, the expectations unclear.

"No. You go ahead. I'll finish up here," she finally said.

He looked at her a moment. "Okay."

When he left the room she felt her insides loosen and her lungs inflate with air. Alone with her thoughts, she wondered if Nick felt the same level of uncertainty that she did. But, of course, he wouldn't. There was nothing uncertain about Nick Hunter. He knew his mind and he knew himself. He wasn't one to question himself or his actions.

She'd been the same way until recently, when the thread of her life was pulled and she began to unravel. The fabric of her being now pooled around her feet, tripping her up at every turn.

The only thing she was sure of was that daylight comes in

the morning. It was her grandmother's favorite saying. The answers were within her and when she put her troubles to rest she'd see the answers clearly in the morning.

## Chapter Three

Parris was lifted from sleep and carried into consciousness on a distant bluesy melody. The dim light of the winter morning cast shadows across things that she didn't recognize. It took her a moment to realize where she was and why.

By degrees the sense of unfamiliarity lessened. She tossed the sheet and blanket aside and sat up. This was Nick's apartment. She'd come here to stay after leaving Mississippi. Her grandmother was dead. Her mother was alive. Her reality took shape as the song beckoned her. She reached for her robe at the foot of the bed and tiptoed to the door. She cracked it open and the highs and lows guided her to its origin.

Parris stood in the archway of the living room. Nick was perched on the edge of the windowsill. His eyes were closed as he raised and lowered the sax in time to the rhythm that moved through his soul. The song strolled to its conclusion.

And as if rising from the depths of unspeakable pleasure, his eyes slowly opened. A look of ecstasy haloed his face, and when his gaze rested on her it stroked her.

A shiver moved through her limbs.

"Mornin'." He hopped down from the sill and placed the sax on its stand.

He came toward her in that slow easy way that reminded her of a prowling panther. Sensual to watch, but deadly.

"Sleep okay?"

Parris could only nod as her eyes clung to the sky-blue T-shirt that outlined his chest.

"You can hang out here today if you want. I have some business to take care of. A friend of mine located a space for me."

"A space?"

He grinned. "For my new club. I have to meet her at ten. She says it's perfect for what I want."

"I didn't realize you were actively looking."

"When I said I cut ties with Percy Davis, I meant it. This will be all mine, no strings. I'll be in hock up to my eyeballs for a while but I think I'll be okay."

"Wow," she said on a breath. "That is so exciting." Her eyes widened in delight. "Mind if I tag along? I mean…if you don't mind."

"Since you're going to be my headliner I guess you should see where you're going to perform."

"Headliner? You're kidding, right?"

"I wouldn't dare." He chuckled at the open look of awe on her face. "You did say you needed a job," he teased.

"Sure…" Her body shifted, adjusting to the news. "I guess I never thought…"

"What, that you were star material? The contract that's

burning a hole in my briefcase says different. The way you packed the house at Downbeat says different." He leaned against the frame of the wall, inches away from her. "I know you haven't had time to think about it, but you need to. Deals like that don't come often."

"I know." She thought about what her grandfather had said about the hole in her music that would remain there until she got the answers she needed to fill it. She looked into Nick's eyes, seeing nothing but promise and possibility there. "I'll need some time." She drew in a breath. "I'm going to see my mother."

Suddenly she found herself wrapped in a gentle embrace.

"It's the right decision," he said into the softness of her hair. "And I'll be here when you return."

She was imbued with anticipation now that she'd said the words out loud.

Nick kissed her lightly on the lips. "When are you planning on going?"

"I haven't figured that part out yet," she said, her voice tremulous. "But soon. I need to look into flights."

Nick took a breath. "No time like the present. You can use my computer and see what kinds of deals are out there."

Now that the decision was made she felt a sense of calmness and control reenter her spirit. For weeks she'd been adrift, at the mercy of events. It was time for her to take back her life, twist and reshape it into something that was recognizable, albeit new. "Let me get cleaned up and then you can show me the way."

Nick's computer was on a small wooden desk next to his bed. The room resembled him. That was her immediate impression. Strong, decisive, dark and comforting. His scent lingered in the air. She inhaled him.

He went to the desk and pushed on the power button. "All yours."

The screen lit up with a picture of Dizzy Gillespie, cheeks full blown and his horn at its trademark askew angle.

"I use Firefox."

She glanced up over her shoulder as he leaned across her to move the mouse. Blue cotton met caramel skin for an electric instant. The charge splashed on the screen in a burst of musical notes. But of course it wasn't the almost-there contact between them that caused the Fourth of July to arrive four months early, she thought.

"Like my screensaver?" he asked, moving back.

*Of course it wasn't the Fourth of July. Screensaver.* "It's definitely you." The thrill lingered on her arm, trembling her fingers. She placed her hands on the keys to steady them.

"See what you can find. I'll be back in a few. Need to make a couple of calls."

"Okay."

His leaving cooled the air around her, as if his presence was the life force that flowed through her veins. When did that happen? Better, why had she not realized it until now? Perhaps she did, she thought as her fingers found their way, but refused to acknowledge it because, of course, if she did she would have been forced to accept an emotion that was unavailable to her.

The Web site to the airline reservations opened and she keyed in Kennedy airport as her starting point. The tips of her fingers hovered over the keys. The hide-and-seek game that the cursor played dared her to stop its frivolity. She could do it. She could make it stop and the game would end. But if she did her future would line up in front of her in perfect formation of date, time, aisle or window. Pick one. Any one.

She blinked to clear her head and vision.

*Paris, France.*

Her heart thumped. The screen filled. Her questions could be answered in a week or tomorrow.

*Tomorrow. Too soon. Not soon enough. March 15. The Ides of March. Caesar met his fate.*

"Find anything?"

Parris jumped.

"Sorry, didn't mean to scare you." Nick sat on the edge of the desk. He draped his long fingers loosely on his lap.

"There's a flight leaving next week."

"Next week?" The immediacy of it set him back. Of course she'd want to leave as soon as possible, once she'd made up her mind. But she wasn't ready. How could she be when she'd only just arrived? There'd been no time to prepare.

"If I book it now the fare is manageable," she said, her declaration filtering through the twists and turns of his thoughts.

Nick's fingers entwined. "How long?"

Parris stared at the screen. "A week, maybe two." Perhaps she'd never come back. Of course, when her mother saw her for the first time she'd want her daughter to stay with her forever, make up for all the years they'd missed. She refused to accept that Emma wouldn't see her, wouldn't want to open her arms and beg to be forgiven. "I thought I'd stay with...my mother...if she has room," she added quickly. "But I can always stay in a hotel, if not."

Nick squeezed the words between his fingers, hoping to crush them. But they were coming so fast. He couldn't stop them and they began to slip through his fingers and spread across the screen. "Confirmation."

There, she'd done it, and in response every nerve in her body shook and danced, thankful to be freed from the captivity of her indecision.

Parris pushed back from the desk. Her gaze became tangled up with Nick's, both asking questions that couldn't be answered, saying so much that couldn't be heard. Not now anyway.

Nick stretched out his hand and she put hers in it. His fingers, slender but strong, wrapped around hers. She felt a wave of comforting warmth, a sense that whatever it was, it would be all right. It simply would.

"Probably should call your grandfather..."

"He must be worried."

"Use the phone in the kitchen."

"Thanks." She stood. He didn't give her any space.

She smelled of softness and morning, her hair a tumble of tight abstract spirals that framed promise, hope and trepidation. His body barely teased hers, yet he could feel every dip, curve and swell. He wanted her to stay but understood her need to leave, to find what she believed she was missing. He understood all too well being half of a whole, his own life a picture of missing pieces.

"Don't stay too long."

She wanted to tell him she knew what he meant, but instead she said, "I won't. Granddad hates phones."

Nick stepped aside to let her pass then glanced at the screen that still held her key to the answers she sought. He only hoped that they were kind.

Nick and Parris pulled up in front of a storefront tucked between a boarded-up used bookstore to the left and a thriving liquor store to the right. Across the street was the Church of the Everlasting. At least that's what the makeshift sign said on the stark white door that looked totally out of place among the grayness. The corner bodega had the usual assemblage of "not sure where my life is going" black men huddled together for comfort as much as warmth. Holding on to their manhood and a patch of concrete they called their own, shooting the breeze and filling the air with puffs from Kools and Newports.

Young women dragged reluctant toddlers with one hand and pushed strollers with the other, heading toward the hope of something better, immune to the "hey, babies" that trailed their sashays, having heard it far too often and knowing that no one called them *baby* and meant it. Only their own daddies, who were more hope than reality.

*Two ree Movies with Membership* flashed obscenely in the window of the video store, hoping to entice the passersby. But these people who bartered for their daily existence knew that nothing in life was free and continued on their way.

Nick put the Navigator in Park, and peered through the passenger window at his possible future.

"Plenty of foot traffic," Parris said, trying to sound hopeful over the rumble of a delivery truck that banged down the tattered blacktop.

Just then a burgundy Jaguar pulled up and parked in front of them. The driver stepped out. Assurance and a sense of entitlement dressed the woman, who clearly was not of the neighborhood. Honey-blond hair framed a peaches-and-cream complexion, her cheeks a pale red from the slap of cold air. She looked neither left nor right as she walked straight to the storefront and stood sentinel. Her bearing and oversized Kate Spade purse were her only weapons against the odd looks tossed her way. The platinum of her watch caught the rays of the sun. Her lips pinched into a thin line that dared someone to cross them. But her green eyes belied the outward confidence. They jumped and darted at every puff of smoke, burst of laughter and flow of curses.

"That must be her," Nick said. He hopped out and came around to open Parris's door then set the alarm. They approached and the wary eyes took on an almost feral glare, fingers clutching her purse a little tighter.

"'Morning. I'm Nick Hunter. And this is Parris McKay."

He extended his hand and the tight lines around her mouth slowly dissolved. A smile of welcome relief stretched across her mouth, revealing perfect off-white teeth.

"So glad to meet you. I'm Celeste Shaw." She shook each of their hands and registered the look of apprehension in their eyes. She needed this sale, this way of proving herself separate from her socialite mother and money broker father. Corrine and Ellis Shaw deplored the notion that their Ivy League daughter, who they'd spent a fortune educating and grooming, had reduced her potential to this lowly lifestyle. And Celeste relished their disdain. "Before you say anything, I know the neighborhood isn't the best. But the entire area is slated for revitalization. The developers have already begun buying up the vacant property. In another five years you won't recognize the place."

As if that's a good thing, Nick thought but didn't say. Just like you couldn't recognize most of Harlem these days. The verve and vitality, the thing that gave Harlem its rhythm, had been replaced with superstores and condos, and people who made more money than most black folk ever dreamed of. What she meant, but didn't dare say, was a *new* Harlem. A Harlem that was safe for folks who looked like her, who could take over the historic brownstones, add outdoor cafés and coffee shops, get rid of mom-and-pop stores and replace them with stores where no one knew your name and didn't care to find out. Nick had other plans. "Let's take a look."

"Great," Celeste answered, beaming. She dug into her overpriced purse to retrieve the keys. "So how do you know Leslie?" she asked into the depths of her bag.

"Leslie and I met about a year ago when I managed a club called Downbeat. She did some renovations for us."

"Leslie is a doll."

"How do *you* know Leslie?" he asked, curious about the odd-couple combination. Leslie Evans was a product of the notorious Red Hook projects in Brooklyn, raised by a single mother, and the polar opposite of this ultrathin, Upper East Side pampered diva who slummed in her off hours to rid herself of echelon guilt.

"Leslie and I met during a theater class in the Village about ten years ago and we clicked." She looked up with the most endearing smile on her face, holding up the keys like a prize. "Sometimes you meet people that change your life. That's what Leslie did for me." She turned, fumbled with the rusty lock and finally got it open.

"Here, let me do that."

Nick came around her to lift the heavy metal gate. He pushed it up above their heads and Celeste opened what used to be a glass door. She went in first.

"I know it's not much to look at but it has plenty of potential."

Celeste crossed the open space of the entryway into the dusty dankness of the interior, knocking a cobweb out of her way without flinching. That earned points with Nick.

Big black garbage bags of refuse sat like brooding Buddas along a peeling wall that might have been tan at one time. A horseshoe-shaped bar held countless stories of days gone by. Wobbly wooden tables that were once draped with revelers sat forlorn, surrounded by empty seats filled now with the ghosts of the past.

You could almost hear the raucous laughter over the sound of clinking glasses and the four-piece combo; smell the scent of expensive perfumes and manly colognes, accenting the well-heeled crowd. The long necks arched in laughter while thick fingers sought soft skin and a chance for a little more with the right turn of phrase…*you sure look good tonight*…and a glass of something warm and dark…*another one for the lady*…to wash it down easy.

Nick drifted through the space, absorbing the memories, the melody, not seeing the disrepair or the angst of what was, but what he knew it could be.

Celeste started toward him. "There's a full kitchen in the back and a large storage room. And as I mentioned the price is right. With renovations this could be a treasure. And—"

He held up his hand to stop her talk and approach. He wanted to do this alone, not distracted by the practiced come-on, but seduced by things she couldn't possibly see or know.

Celeste, pink-faced, stopped in midstep. She knew she sounded naive but she did believe that in the right hands and with enough work this forgotten wasteland could really be something.

"How many people have you shown this to?" Parris asked as Nick disappeared in the back.

Celeste hitched her purse higher up on her shoulder. "Mr. Hunter is only the second one," she admitted. "The first guy never got past the entrance. He took one look and walked away." She sputtered a nervous laugh, her cheeks warming. "I'm still kind of new at this," she confessed.

"Although it's not my decision to make, I agree with you. It has potential."

Celeste brightened. "You really think so?"

Parris cocked a brow and a half smile. "Don't you?"

Celeste blushed. "Yes, I really think so and I'm sure Leslie would love to get her hands on this place." She caught herself and looked at Parris. "I mean if he takes it. I don't want you to think…"

Parris gently placed her hand on Celeste's shoulder. "Relax." She bent close. "It'll be fine."

A flash of gratitude settled the lines of worry around Celeste's eyes that allowed Parris to see beyond the armor of her designer suit and the odor of money that held lesser ones at bay, to a vulnerable young woman who was as uncertain about what she was doing as Parris was. The clothes, the car and the practiced attitude of superiority were all part of the elaborate camouflage of one who needed props to help them be somebody. Stripped away of artifice, Celeste Shaw was as ordinary as anyone else.

"Do you live in the city?" Celeste asked, *city* being the euphemism for Manhattan.

"Yes and no."

Brows rose in query.

"I'm sort of staying with Nick…temporarily until I can find a place."

"Oh, I see."

But Parris knew that she didn't see. No one would. They would all assume that something was going on. That at night they slipped into each other's bed, shared hot, wet kisses in a tangle of arms and legs, hers spread to give him room. And they'd cry out each other's names in a language that only they could understand. That's what everyone would think. And she would look only at the ground when she came out in the morning barely saying hello to the neighbors who sat in judgment about things they didn't know.

"Roommates?"

Parris's neck burned. The heat rose to her cheeks. "Yes, roommates." She should go find Nick.

"I got the impression it was more than that."

"Why!" Her voice crested in agitation. "Is it so hard to believe that a man and woman can share a space and not be involved?"

"I'm sorry. I'm sorry. I didn't mean to imply anything. Sometimes I talk before I think. Bad habit." She drew in a breath and released her apology. "It's just that the way you are with each other." With a short huff she adjusted her bag again as if it had gained weight.

The words were delivered as a statement of fact. An undeniable truth, direct and sincere, leaving Parris no choice but to accept it. In doing so she allowed a seed of trust to take root.

"Why do you say that?"

Celeste glanced up. She looked Parris directly in the eyes, so intensely that Parris took an involuntary step back. "The way you move in unison, but still apart. You're together and still give each other space. Symbiotic." The corner of her thin mouth jerked in time to the shrug of her shoulder. "A vibe, that's all." She began foraging around in her purse again.

"What are you looking for?" she asked, amusement in each distinct word.

Celeste flushed. "Truthfully? Nothing really. I always start digging in my bag when I'm nervous and blurt out stupid crap that's none of my business."

The guileless confession reached down inside Parris and wiggled around between her ribs until she broke out in bottomless laughter. The sound was so sudden and alive that it leaped into Celeste's opened mouth of surprise.

Their laughter rippled and danced the two-step around the overturned chairs and tables, doubling them over from the simple pleasure of it.

"What's so funny?" Nick looked from one face to the other—both were almost identical in joy.

Their laughter simmered to bursts of bubbles as they sniffed and wiped damp eyes.

"I don't know," they said in unison, looked at each other and took up the chorus again.

Nick shook his head. "Some kind of woman thing," he muttered.

"Ooooh, whew." Parris dabbed at her damp eyes.

"I haven't had a good one like that in ages." Celeste sniffed. "Humph." She drew in a breath to steady herself then turned her amused gaze on Nick. "What do you think?"

He took a step over to Parris, who was slowly pulling herself together, and looked down at her a moment before sliding his arm possessively around her waist. She gazed up at him, her brows knitted in question. Nick focused on Celeste.

"We'll take it."

It took every ounce of self-discipline and years of "coming out" classes and daily admonishments from her mother on proper decorum to keep Celeste from leaping right up in Nick's arms.

"You're sure?" she asked instead of something appropriate to the joy of her first sale.

"Yes, very sure."

Parris's subtle "I told you so" smile settled the raging butterflies and confirmed that his answer was real and not imagined.

"I'll get the papers drawn up and give you a call when

they're ready." She stuck out her hand. "Congratulations." She pumped his hand. "It shouldn't take more than a week."

"Great."

Parris leaned up and kissed him on the cheek. "Congratulations," she whispered. "I think it's perfect."

His gaze dipped into her soul and stirred it. "So do I."

Celeste stood a bit to the side, watching the exchange, nothing sexual but more intimate than if they'd stripped bare for each other. It was natural and easy and she envied the moment. She and Clinton Avery had been a couple for three years. They were engaged to be married and never in all that time did she ever feel what she felt in Nick and Parris's presence.

The sudden realization startled her before settling down to an acute sadness. Her life had been spent in the requisite two-parent home. Anything she'd ever wanted was hers for simply being the only daughter of Corrine and Ellis Shaw. Although she'd been showered with clothes, the best education, the right friends, cars and money, affection—at least outward affection—had been missing.

But until now she didn't know or care. Her parents never touched or passed soft looks between them and she mimicked their life with her own. And it was then that something flared inside her. An emotion so foreign she couldn't give it a name. She'd never wanted for anything in her life. But she wanted what they had. She wanted to know what it felt like to have someone look at her with adoration—not possession—to hold her as if she might break, not because it looked good on camera. She wanted laughter to bubble up like uncorked champagne, not the artificial sound of practiced humor with delicate hands covering mouths. Laughter like the kind she'd shared with Parris and sometimes Leslie. And she thought perhaps being with them, that what they had, the magic that she coveted, could be hers, too.

They both turned toward her and the spell was broken. Celeste blinked away the hunger in her eyes and spoke into her purse.

"If you're done looking around I guess we can go." She glanced up.

Nick checked his watch. "Wow, I didn't realize how late it was." He turned to Parris. "I need to catch up with Sammy. I can drop you off at the apartment if you want."

Samuel "Sammy" Blackstone was one of Nick's best friends and a member of the band since its inception. Their years together dated back further than either could remember. They each had a different version of how they'd met that varied with the occasion and the company they were in.

"If you're in a hurry I can take Parris. If it's okay," she said to Parris.

"Sure, if you don't mind." Parris offered a smile of surprised gratitude.

"Not a problem."

They walked out, almost in step.

# Chapter Four

Parris settled herself into the lush interior of the Jaguar that still smelled like the showroom. "This was really nice of you to drive me."

"It's not a problem. I'm done for today."

"I'm pretty much on my own, too."

Celeste flashed her a look as she pulled out into traffic. "Hungry?"

"Starved."

They laughed in time to a Billy Joel tune that Parris realized she liked.

The wind had kicked up a notch and the clouds overhead were thick pearl-gray threats by the time they found a parking spot at Amsterdam Avenue and 110th Street. They stepped out of the cozy warmth of the car and the easy conversation

into the backhand of cold air that lifted skirts and sent ciga-
rette butts flipping and tumbling down the street like un-
trained acrobats.

Parris pulled the collar of her short wool jacket up around
her neck. Even though she'd lived in New York for a few years,
she still hadn't gotten used to the onset of the bitter winters
and days so cold that people could actually freeze to death on
the street. Those lost souls, whose only source of warmth was
the grates that covered the underground railroad, a macabre
symbol of freedom in a way that could be as treacherous as life-
saving. Ironic if you thought about it.

Celeste hooked her arm through Parris's as if they were good
old best girlfriends and led her toward Mira's, a bistro where
students from Columbia University hung out between classes.

The heavy glass-and-wood door swooshed closed behind
them, securing them in a warm vacuum. Voices buzzed and
forks clinked against plates at tables populated by bespectacled
and studious types mixed in with those who wandered the halls
of ivy simply because they could afford to do so.

The air held the aroma of well-done burgers and fries
drowned in ketchup, and there were conversations of politics,
unreasonable professors, ski junkets to Aspen, celebrity falls
from grace and dreams of summer.

"Stay or go?" a worn-out-looking waitress asked.

"Staying," Celeste said.

"Right this way." She led them around the table to a vacant
two-seater in the rear, giving them a bird's-eye view of the
comings and goings.

Parris and Celeste shrugged out of their coats and settled
into their seats.

The reluctant hostess placed two plastic-coated menus in front of them. "Someone will take your orders shortly."

Celeste leaned across the table, her voice a pseudo whisper. "The food is much better than the service. I promise. I used to come here when I was an undergrad. Not much has changed." She opened her menu.

"You attended Columbia?"

Celeste nodded. "Yep. Class of '02. Barely," she added with a wink.

"I sense there's a story behind that." Parris checked out the menu while waiting for Celeste's response.

"Let's just say that my stay at Columbia was checkered at best. I could have been a good student but I didn't need to be. My parents paid for one of the libraries, the Shaw Research Center."

Parris's eyes widened. "Oh."

"Hmm. So needless to say many of my professors turned a blind eye to my barely passing grades and missing reports, excessive absences…"

Parris's sense of perfect pitch registered that the cavalier statement held undertones of melancholy and possibly regret. She angled her head to the side. "Why, Celeste? I mean, so many people would love the chance to go to a university like Columbia."

Celeste sighed and put down the menu that separated them. "I've asked myself that question a million times." She raised and lowered her shoulders while slowly shaking her head, the combination an outward display of her inner confusion.

"Any answers?"

"What can I get you ladies?" the waitress asked, cutting off Celeste's response.

"The burgers are the best," Celeste recommended.

"Fine. I'll have mine medium well with cheddar cheese and a side of fries."

"Make that two."

The waitress picked up the menus with a promise that the wait would not be long.

Parris turned her attention back to Celeste, curious about this woman who had so much and couldn't care less. She didn't want to believe that she was like so many that floated through life on a pass and on the backs of those who were truly deserving.

"Tell me why an obviously rich kid is skulking around in depressed neighborhoods peddling property when you could be doing a million other things?" Parris asked, sensing that she wasn't going to get an answer to her first question.

Celeste reached for the comfort of her purse. "I wanted to do something meaningful."

Parris arched a brow of doubt. "Then why not work in a shelter, or travel to the Sudan, or build a school or something?"

Celeste huffed. "I do what I do because it makes my parents cringe." She laughed.

"What? You're kidding."

"No. Not at all." She took a long swallow from her glass of lukewarm water. She glanced at Parris above the rim. "What?"

"Are they that bad?" She couldn't imagine herself doing something intentionally spiteful to upset Cora or David.

"My parents are the poster children for 'upper crust.' Their entire world revolves around appearances and protocol," she said with disgust.

Parris leaned back. "But you benefit from all of it."

Celeste didn't flinch. "I do and I'm not ashamed of it. My family's money has provided me with things that most people only read about or see on television. The best schools, clothes, my own car and apartment at eighteen. I've always had the right *things* in my life." Her intense gaze drifted off, her expression settled to one of resignation. She drew in a breath, pushing the images aside, and turned her head slowly toward Parris. She wrapped her hands around her glass. "I suppose in these days of terrorism," she whispered, "I would be considered a subversive." She sputtered a light laugh. "Dismantling the system from within so to speak. The system being my family." She raised the glass, as if in a toast, before finishing off the water.

"You're serious?"

"Very. Look around you. Look at what's happening to families, the country. That's not the doing of those guys on the street corner or the local grocer who can barely make his lease payment just to be able to stock rotten vegetables. Or the family who lost their home and their savings. It's because of people like Corrine and Ellis Shaw. My family owns several luxury hotels and a string of run-down apartments. They help to keep down the very people they claim to abhor. What I do, trying to bring life back to some of these areas, is to return what the Shaws have taken."

She spewed her parents' names with such contempt that Parris almost felt sorry for them, sorry for parents who'd given birth to a child that obviously loathed them or at the very least what they stood for.

"I can't change every household but I can sure as hell put mine through the ringer. I want to be for my mother and father a shining example of what money can't buy."

Celeste tossed her blond hair away from her face and Parris would have sworn she saw the sparkle of tears in her eyes. But Celeste, she was quickly beginning to see, was a master of disguise. She wondered if Corrine and Ellis had any idea who their daughter really was.

"What about your folks?" Celeste dipped a French fry in a tiny pool of ketchup that she'd meticulously crafted around the rim of her plate that led to thick red rivers surrounding her burger, pickle and coleslaw.

Parris tore her gaze away from the Picasso-like concoction and focused on Celeste. All her life the question that had been asked so many times only required the same practiced answers. My mother gave up her life for me, 'cause she loved me so much. And my daddy couldn't live without her and disappeared. My Grandma Cora and Granddad David raised me with more love that any one child could ever need.

That was the story she'd told from the time she was old enough to tell it, until she became too old for most folks she ran across to ask or care.

None of the lie was true any longer. She had yet to say the words out loud to anyone besides Granddad and Nick. No one. Not even her best friend Gina, who she'd yet to call and tell of her return.

The letters had a hard time finding their way together to form words that made sense to a stranger. But maybe this stranger, who was a mass of contradictions and misfit pieces, who thrived on comeuppance, would be the one person to understand her rage, her shame and her guilt.

Celeste sipped loudly through her straw, a polite slap in the face to Ms. Manners. "You don't have to answer. To tell you the truth, I dislike talking about my parents almost as much as I dislike them, period." She popped an ice cube in her mouth and crunched.

"Actually I believed my mother was dead until about a month ago."

Celeste stopped chewing. She picked up her napkin and daintily dabbed at the corners of her mouth. "Why?"

That was the question that crept up on her, that sat on her shoulder, whispered in her ear, formed the images of her dreams. It was the question she sought the answer to between the fine lines on the yellowed, cracked pages, in the bottom of the red tin can, on the last fleeting breath that Cora took, in the solace of the church. She'd looked everywhere. Until she finally accepted that any hope for an answer would only be found thousands of miles away.

"It's what I need to find out."

"O-kay." The pendulum of her gaze finally settled and squinted at Parris as if to get her response in line with the image in front of her. "The Shaws paid a small fortune to educate their little girl. I have to brag, I'm no dummy, but I must have missed something."

Parris tightened her lips in contemplation. She'd already said enough to have the question remain a lingering epitaph to whatever relationship they may or may not forge. She was bound to run into Celeste again, even if only in her thoughts.

She began slowly revealing as much as she could from the fragments of letters, and her grandmother's halting words, to mesh with what she'd always imagined.

Celeste remained attentively silent while Parris spoke, carried along by the filaments of hope and wistful longing that strung together the painful tale of rejection. As she listened she heard her own story. The story of a girl turned woman, who desperately wanted the love and acceptance of the only person who really mattered. Perhaps together they could find what they sought—meaning for their existence.

"Can I get you anything else?" The waitress hovered, breaking the tenuous bond that had formed.

Identical looks fell upon the inquiring face. "No," they responded in unison. She dropped the check in the center of the table, which they both ignored.

"What if you can't find her?" Celeste asked.

Parris settled back into her seat, pushed the remnants of her food around on her plate. "I can't think that I won't."

The intensity of Parris's gaze and the strength of her conviction, like magnets, drew Celeste forward. "What if she tells you what you don't want to hear?"

"Like what?"

"That she chose her way of life over you. Are you prepared for that?"

Parris looked away. It was a question she'd asked herself but never listened for the answer. "I don't know."

Celeste placed her hands on the table. Her fingertips pressed into the plastic place mat. "I asked my mother once."

"Asked her what?"

"Why she didn't love me."

Parris's stomach knotted. "What did she say?"

"She just looked at me with that superior expression, laughed and told me I was being dramatic."

The pain of rejection fluttered beneath the pale cheeks, drew the lips into a line of resolution and the eyes into wells of acceptance.

Parris reached across the table and stilled the drumming fingers. "Some people find it hard to say how they feel."

Celeste forced a smile. She tugged in a long breath. "When do you leave?"

"Next week."

Celeste took her wallet out of her bag. "I hope everything works out for you." She placed two twenties on top of the bill. "Ready?"

No, not really, she thought. But it was too late now.

"Thanks for lunch," Parris said once they'd pulled in front of Nick's apartment building.

Celeste turned halfway in her seat. "I should be thanking you."

Parris frowned. "For what?"

"For listening to my rants." She tucked a lock of hair behind her ear. "And not saying I was crazy even if you thought so."

"My grandmother taught me better than that," she teased.

Their laughter bound them in understanding.

"Hey," Celeste said softly, her words embraced by uncertainty, "when you get back…and get everything straight with your mother…maybe we can get together."

"I'd like that," Parris said without hesitation, pleasantly surprising them both.

Celeste glowed. She dug in her bag for her wallet, pulled out a business card and wrote her cell number on the back. She handed it to Parris. "Call. Whenever you're ready."

Parris took the act of friendship and tucked it in her bag. "I will." She opened the car door and stepped out, then turned back to Celeste. "Don't do anything crazy while I'm gone."

"Me!" she said, feigning offense. "I wouldn't dream of it."

Parris used the spare key that Nick had given her and let herself in. It was so strange walking into his apartment as if she really lived there. Although it had only been one night she felt a comfort in the newness.

She placed the key on the rectangular table beneath the

black-and-white photograph of Miles Davis at the Newport Jazz Festival as she'd noticed Nick do the night before. She didn't know quite what to make of Celeste Shaw. She was certainly different from anyone she'd met before. And she didn't think it had anything to do with her being white. Although her limited relationships with white women were relegated to the workplace and on television, it wasn't that. Celeste Shaw was simply different—in an interesting way. She was an amalgam of contradictions that made her often outrageous declarations all the more fascinating.

Parris shook her head in mild amusement as she took off her coat. Now what to do with herself, she wondered as she walked in the direction of her room. She wasn't hungry. She wasn't sleepy. She turned halfway and went back toward the front where Nick kept all of his stereo equipment and incredible collection of music.

She browsed the shelves of albums and CDs. She found *Betty Carter's Greatest Hits,* which included duets with Ray Charles. She put the album on the turntable. The grooves hissed seductively beneath the tease of the needle and the husky timbre of the Godmother of Jazz filtered into the room and wrapped her in the security blanket of every perfect note.

Parris wandered over to the well-worn couch that had a faded cream-colored fabric. She sank down into the surprisingly cushiony pillows, kicked off her shoes and tucked her feet beneath her.

Humming along to the familiar refrain, "Baby, It's Cold Outside," she rested her head on the armrest and closed her eyes. The lyrics played with her, taunted, soothed and carried her off to that place that was all her own. The world she'd created as a child sitting by the Left Hand River listening to the melody of the cicadas, making time with the bass beat of the bullfrog, serenaded by the sweet soprano of the mockingbird, smoothed and blended by the gentle brush of water over rocks and the rustling leaves of the willow sizzling under the Mississippi sun.

*Parris…Parris…*

The light was so bright against her eyes. Her eyes flickered open.

"Hey, sleepyhead."

It took a moment for her thoughts to clear. She struggled to sit up.

She ran her fingers through the spirals as the final notes of Betty Carter's "People Will Say We're In Love" drifted away.

Nick lowered himself down next to her.

"So Celeste got you back here safe and sound," he said.

"We went to lunch."

"Lunch?" His brows rose. "Really? How did that happen?"

Parris smiled at the look of disbelief on his face. "We were both hungry so we went to get something to eat."

Nick's brow wrinkled.

"She's really…interesting, for lack of a better word."

"I kind of picked up on that. What I'm trying to figure out is what you two could possibly have to talk about."

The confessions and secrets that they'd shared over juicy burgers and crispy fries drowning in rivers of red would only be understood by the ones who'd spoken them.

"Hmm, girl stuff." She stood and stretched her tight limbs. "So aren't you excited about your new place? What did Sammy say?" she asked, steering the conversation.

Nick's dark eyes lit from beneath. "He's probably more excited than I am. He'd always been pushing me to get out from under Percy." He stood and paced the room as he spoke. "This is what I've dreamed of, worked for." He shook his head. "I still can't believe it. And I probably won't until the papers are signed and we have our grand opening." He turned to her. "With you as the star."

Parris stuck her hands in the back pockets of her jeans. "There's a lot of work to be done before then."

"I know. But if we can get everything in place, a contractor, proper licenses, I think we can be ready by July. That's what I'm aiming for. Sammy knows some people and I'm sure Leslie will be on board. We're going to need a staff…."

Parris held up her hand. "Let's figure out the staff thing and how you're going to advertise and where. And you need to apply for your liquor license immediately."

Nick blew out a breath. "I know, I'm running ahead of myself. Did Celeste mention when the paperwork would be ready while you two were having your 'girl talk'?"

Parris chuckled. "Let's go over your business plan and work out a checklist in order of priority."

Nick spread his arms wide. "I'm all yours."

Her neck heated.

He moved toward her and the world around them seemed to vanish. All she could see was Nick. The bottomless darkness of his eyes, the soft shadow of his beard that outlined his rugged jaw, the expanse of his chest barely contained in the black T-shirt, and the scent of him that loosened her muscles and lightened her head.

Nick touched that hot spot on her neck, sending heat rushing through her limbs.

"This is for us," he said, his voice low and thick, like the bottom note on the sax. "Everything I do now is for us. Me and you. You need to know that, understand what it is that I'm saying."

Her heart hammered, raising her shirt up off her chest with its pounding. "Tell me."

His eyes glided over her face. His lips parted. "In time." He kissed her lightly on the mouth. "In time." He took her hand. "Come on, let's make that list."

As he led her down the hall toward his office, Parris wasn't sure if she was relieved or disappointed; only that one day the time would be right for both of them.

"You're staying with Nick?" Gina squealed through the phone. "I can't believe it."

"Me, either," Parris confessed. She leaned against the headboard and crossed her ankles. It was so good hearing Gina's voice again. They'd been the two most unlikely people to become friends but they had, much to the delight of the office gossips, as it provided them with more watercooler fodder. Gina had developed a reputation for being "loose," because she always boasted about her hot dates. No one really knows when all the rumors started, but Parris discovered it was far from the truth. If anything Gina was simply lonely and looking for attention, and a real friend. Parris and Gina didn't care what other people thought. If anything the alienation from the staffers drew the two closer together.

"So...have you two...you know?"

Parris giggled. "No. We haven't...you know," she replied to her friend.

Gina sighed. "Girl, that fine man gave up a business, packed his bags and came way the hell down to nobody never heard of Rudell, Mississippi, to be with you during one of the hardest times of your life and you haven't jumped all over him! Girl," she admonished.

Parris chuckled even as she realized how right Gina was. But so much had been happening to both of them, and she was sure that when the time was right they would both know it. The last thing she wanted to do was tumble into a physical relationship with Nick for all the wrong reasons.

Gina switched gears and brought Parris up to date on the happenings at the office. "Frank is still obnoxious. You don't know how happy I am that you're out of that relationship. No good would have ever come from it. He wanted to control you, control your life."

Even while Parris was in the short-lived relationship with Frank, the warning bells of trouble were like oncoming head-lights destined for a collision. The end was tragic and inevitable. "All water under the bridge."

"Which is why I can't understand why you haven't crossed the line with Nick."

"I told you why."

"Uh, beep, wrong answer. No, you didn't."

Parris emitted an exaggerated sigh. "For the better part of the time that I've known Nick, his life has been entangled with someone else's. You know that. He was seeing Tara when we met, not to mention that he was in partnership with her father, Percy. The both of them were pulling strings from every angle. And I was dating Frank—for all that was worth," she added with disgust in her voice. It was true that the tug between her and Nick was undeniable from the moment she laid eyes on him. They'd done everything short of draw a line in the sand to keep them from acting on how they felt. Until that one time. It was innocent. She'd just come off the stage totally elated from her performance and the thundering response from the audience...

*They'd opened with a jazz medley of tunes by Cole Porter, then segued to a collection of songs by Duke Ellington, tossed in some classics from the pen of Gershwin, then changed the tempo with a Chaka Khan ballad, "Your Love is All I Know," and closed with an original composition by Nick, written especially for Parris's range and versatility, called "Since I Met You, Nothing Seems the Same."*

*The applause was deafening, vibrating the walls, the glass, then slipping out the door to dance on the street and finally running back inside to start all over again.*

*Parris did three encores, and the crowd couldn't seem to get enough. Finally she made it to her dressing room as the band played their closing theme, elation running through her in waves that kept her pacing back and forth across the floor, reliving every instant of the set. Something had happened out there. She'd felt it. She'd become one with every note, every dip and curve. She was the music.*

*"Parris, Parris." Nick rushed through the door. "Baby, you did it. I just finished talking with Newhouse. He wants to meet you on Monday."*

*"Oh, Nick. I can't believe it." Her voice cracked with emotion.*

*"Believe it. Here's his card." He handed the card to her, and she stared at it in wonder.*

*"This is for real, Parris. I told you that you would do it. I knew it!"*

*Spontaneously, Parris threw her arms around him, and he hugged her to him in return. The moment was simple and pure as they let their happiness spill from one to the other. Then suddenly, the mood, the reason for the embrace, shifted. They were no longer two people simply sharing a moment, they were a man and woman who had fought day in and out to keep a seal on their emotions for each other.*

*He held her a bit tighter, burying his face in the pillow of her hair.... She trembled in his arms...a soft moan escaped her lips. He leaned back and looked down into her face.*

*"Parris, I—"*

*"What the hell is this!"*

*Nick pulled back, not completely releasing Parris's waist.*

*Tara stood in the doorway, her face a mask of injured fury. She stalked across the room.*

*"Tara, it's not what you think," Parris began.*

*"Shut the hell up, bitch. I've had about enough of your shit since you and your country ass came to town."*

*"Tara!" Nick shouted, his face contorted into barely contained rage.*

*"You—don't you dare. You have the nerve to do this to me—with her." Tara's voice rose to a screeching pitch. "If it wasn't for me and my daddy's money, you would still be a no-name musician running from club to club trying to put two dimes together."*

*"That's enough, Tara."*

*"You wasn't nothin' then, and you still ain't nothin'," she ranted on, pacing back and forth in front of them, pointing and tossing her head in dramatic fashion. "I made you, and I can unmake you. One call from me to my father and you're finished, do you hear me! You think I'm gonna sit still and watch this little no-talent, country hick mess up my life, take what's mine. Hell, no. I'd rather see you dead first."*

*"There's nothing going on between me and Nick, Tara. There never was and never will be. You can't always believe what you see," she said, with a calmness that belied the fury and humiliation she felt for herself and for Nick. "I came here for one reason and one reason alone, but you'd never understand that."*

*She snatched up her coat and purse and brushed past Tara and out the door.*

*"Parris, wait."*

*She turned, looked from one to the other. "I think you both have some things to work out." She closed the door quietly behind her and slipped out of the club unnoticed....*

The next time she saw Nick was when he'd arrived in

Rudell for her grandmother's funeral. He'd severed his ties with both of them the same night. Her only regret was that she hadn't been there to see it.

"I suppose you're right," Gina said, easing into Parris's thoughts and pushing them aside. "It does show what kind of man Nick is."

Parris drew in a short breath, cleared her head.

"It does." Nick was a man like her grandfather—hardworking, determined, a man of loyalty and principles. Even in the murkiness that her life had dissolved into it was clear that she'd been blessed with examples to live up to, base her opinions and ideals on, know what she should and should not accept in life and in love. She also knew that the very same examples and teachings were the shackles that were holding her in place.

"While I was back home I found out some things about… my mother."

"Your mother? What kind of things?"

"She's not dead," she began and unwound her story over Gina's stunned gasp. She told about the letters and the revelations her grandmother made.

"Oh, Parris. I don't know what to say. All this time…" Her voice drifted off and in the momentary pause Parris sensed that her friend was thinking the same thing she was; how could a mother do that to her child and why?

"What are you going to do?"

"I leave for France next week."

"What! Just like that? Does she even know you're coming?"

"No."

"Do you know where she lives?"

"No. Not exactly."

"Well, is Nick going with you at least?"

"No."

"Parris! You can't just fly off in search of your long lost mother all alone. I know this is important to you but be realistic. What if you can't find her? You have no way of knowing if that address is any good." Her voice continued to climb the scales. "And if you are lucky enough to find her, what if she won't see you? Have you thought of that?"

She'd thought of all those things. In her dreams she enacted every possible scenario, except the ending. It was like those falling-off-a-cliff dreams. You fall and fall, hurtling through the dark unknown, only to be awakened seconds before what would seem inevitable. You survive the fall. And whatever this trip did or didn't do she would survive the fall.

"I know there's no point in wasting my time trying to change your mind especially since you have a nonrefundable ticket."

They laughed.

"You just make sure you see me before you go head off to parts unknown."

"I will."

"And try to get some for the road."

"Gina! You haven't changed a bit."

"That's why you love me. Talk to you soon."

Parris was getting the hang of this playing house thing. She looked forward to Nick's music coaxing her out of sleep. The scent of him. His laughter. The weight of his presence that took up space that she wanted to share with him.

They talked every chance they got, about anything and nothing. It didn't matter. They riffed off the sound of each other's voices.

When she went to bed at night, she'd watch the light beneath her door blocked by the shadow of his footfalls. "'Night," he would call out but never come in. "'Night," she'd reply and wish that he would. He was waiting for a sign from her telling him that it was all right, that she wanted more than the platonic ideal they'd created. She knew that even as she tentatively knocked on his door the night before she was to leave.

Nick opened the door and her heart stopped beating. The air stumbled in her lungs. The darkness of his eyes was that endless stretch of blackness as she fell through the night toward the inevitable. She would survive. Nick would catch her.

"I…"

He took her hand. "Don't talk. Don't explain."

Gently he pulled her inside and shut the door behind them.

Parris awoke not to the strains of Coltrane but the steady beat of Nick's heart. A flood of peaceful warmth flowed through her, delivering a smile of raw happiness to her mouth. His hard, muscled thigh was draped over her, pinning her to bare flesh. Her senses preened. The air was filled with the scent of them. Heady, muggy, telling.

Nick groaned softly. He nestled her closer. The heat between her thighs pulsed like live wires. She still felt him there, memorized the way he'd loved her—slow, urgent, deep and long. Her muscles hummed with pleasure and as she drifted off to the rhythm of his heart and the warmth of his breath brushing against her hair, she knew why she'd waited.

Parris squeezed Nick's hand as they walked through the doors of JFK airport. Her flight was due to leave in two hours. She wanted to spend every second of it with him, but that was impossible.

"Sure you have everything—passport, wallet, cell phone, something to read?" he added with a half smile.

"Yes." She gripped his hand tighter.

"You'll call me as soon as you land?"

"I promise." She struggled not to cry.

They were next in line.

"Where will you be flying to today?" the cheery reservationist asked.

Parris swallowed over the sting in her throat. "France."

"Are you traveling also, sir?"

Nick and Parris exchanged a look filled with a million questions. "No," he answered.

He curled his arm around her waist and tenderly kissed the top of her head as she handed over her documents and got her boarding pass in return.

They walked together as far as security would allow him to go.

"I'll call you as soon as I can."

He brushed her cheek with his fingertips and her eyes fluttered for a moment. "I'll be waiting."

Parris joined the security line, glancing back over her shoulder as Nick's image drew farther away until she couldn't see him at all. A moment of panic gripped her. What was she doing? This was crazy and impulsive. There was no guarantee that Emma still lived in Paris at the thirty-year-old address. This was a mistake. But like lemmings drawn to the edge, she kept moving until she was walking down the aisle, finding her seat, holding her breath as the world disappeared and she soared into the clouds.

## Chapter Five

Celeste turned the key, opening the door to exquisite nothingness. The abyss was alive, traveling along the champagne-toned silk drapes, woven into the threads of the imported Turkish rugs that drew one's attention to the gleaming teak wood floors, out to the imported antique furniture, upward to the vaulted ceilings. Her emptiness echoed with each footstep, leaving a scent of Chanel in its wake.

Most days the void didn't consume her. Today wasn't a sensation, it was a physical weight that draped her shoulders and clung to her ankles, curving her back and sucking her feet into the mire.

Thunder rumbled in the distance, muffling the sound of the phone. It took a moment for her to register the ringing. She dropped her bag on the oxblood leather couch and reached for the phone on the end table. The caller ID highlighted the number. Briefly she shut her eyes in annoyance, steeled her emotions and picked up the receiver.

"Hello, Mother."

"You would think that with caller ID you could at least pretend to sound happy to hear from me," Corrine Shaw chastised.

There was no point in debating the issue or insisting that Corrine was wrong. She wasn't. Celeste opted for silence, her strongest weapon.

"I'm calling to remind you about tomorrow night."

Celeste fought and failed to contain her sigh.

"It's important for both you and Clinton to meet these people."

"Important to who, you and Dad? Not me."

"You have no idea what's important."

*Here it comes.*

"That's apparent by this...this job." Her mother sputtered the word as if she'd eaten dirt. "It's beneath you. Beneath us. What will my friends say? Of course you don't care," she continued, stealing Celeste's retort. "But I do. Your father does. We have a reputation. This family has a legacy to uphold."

*Begun by your grandfather,* Celeste recited in her mind, rolling her eyes. She'd stopped listening to her mother's rant. It never changed. *The legacy, the reputation, popular opinion, her disrespect, worthlessness, on and on.*

"Celeste!"

Celeste flinched. "Yes?"

"Eight tomorrow. And please be on time."

"Goodbye, Mother. I'll see you tomorrow." She hung up before Corrine could launch into another monologue. The five-minute conversation had successfully drained her of whatever strength she had left.

She took off her shoes and went down the long corridor that featured a Rembrandt, a Picasso and a John Biggers just to piss off her mother.

Maybe a glass of wine and a mindless evening of surfing the cable stations would lift her from her growing malaise.

She should be ecstatic. She'd landed her first deal. The papers were all but signed. Money would change hands soon. She'd finally accomplished something on her own, without the prerequisite of her family name.

Suddenly weary she turned toward her bed and noticed the flashing red light. She pressed the message button and Clinton's voice reached out through the phone lines.

"I'll be working late tonight, sweetheart, but I thought I'd stop by, stay over. Call me."

Next to her mother, her fiancé Clinton was the last person she was in the mood to see. The heavy sigh took what little she had left and dumped her on the bed. She stretched out and stared at the off-white ceiling. She tried to pinpoint when she'd begun to feel so utterly disconnected, her usual fire reduced to soot. She knew Corrine was partly to blame. She had a knack for bringing out the worst in her, which didn't take much. Corrine also knew how to make her feel like an incompetent child again, one constantly in the throes of a temper tantrum.

But it was more than that. She'd lived within the vise of her mother's grasp for nearly three decades. She was only able to break free during her college years by getting to know other cultures, different ethnicities, people from all walks of life, something that her grandfather had quietly encouraged, much to her mother's dismay. She'd often question the credo that her parents and their circle lived by—those that didn't have, weren't worthy of attention. In the minds of the Shaws, wealth was privilege without responsibility. She'd learned how to protect herself from being punctured too deeply by her mother's caustic tongue. So it wasn't that. What she'd begun to realize during the past few days was that this engulfing sensation of doubt about the validity of her life and her own happiness had come into question again after meeting Parris McKay and Nick Hunter. What she saw in them was a possibility that she'd never imagined, a realness that for her entire existence had eluded her.

Over the years, she'd thrown stones at the glass window of her wealth and status, from her choice of friends to working a real job. She hadn't walked away from the shards of glass but pretended to walk over them, like some mystic traversing a bed of nails and not getting hurt. But she had been hurt, little by little, and as she was diminished her resentment at herself grew. Resentment over her weakness to leave behind the things she professed to deplore. She was trapped by the trappings, and the fear of what life would be like without them held her in place.

When she met Nick and Parris she also met an unrecognizable part of herself—envy, an emotion that never before had a place in her life. She wanted what they had and she wanted Parris's courage to face the unknown.

She had neither. That realization was at the core of her current state of ambivalence. Until she found the way and the will to combat it she'd continue to dance off beat to their music.

The doorbell rang at ten. Since Celeste had arrived home she'd gone through the rituals of preparing for Clinton's arrival. When she opened the door she transformed into the only Celeste that he knew.

"Hello, sweetheart." He leaned down from his six-foot height and kissed her briefly on the lips, before breezing inside.

Clinton Avery was the only son of William and Phyllis Avery, heir to a multimillion dollar fortune built on oil and shipping that dated back three generations. Clinton, like Celeste, had been groomed in the world of "better than." His education had been mapped out before he was born. When William and Phyllis decided the time was right for a child, they'd begun the application process to all of the elite nursery schools in the city. Nothing would ever be too good for their child. It never was. Up to and including forging an alliance with his golf and country club buddy Ellis Shaw and the promise they'd made to each other on the eighteenth hole to wed their children and secure their fortunes.

And Clinton reeked of Ivy League privilege from the cut of his naturally blond hair and his tailored Italian suits, down to the spit polish of his wingtips. Clinton, easily mistaken for a young Robert Redford or a Brad Pitt of *Troy* fame, was, if nothing else, good to look at. He was highly versed in the most obscure facts, which would make him an ideal candidate for *Jeopardy!*, but of course that wasn't becoming of an Avery. His family's inherent snobbishness was inextricably tied to old Connecticut money, the musty smell an aphrodisiac to the nouveau riche. However, beneath the expensive suits and two-hundred-dollar haircuts, and a zealous belief that money can buy you everything, he was really a good guy. And all the money he spent on mastering the art of tantric sex was worth his company.

They'd been officially seeing each other for three years. In their world of rarified air, "seeing each other" meant that you'd been photographed by the press, seen at all the major events together and shared a secret getaway that all the right people knew about. When asked if "you're an item," you look at each other adoringly and say "no comment." The goal, of course, was not to quell curiosity but to stoke it.

Her best friend, Leslie, barely tolerated Clinton "and his ilk," although she barely tolerated anyone. But according to her, Clinton was too full of his own nonimportance.

"I'm bushed." Clinton loosened his tie, dropped his brief-case in the foyer and went straight for the bar. "Bitch of a day," he groused, moving bottles to find the cognac, his drink of choice. "Fix you one?" He held up a short tumbler in question.

"No, thanks."

"Do you know that in less than a decade the white race will be the minority?" He tossed down a deep swallow and she watched his cheeks glow from the inside. His lips pursed.

Celeste knew that the question, like most of Clinton's questions, was rhetorical. He simply phrased his statements as questions to give one the impression of being included in the conversation.

"Hmm," she murmured before staking out her spot on the couch. Clinton loved making love on the couch. It was almost as if he considered it somehow decadent. She watched his sea-blue eyes darken as he approached her. "I saw on the news that the market took another dive."

He nodded. His jaw clenched. "A bloody mess." He took another swallow of his drink and sat down beside her. His hand caressed her bare thigh. "Things are bad all over. Even with all of our diversification we've already been hit hard." His hand inched higher.

Celeste allowed her mind to wander while Clinton prattled on about futures and industrial averages. She had no intention of interrupting him as long as he was making every nerve ending of her body jump and sizzle. She couldn't conceive of being without. It didn't factor into her train of thought. But she sensed more than heard Clinton's deep fears of impending doom. His touch, which had been featherlight and electrifying, had become tight and tense with unspoken urgency.

Her gaze settled on him and she saw the tight line of worry that crossed his brow right between the silken locks of hair that dappled his forehead. Clinton was not one to worry about much of anything. Like her he'd been born into wealth and privilege. However, where they differed was that he was deeply invested in the future of his fortune. She simply accepted that hers would always be there. But seeing the distant look in his eyes, and succumbing to the unfamiliar pressure of his touch, perhaps it was time that she paid more attention.

At some point they'd made it to Celeste's bedroom and while she listened to his soft snores of satisfaction, she stared out at nothingness. Sex with Clinton was the one worthwhile perk of their relationship. Tonight even that fell short and she had no idea why. Her feelings of disconnect had invaded her last refuge.

Clinton turned on his side, burying his head in the curve of her neck. She smiled. He was sweet and charming, smart and rich, and from everything that he said and did, he loved her.

Of course, she'd told him as much herself, and at times she almost believed it. But Celeste had no idea what real love felt like, what it looked like. She imagined it was what she saw on television and in the movies and between Parris and Nick. It was an aura, an energy that couldn't be manufactured.

What was that like? Clinton draped his arm across her waist. She closed her eyes and ran a rapid-fire movie of her life with

Clinton, waiting for the spark, that feeling in the center of her being. The movie drifted off without fanfare, without applause, and she'd felt nothing. She needed to know and it suddenly frightened her to think that she may never find out.

The muscles in her stomach clenched and the overwhelming urge to push Clinton to the floor and scream at the top of her lungs was so overwhelming that she trembled. The nerves beneath her skin popped and vibrated. Her heart raced and heat engulfed her. Clinton moaned, turned on his side and away from her. She drew in a strangled breath of freedom.

Tossing the covers aside she eased out of the bed and tiptoed into the bathroom, shutting the door in silence. She leaned against the door, pressed her fist to her mouth and wept.

Celeste braked her Jag at the red light on Lenox Avenue. She pressed speed dial on her cell phone, which was mounted on the dashboard. The phone trilled.

"Hello?"

"Hey, Leslie."

"You just caught me."

Celeste could hear Leslie huffing and wished that she would do something about the extra weight.

"I have to meet a client in about twenty minutes and I'm running late. Another bad morning."

Celeste knew what she meant without having to ask for an explanation. Leslie Evans lived with her mother, Theresa—or rather Theresa lived with her daughter—after Theresa had suffered a stroke a year earlier. The dynamics between mother and daughter had always been strained and this most recent alteration in their relationship put it at the breaking point.

"Have you heard from Nick Hunter?"

"No, should I have?"

"I'm pretty sure he's going to contact you."

"You got it!"

"Yes." She laughed. The light turned green and she moved across the intersection.

"Oh, Celeste, congrats. I'm so happy for you. I knew you could do it. What did Clinton say?"

Her buoyant mood spiraled back down with a crash. "I didn't tell him."

"Cel…" She sighed, heavily. "Anyway, we'll talk. I'll call you tonight."

"Not tonight. Mother has arranged one of her 'festive' gatherings."

They both snorted their disgust. Neither of them would ever forget the disastrous night that Celeste convinced Leslie to come to one of the Shaws' gatherings. She hadn't wanted to go, swore she didn't have anything to wear. Celeste would not be deterred and took Leslie shopping. When they walked in, heads and eyes turned in their direction. The entire evening was filled with condescending questions and comments from where a woman of her size did her shopping, what her parents did for a living, where she had her hair done, to the appalling revelation that Leslie didn't summer in the Hamptons, but rather Coney Island or not at all.

Leslie had never been so humiliated or furious in her life. Celeste was mortified. Needless to say, Leslie made her excuses, claiming a headache, and left early. Celeste spent the next week trying to make it up to her friend, until Leslie clearly informed her that her family and friends were pompous assholes, but she wouldn't hold it against her if she swore never to invite her to anything like that again.

"Try to get through it."

"Don't I always?"

"Call me tomorrow," Leslie said, not missing the lack of bite that usually underscored any mention of "The Shaws" coming from Celeste.

"I will." She disconnected the call. She didn't want to think about the evening ahead. The hours of pomp and circumstance, air kisses and enough food to feed a third world country. All the while she would perform as expected, keep her chin lifted to the right height, her eyes sparkling with interest and her laughter pitch perfect. And for her Oscar-winning performance her bank account would receive its monthly infusion of capital, and she would continue to live the life of the consummate hypocrite.

Celeste turned onto the block of the would-be club and looked for a parking space. She was able to squeeze in between a U-Haul truck and a vandalized Volkswagen with missing plates. She turned off the ignition and looked around at the breath of despair that filled the lungs of the corner trio and pushed the residents unwillingly up and down the street.

Her existence, so far removed from this that the experience of being here in the midst of a language and a life she couldn't fathom was equivalent to walking into a foreign land where you were an illegal immigrant. Her gratuitous attempt to bring life back to the dead was only to ease her own conscience so that she could sleep at night in her queen-sized bed nestled on fluffy down pillows and imported cotton sheets.

*You still benefit…why aren't you in the Sudan or building houses…?*

Parris's question buzzed around her like a mosquito. No amount of swatting, ducking or moving from its path could still the insistent, incessant demand for attention.

In her rearview mirror she spotted Nick's car pull onto the block. She took her safety net from the seat and got out, draping the strap over her shoulder. They met in front of the club.

"This is my friend and business partner, Sam Blackstone. Sam, Celeste Shaw."

Sam stuck out his hand and hers was enveloped in a bed of gentle strength and warmth. A flutter danced in the center of her chest when she stumbled into the invitation of his brown eyes and teasing smile.

"Nice to meet you."

"You, too." She buried her gaze in the depths of her purse in search of the key. Her fingers shook as she fumbled with the lock.

Sam took the key from her fingers. "I can do that."

Her heart pounded. She took a step back, feeling foolish and giddy at the same time.

Sam released the locks and opened the door, allowing Celeste to enter first. Her shoulder brushed his chest. The jolt quickened her step. He was right behind her. She felt the heat of his presence press against her back, tickle the hair on her neck.

All of her patented sales lines drifted in and out of her head like a bad cell-phone connection. She opted for silence lest she say something totally inane. She came to the center of the space and turned, only to come face-to-chest with Sam. Her gaze rose upward and his probed her, picking away at the thin layer of facade. She knew standing there would allow him to strip her raw, but she could not move. Maybe she didn't want to.

"What do you think?" Nick asked, coming up on them, giving her the escape she needed but couldn't find on her own. He blew into his cupped hands.

"I'm thinking it has potential." Finally he turned away from Celeste and followed Nick to the back.

Celeste allowed herself to breathe and followed them with her eyes, not trusting her legs, which were suddenly weak. She'd never reacted that way to a man before. Not to Clinton. Not anyone. He was nothing special. An ordinary man. Yet the sweet honey of his eyes, the generous curve of his mouth, the rough-hewed texture of his brown-sugar complexion stirred her deep below the surface. Absently she rubbed her hand where his thumb had brushed her knuckles when he held it.

She adjusted the strap on her purse and jammed her hands in her pockets, then crossed the dimly lit room and took a chair down from a three-legged table and placed it by the murky window. Professionalism dictated that she at least give a semblance of a tour and do her spiel. Nothing was working—her brain or her limbs.

Voices deep and rich drifted toward her, their harmonized camaraderie gave life to the peeling walls and cracked ceiling. They were laughing as they approached, laughing the way only people who know the worst about you can, and still care.

She pushed herself up from her seat, straightened her shoulders. "So," she said on a breath, "what do you think?"

"I think my man here made a good deal." Sam tilted his head to the side. "It's going to need some work." Sweet honey settled on her. "But we can make it work." The corner of his mouth tipped upward. "Neighborhood leaves a lot to be desired."

"It's the same thing I was saying to Nick…Mr. Hunter. This entire area is set for revitalization," she rambled, knowing that she was but unable to stop herself. "In a few more years, you won't be able to buy your way into this neighborhood."

"Time will tell, I'm sure." He turned to Nick. "When is Parris due back?"

Nick's buoyant expression became solemn. "Not really sure."

"Have you heard from her?" Celeste asked.

"No."

"You will." She offered an encouraging smile.

Nick exhaled. "Well, we better get out of here. When will the papers be ready? I can't make a move until they are."

"I'm expecting everything to come through this week. I'll call as soon as they do so that you can come into the office. I know how anxious you are to get started."

"Sam will be coming with me, if he's in town."

She snatched a glance at Sam. "Of course." She ducked into her purse. "If you're ready, I'll lock up." She let them out in front of her while she secured the locks. When she turned, Sam was right behind her.

"Good to meet you."

"You, too."

He extended his hand and she placed hers inside it. Her heart thumped so hard in her chest she grew light-headed.

"I'm sure we'll see each other again." He released her hand and she was able to breathe as she watched him walk toward Nick's car and get in.

For several moments she stood there, even as they drove off, working to get her bearings. Finally, in a state of mild confusion she got in her car, focused on the mechanics of driving and pulled away.

# Chapter Six

As Celeste prepared for her evening under siege with her parents she held on to the wicked image of their appalled expressions if she walked in with Sam Blackstone on her arm instead of Clinton Avery. The smile that she would be able to maintain throughout the ritualistic evening would certainly be due to the anarchy she held in her heart.

Clinton was impeccable as always and for a moment when he stood in the threshold of her doorway, there was a second that Celeste's heart softened, her stomach lifted and a fleeting warmth filled her.

"Hello, sweetheart." The perfunctory kiss on the cheek—something that she'd encouraged long ago to avoid smudging her lipstick—broke the temporary spell of "just imagine." "Ready?" He brushed by her in that long-legged loping stride, simultaneously checking his Rolex watch.

Celeste drew in a breath of resolved frustration, closed the door and followed him inside. He turned upon her approach, his sea-blue eyes cool and discerning.

"You seem happy."

He said the words with the same unfamiliarity that its association had with his fiancée. In the years that he'd known Celeste, been intimate with her in ways he'd never been with another woman, he would describe her in many ways: pretty, intelligent, highly sexual, at times complex, opinionated, but never happy. Celeste was content, if anything. At ease with her life and what her station in life could afford her, much like himself. He supposed that was the equivalent of happy, something they simply took for granted. But he'd never *seen* Celeste *happy.*

"I don't know what you mean." She plucked her mink jacket from the chair and draped it over her arm.

Clinton's brows shrugged off the momentary glitch and he settled back into his comfort zone. "I decided to get a driver for tonight," he said, his breath warm on the back of her neck as he helped her on with her jacket. "So we can really enjoy the evening."

Celeste smiled to herself. That may be the obvious reason, but the real reason was that Clinton was angling to make an impression at her parents' soiree. She couldn't blame him. It's what they did. She turned out the lights and with his guiding hand at the small of her back they started on their evening of predictability.

When the black Lincoln pulled up in front of the Shaws' Park Avenue town house, they were greeted by red-vested valets and a long line of luxury cars. The party was in full swing although Celeste and Clinton had arrived only an hour beyond its start time.

"Your parents always know how to throw a party," Clinton said. "I think I just saw the finance chairman speaking with Senator Collins." The excitement in his voice was barely contained.

"Probably," she said absently. "They're always around." She'd grown up calling most of her parents' inner circle "aunt and uncle" so-and-so. To see the eclectic blend of who's who in the house where she grew up was tantamount to Sunday dinner at Grandma's—no big deal.

Although they'd both come of age under the umbrella of wealth and all it entailed, the Shaws also had political capital where the Averys did not. This salient fact still brought a glimmer of awe to Clinton's eyes.

Celeste glanced across the crowded floor of the main room. There were at least sixty guests milling about, chatting in the airy way that rich people did; all smiles and knowing nods, flashing diamonds, platinum and new figures courtesy of very expensive Park Avenue surgeons.

Corrine gave her daughter a finger wave above the heads of the gathering and motioned for her.

"We're being summoned," Celeste murmured.

He dipped his head in her direction then followed the lift of her chin. "Who's that with your mother?"

"Richard Phillips, he's running for senate."

Clinton straightened his shoulders. "Let's not keep them waiting."

While Celeste smiled and nodded in all the right places, her mother—always the consummate hostess—extolled Clinton's virtues and how well he would one day do in politics.

"What line of work are you in now?" Richard Phillips asked.

"I'm a financial consultant for Ameritrade. My fourth year. I handle the corporate accounts and acquisitions."

He nodded his approval then dug in the breast pocket of his suit jacket and extracted a card. "Stay in touch. Depending on how things go, I may be able to use someone like you on my team."

"Thank you, sir, I like the sound of that." He took the card and gave Phillips one of his own.

"I'd better go mingle," he said to the trio. "Good meeting you, Clinton, and as always it's a pleasure to see you, Celeste."

Corrine turned to the two young people. "These are the kinds of people you need to know, Clinton, if you plan to get ahead in this world."

"I totally agree. I appreciate all of the introductions."

"Have you spoken to your father?"

"We only arrived a few moments before you saw me," Celeste said, feeling immediately defensive. And knowing her mother she was being set up for the onslaught.

"Had you arrived when I asked you to arrive you would have had the opportunity to speak with him before he was bombarded with all of these people vying for his attention. But of course that would never occur to you—to do anything that I ask."

The flame of ridicule began in her ears, spread to her face and down the center of her chest until the heat of her embarrassment engulfed her. Her eyes burned. "I'll go find him."

"I'm sure he's out on the terrace. Heaven only knows why in this chilly weather. I'm sure he's smoking one of those damned cigars." She turned her back on Celeste and hooked her arm through Clinton's, telling him who she wanted him to meet as they walked off. As if Celeste no longer mattered. Maybe she didn't.

As she made her way through the knots of guests, Celeste

was stopped by her "Aunt" Anne, who was happy to see that she hadn't brought that "friend" of hers. "She really doesn't fit in, if you know what I mean," she said in a conspiratorial whisper.

Celeste lifted her chin. "Actually, I don't." She offered a tight smile to the startled expression of her "aunt" and escaped.

Celeste found her father on the terrace in deep conversation with the head of one of the computer giants. Ellis Shaw was a handsome man, one who commanded attention the moment he entered a room. He was still tall, even at sixty. His full head of black and gray hair was the envy of many of his associates. But it was also the power he wielded that drew lesser men to him—they wanted what he had to rub off on them somehow. Her mother carried the fortune. But her father was the real rainmaker of the family. He had the ear of anyone who was important, from one end of the country up to the highest office in the land. That was his gift.

"Hi, Daddy."

He blew a cloud of smoke into the air before turning to the sound of her voice. Something mildly resembling a smile tugged the corners of his mouth. "Did your mother send you?" His gray eyes glimmered against the backdrop of the night sky.

"Something like that." She stepped up to him and kissed him lightly on the cheek.

"Clinton's here, I'm sure."

"Mother is introducing him around…like a pet," she added with disdain.

Ellis made a noise in his throat. "That's how you get ahead in the world, by who you know." He tugged on the cigar and let the smoke drift along the night air.

Another lecture on social networking she did not need. "You're right, of course. I suppose I should get back inside and mingle. Especially since I already know you," she teased, in an attempt to lighten the weight of the mood.

"I'll be in as soon as I'm done."

Celeste nodded, opened the sliding glass doors and stepped back inside, closing them behind her. In the few short minutes that she'd taken to speak with her father, the number of guests had multiplied. The noise level ballooned and food, drink and music flowed with the gusto of rushing water after a heavy rain.

"They should gather up all the poor, the blacks and the Jews and ship them off," one man was saying to another.

"Aren't they all the same?" his friend quipped.

They laughed at the joke and raised their glasses in a toast.

"The problem is the Democrats."

"They'd love to have the whole country on welfare and have *us* pay for it."

Celeste cringed and kept walking.

She didn't see Clinton or her mother and that was a good thing. She threaded her way around the bodies until she'd reached the front door, where she'd been ceremoniously relieved of her coat upon her arrival. She dug in her evening bag, took out a ticket stub and handed it to the young girl on coat duty. Shortly her coat was given to her and Celeste took one last look over her shoulder before slipping out. Of course, she'd never hear the end of it from her mother but her mother's diatribe would be the punishment she was willing to accept simply to get away from the oppressive scent of success.

Celeste stepped out into the chilly March night, drew her mink jacket around her and began walking.

★ ★ ★

Leslie Evans lay curled up on the well-worn couch. A half-eaten bowl of potato chips rested on the smudged glass coffee table. CNN played in the background rehashing the latest on the political landscape. Since the election of President Obama, she'd become addicted to politics after years of malaise. It had become her refuge, a way of turning her mind onto the problems of the world and away from her own—the life that she'd come to dread waking up to day after day.

Anderson Cooper was in the middle of discussing the plummeting stock market prices when the doorbell rang. She glanced at the clock that hung above the mantel. Five more minutes and it would be time for MSNBC, she thought absently. The bell rang again. Annoyed at being disturbed and by the fact that she had to get up or else the next ring would surely wake her mother, she pulled herself up and padded barefoot across the cold tiled floor to the door. She drew her robe tighter around her.

"Who is it?"

"Les, it's me, Celeste."

Leslie frowned and opened the door. "Cee, what in the world are you doing here? I thought you had that thing with your mother tonight."

"I did. I should have called…."

"Girl, please, come on in. You're letting in the cold air." She shivered.

Celeste stepped in. "Thanks."

"I was watching—"

"CNN." Celeste finished the sentence, knowing her friend all too well.

"So how bad was it?" Leslie asked, leading the way to the living room.

"As bad as I expected." She slipped out of her expensive fur and tossed it to the side like a pair of dirty gym socks. She plopped down on the love seat and kicked off her shoes, wiggling her toes in relief.

Leslie resumed her position and tucked her bare feet beneath her. "What did you do with Clinton?"

Celeste waved off the question. "He'll be fine. By the time he realizes I'm gone, it won't really matter. I'll simply tell him I came down with a splitting headache and didn't want to pull him away."

Leslie pursed her lips, flattening their plumpness into a tight line of concern. Her dark eyes rested on Celeste. "Why do you put yourself through all this? I could never understand. You are so unlike *them*." She uttered the last word with the puckered bite of one who'd sucked on a lemon.

Leslie and Celeste's lifestyles were polar opposites. Yet it was their differences that bound them in a way that was incomprehensible to those outside of their intimate twosome. It was the inconsistencies about their lives, the cracks in their personalities and the internal angst that they shared that strengthened their fledgling sisterhood. One black, one white, one wealthy, one poor.

Celeste could only imagine what life must have been like living in the projects of New York City. She'd only seen pictures and heard commentary by those who'd laid the foundation for generation upon generation to be entrapped there. Of course their perspective was couched in myth and sanctimonious rhetoric. But if there was any truth in the notion that you are a product of your environment, it was certainly true, at least in part, about Leslie. She had a hard edge to her soft roundness, a wariness and often pessimistic view of the world and a resiliency that Celeste often marveled at. Although she wouldn't want to change lives with Leslie, she respected where her friend had come from and how far she'd taken herself...at least on the surface.

Leslie reached for a potato chip then changed her mind. "Go on and say it."

Celeste's green eyes glanced up. "Say what?"

Leslie huffed. "That I don't have any business laying around wolfing down a bowl of potato chips. Why don't I have something healthy, like a yogurt or some carrots?" she singsonged in a mocking voice.

Celeste screwed up her nose. "Do I really sound like that?"

"Yes. You do." She rolled her eyes.

"You know I don't mean any harm. I'm just worried about you. We already had a scare with your blood pressure and that fainting spell a couple of months back. And your mother..."

The albatross had entered the room with the mention of her mother. Theresa Evans had been a strong, dominating force, wielding and molding Leslie into a mere caricature of the woman she might have been. That woman was now a shadow of her former self, confined to bed and a wheelchair, needing assistance to eat, wash, dress and even speak. Some days Leslie was so overwhelmed with the enormity of the responsibility that she often felt that this was yet another way for her mother to control her life. The resentment battled constantly with the guilt of her ugly thoughts. Depending on the day and her mood, one or the other won out. Today resentment clinched the title.

"How is she today?"

Leslie's gaze drifted away. "The same." Her eyes suddenly filled. "I'm just so tired." She pressed her fist to her mouth.

"Leslie, you need a break. I told you I would help you pay for someone to come in and take care of her."

Vigorously she shook her head, the tumble of naturally curly hair spilling back and forth across her shoulders. "I need to do it. It's my responsibility. And I still have her home attendant Gracie at least for a little while longer."

They'd had this conversation a least a dozen times since Theresa had been felled by a devastating stroke nearly a year earlier that left her trapped in a shell of her former self. It was incomprehensible to Celeste that someone would want to take on that role of nurse when you could easily pay someone else to do it. She couldn't imagine taking care of Corrine Shaw on an everyday basis. Being in her repressive presence when she was well was exhausting enough. But Leslie had been adamant from the beginning. Her mother's insurance only covered someone coming in twice per week for four hours, which was the tiny window that allowed Leslie to try to run her design business, take meetings and deal with clients. The rest of the time she was as trapped in this two-bedroom apartment as her mother. And she comforted herself with eating. While Theresa seemed to shrink week by week, Leslie mushroomed, seeming to take on every pound that Theresa lost. And their already adversarial relationship only added to the strain that lived in the apartment as the rent-free third tenant.

"Let's talk about something else, okay?" Leslie adjusted herself on the couch. She reached for the remote and turned off the television. "So, tell me all about the deal?"

Celeste's expression brightened. She sat up straighter in the seat and gave Leslie all the details about the place and how excited she was to have closed such a major project. "I know that Nick is going to ask you to come in and work your magic. He said as much. Well, I actually suggested it to his girlfriend, Parris."

"Girlfriend? Don't you mean Tara?"

Celeste frowned. "I don't know about anyone named Tara, but there is something definitely going on with the woman he was with—Parris. She's apparently staying at his place."

Leslie's tapered brows shot up. "You're kidding. Parris McKay, the singer?"

"You know her?"

"I've heard her sing in the club. Phenomenal. I thought there might have been a vibe going on between them, but I was pretty sure Tara wouldn't let that happen." She slowly bobbed her head as the images and pieces came together. "They make a great couple. Wow. Good for them." She focused on Celeste. "What did you think of Parris?"

"Actually, I think she's really great. Kind of reserved with a little bit of Southern naiveté, friendly, very pretty." She leaned forward, resting her arms on her thighs. "I thought maybe the three of us could get together when she gets back."

"Back from where?"

"She went to find her mother."

Leslie frowned. "What do you mean, 'find her mother'?"

"Apparently she'd spent her entire life thinking that her mother was dead and only found out recently that she was alive and well and living in France."

"You're kidding."

Celeste shook her head. "Nope. That's what she told me."

"That must have been a shock."

Silence joined them and they contemplated what life would be like for each of them had their own mothers not been in them.

Her rudimentary high school French came to her in bits and pieces, after she'd landed at Nantes airport southwest of Paris, at least enough to tell the cab driver to take her to the town of Amboise in the Loire Valley.

"I'm going to Ninety-Eight rue Pascal."

"Ah, in Amboise, Loire Valley."

"Yes," she said on a breath of relief, cringing as she'd listened to herself mangle the language.

As the cab wound its way through the early evening traffic, Parris's heart thudded and banged in time to the bounce and roll of the cab along narrow cobblestone streets before darting out onto the A10 motorway. She smoothed the yellowed envelope with her mother's last known address across her lap. The lamplight from the street intermittently streamed in through the window, casting short shadows and bits of illumination upon her destiny. Her fingers shook. She gripped her knees and concentrated on breathing slowly and deeply. She peered out of the window as the city of lights flickered and grew dim and the rolling landscape of countryside took its place. She had no idea how long the trip would take but surely an eternity had passed.

It began to rain, slowly at first and then with torrential force. The wipers slashed furiously against the window. The driver slowed as the road disappeared in front of them. She barely made out the sign that read Entering Loire Valley, exit No. 18. Her breath caught. She gripped her knees tighter as the pounding in her chest reverberated in her head. After about another fifteen minutes the driver drew to a stop along a winding path braced on both sides with cottage houses in varying sizes and degrees of splendor with overhanging trees silhouetted against the deep purple sky. At the end of the path cushioned in a cul-de-sac was a three-story structure with a wraparound terrace, towering trees and a sprawling lawn. Lights glowed on the upper floor illuminating the rain.

"Ninety-eight rue Pascal. This is your address."

Parris could not move.

"Madame? Your address."

She nodded numbly. What if her mother wasn't there and this was no longer her address? She had no plan. No way of getting around or even a clue as to where to stay.

She gripped the back of his seat. "Can you...wait?"

The driver glanced at her over his shoulder. He held up his hand. "Five minutes."

She made a move to get out.

"You pay now."

She fumbled around in her purse and took out twenty dollars. "Is this enough?"

He looked at the American money and bobbed his head once. Parris opened the car door and stepped out. For a moment she stood stock-still, the rain tumbling down around her, plastering her clothes to her body. She shivered, reached back into the cab for her umbrella and cautiously moved toward the front door. She unlatched the fence and walked forward.

Three steps separated her from all the answers that had eluded her. She put one foot in front of the other, reached out and rang the bell.

In the distance she could hear the chime but no movement, no voices, when suddenly the door was pulled partially open. A woman of medium height with dark sleek hair pulled back into a tight bun at the nape of her neck, peered at her with suspicion from the crack in the opened door.

"Yes, may I help you?" Her lilting French accent was faint, but her English was clear.

Parris swallowed over the tight knot in her throat. "I came to see Emma McKay...Travanti."

"The Mrs. is out with Mr. Travanti. Was she expecting you?"

"Uh, no, she wasn't. Do you know how long she'll be?" Rain slashed against her and her umbrella turned inside out and blew out of her hand, tumbling across the lawn.

"As I said, she is out for the evening. Who should I say you are?"

"She…doesn't know me."

The woman looked closer through the rain, attempting to make out the figure in front of her. A light flickered in her eyes.

Parris turned. Those three steps were like falling from a cliff. A sickening sensation, one of a swelling magnitude, rose to her throat, gagging her as she heard the door shut behind her. Tears of a strange kind of relief flowed and were just as quickly washed away with the rain, only to be replaced with the sorrow of defeat.

Emma squeezed her eyes shut, pressed her back to the door and dragged in long gulps of air. She didn't dare move until she heard the car pull off.

"Em, who was that at the door in this weather?"

Emma opened her eyes. Her husband stood in front of her, looking at her curiously.

"No one," she whispered.

# Chapter Seven

"Do you know of a hotel in the area?" Parris asked the cab driver—Amin—while she struggled to hold onto her composure.

"Back in Town Square." He stole a glance at her in his rearview mirror. "The people were not home?"

"No." She lowered her head. Water dripped from her hair onto her lap.

He peered at her again and the longing that draped her like a cloak caused him to reflect on what had brought him to this foreign land. "When my daughter Mya left our homeland of Senegal to live here to attend the university, I was never so worried about her being away from home and friends and family." He shook his head. "Every night my wife, Akewi— rest her soul—and I prayed that she would be safe. All a parent can do is hope and pray that their grown-up child will remember all the things they've been taught and that life will treat them with kindness. Our Mya believed in the goodness of people, and she was right. Those who were once strangers became friends. And it made me believe, too. When I lost Akewi to the fever, there was nothing to hold me in Senegal. Nothing but memories and loss. So I took my chances, trusted my daughter's instincts. And here I am!" He chuckled lightly. "May I ask who you were looking for? Perhaps I know them."

Parris blinked rapidly to stem the tears that burned her eyes. "Um, her name is Emma Travanti."

"Ah, Ms. Emma!"

Her heart pounded. "You know her?"

"Everyone knows Ms. Emma. She owns Voile Bistro."

Her thoughts raced. "In town…"

"Yes, on Monoir Square. You can't miss it. Perhaps you will find her there tomorrow. They open at noon. I can point it out to you before I take you to your hotel."

"Thank you." She squeezed her hands together on her lap. *Noon. Tomorrow.* Parris turned to stare out of the window. Tomorrow. She would meet her mother tomorrow.

Amin reversed course and drove back toward the center of town. He drove up and down several narrow commercial streets before finally slowing. "There, on your right, Voile Bistro."

Parris peered out the window, memorizing the brown-and-white overhanging awning, the plate glass window that advertised plates of mouthwatering treats—Voile Bistro. Her stomach rolled over and again, mimicking a beach ball kicked across the sand.

She swallowed over the knot in her throat. "What is the name of this street?"

"Rue Venier."

She repeated the name over and over to herself. *Rue Venier.*

After a bumpy twenty-minute ride filled with wondrous stories of Amin's life in a tribal village of Senegal, and talk of the first Black president in America and his impact on the world, Parris had begun to push to the back of her mind her current dilemma and almost imagined herself on an exciting vacation, until they came to a stop in front of Le Moulin du Port, one of several bed-and-breakfast inns that Amin had recommended. Amin hopped out of the cab and helped Parris, holding his own jacket over her head as they ran to the front door. He darted back to get her bags.

"I'll stay and be sure you get a room," he offered.

She looked into his eyes, the caring eyes of a father, his midnight black face lined by years of sun and struggle, and she understood the kindness of strangers. She tilted her head in question. "You never told me where your daughter is now."

Amin smiled. "She works for a local radio station in the city of Paris. Perhaps you will get a chance to meet her."

"I'd like that very much."

He rang the bell and moments later a woman answered. She appeared to be around sixty years old, and was exquisitely dressed in a long sea-blue cotton dress that gently wrapped around her long slender figure. Her silver hair was pulled back into a tight bun, which seemed to be the hairstyle of choice, Parris thought absently. She'd noticed the coif on every other woman she'd seen since she landed in France. The only things that gave any hint to her age were the fine webs at her eyes and the loss of firmness at her exposed neck.

*"Oui?"* She looked from one to the other.

"I was hoping you had a room for the night. I only just

arrived today from the States and...I thought...I'd planned to stay with a...friend." She brushed wet hair away from her face.

"Ah, yet another lost American." She smiled. "You are in luck as I had a cancellation today." She threw a sharp look at Amin. "And you?"

"I'm only the driver. I wanted to be sure she had a place to stay before I left."

She turned to Parris. "There are still kind men in the world that will not take advantage of a young woman." She looked them over one more time. "Come in out of the rain."

Amin carried Parris's bag inside. She turned to him.

"I can't thank you enough." She went into her purse and took out another thirty American dollars. "Will this be enough?"

"More than enough." He dug in his pocket and took out a battered card and handed it to her. "Keep this. Call whenever you need a ride around town."

"I will."

"I hope you find Ms. Emma tomorrow."

Parris swallowed. "Yes, so do I."

He gave her a slight nod of his head and turned to leave. The woman locked the door behind him then returned to Parris.

"Let's get you checked in. My name is Marie."

"Parris."

She glanced at Parris from behind the desk, her fine brows arched in appreciation. "Like our beautiful city of lights?"

"Yes."

Marie looked her over. "It suits you." She opened the register to a blank page and turned the book toward Parris. "The room that I have available is the *Orangerie*. It's on the second floor. It has a lovely balcony with an exquisite view of

the Cher River." She paused. "It is 110 euro. It includes breakfast until noon," she quickly added.

"That's fine." Parris signed her name.

"Perfect!" She took the book with a flourish and swept from
behind the desk as if walking onstage for her close-up, Parris
thought with amusement. She would discover later that Marie
once had a fledgling career in theater before a scandal ran her
out of town.

"Follow me and I'll show you to your room."

Parris trailed in Marie's heavenly scent as she was led to the
end of the hallway on the second floor. Magically, Marie
produced a key and turned it in the lock. Parris smiled inwardly,
trying to recall the last time she'd stayed in any type of hotel
setting where the room required a real key. Her purse was filled
with key cards from an assortment of hotels from her various
out-of-town trips.

Marie opened the door in another grand gesture and
switched on the light. Parris inhaled a soft gasp of delight. The
room was adorned in warm earthy colors of gold, brown and
burnt orange with sprinkles of sunshine yellow. The heavy
drapes were pulled back in an arc on either side of the French
doors that led to the balcony. She could just make out the halo
of the moon from between the rain and clouds setting gingerly
atop the fingers of trees and the curve of the hill in the distance.
The centerpiece was the four-poster bed that stood high above
the floor with dozens of pillows atop a thick satin quilt that
captured all the colors of the room.

"The bath is this way." Marie walked to what Parris thought
was a closet and opened the door.

The bathroom, complete with tub, shower, sink and bidet,
was actually a level below her. Once the door was opened, one

stepped down into the expansive bath that was nearly the length and width of the bedroom.

She turned toward Marie, feeling her first moment of delight since she'd landed hours earlier. "It's wonderful. Thank you."

"Breakfast is served in the dining room from six in the morning to noon. And we offer light refreshments from two until six. There's a heated pool, a car service to take you farther into town or to the rail. The remote for the television is on the nightstand. I'll have your phone turned on in a moment. The charges will be added to your bill. Uh, you didn't mention how long you would be staying?"

The air of her momentary elation was sucked out of her. "I'm not sure. A couple of days."

Marie waved her hand. "That is fine." She looked around. "Well, enjoy the rest of your evening." She swooshed out and closed the door softly behind her.

Parris sat down on the embroidered footstool at the end of the obscenely large bed and looked around at her new home away from home. For the past three months she hadn't been in a place she could actually call her own. Although she'd stayed in her old room back in Rudell, it wasn't the same as having your own. Then it was on to Nick's place and now here. She expelled a long breath, shrugged out of her damp coat, took off her shoes and wiggled her tired toes. What she longed for was a nice hot bath, to ward off the chill and hopefully relax her muscles, which had tangled themselves into bands of anxiety. Then she would call Nick.

Wrapped in the thick white robe provided by Le Moulin, Parris ran a towel through her wild, freshly shampooed hair, feeling renewed after soaking in the lavender-scented water for nearly an hour. She turned on the little heater that sat in the corner near the French doors and within moments the room was warm and toasty. She stripped out of her robe, found her lotion in her suitcase and took her time kneading and stroking her skin until she felt the hours of weariness drift off and true sleepiness settle in. She stretched and yawned before putting on her nightgown and sliding down between the cool sheets. Turning on her side, she reached for the phone and was relieved to hear the dial tone. She dialed the operator and gave him Nick's number.

She curled on her side, listened to the phone ring on the other end and felt the pound of her heart bump back and forth between her chest and the thick mattress. The sound of his voice only escalated the banging.

"Parris!"

"Hi," she said on a breath, wishing she could see the expression on his face.

"I've been going crazy waiting to hear from you. Is everything all right? Are *you* all right?"

The questions were straightforward but they both knew they were laced with a multitude of meanings, from emotions that had yet to be fully verbalized, to the reason why she was a million miles away from anything familiar.

"I'm fine. Tired but fine. I…I'm staying at a bed-and-breakfast. I went to the house," she began, hearing his question in the silence. "She wasn't there. But the cab driver knows her."

"You're kidding."

"Apparently she is well-known in town. She owns a bistro." She felt so odd talking about this woman, her mother, sharing kernels of freshly discovered details about her that others took for granted. Meeting people who knew who Emma was, what she did for a living, and she, flesh and blood, only knew hearsay. It was a sobering sensation.

"At least you have a line on her, and the address that your grandmother gave you is still a good one."

"Yes, that's true." She reached up and turned out the lamp on the nightstand. "Enough about me for now. How is everything with you?"

He told her about taking Sam to the new club location and that he was as excited about it as they were. "Call me crazy," he said after spinning the details of the visit, "but if I didn't know better I'd swear something was popping between Sam and Celeste."

"Get out of here! Sam and Celeste? Mr. 'The revolution will be televised' and Ms. 'Cover model for the uptown girl.'" She laughed at the incongruous image.

Nick joined in the laughter. "I know, I know," he said, still chuckling, "But I was there. It was like watching one of those commercials where the couples are running toward each other across a grassy knoll in slow motion."

Parris broke out into laughter again. "You need to stop."

"I'm serious," he said, laughing even harder.

"So…what did he say? I know you grilled him."

"Actually, I didn't."

Parris propped up on her elbow. "Why not?"

"Sharing my suspicions with you is one thing, saying them to Sammy is a whole other story. He would flip if I was wrong and I'd never hear the end of it. You know how he is about 'crossing the line.'"

"Hmm, that's true, which is why I find it so hard to believe that he would have the slightest interest in Celeste in the first place."

"True. But…I know what I saw. It was the same kind of vibe when you and I are together," he said, his voice lowering.

Parris felt her stomach flutter. "I wish you were here," she said on a breath of longing.

"So do I. I had no idea how deep my missing you was going to get until I walked in this place and you weren't here. It's not the same without you."

"I hope to get back soon. I wasn't sure about that before I left. I had this adolescent feeling that I'd meet my mother and she'd welcome me into her life with open arms and never want me to leave." She breathed deeply. "But after going to the house, having my hopes built up to a point that probably nothing could live up to them, I got brought down to earth…reality. No matter what happens, I have a life, too." Once the words were off her mind and out of her mouth, the truth warmed her like good brandy in front of a fire.

"Baby, I couldn't be happier that you said that. But I want you to know that no matter how long it takes to work it out with your mother, I'll be here when you get back and if you need me, just pucker up your lips and blow."

She giggled. "I'll keep that in mind." She squeezed her thighs together, remembering clutching Nick tightly between them. "I'd better go. No telling how much this call is costing. I'll call again when I can."

"Give me the information of where you're staying. The next call is on me."

Parris switched back on the light and read the information off of the phone.

"Got it. I'll call you tomorrow."

"Okay." She gripped the phone.

"I know everything is going to be fine with you and your mother. So don't worry."

"I'll try not to."

"Good night, sweetheart. Rest well."

"You, too."

Emma paced the polished living room floor, intermittently peeking out from between the curtains to see if the girl had returned. She knew her the instant she saw her silhouetted against the rain and waning light. Why didn't she invite her in? Why did she lie? A strangled sob stumbled in her throat. For weeks since she'd received the letter from her mother, telling her that the decades-old lie had been revealed, she'd expected yet dreaded the moment when she would come face-to-face with her daughter. Parris. That's what Cora said she'd named her.

It was fear that seized her mind and twisted her thoughts. No longer an emotion but an entity, some real thing with a power greater than her own will. The same fear she'd felt the night when she gave birth to her alone in her apartment. Her brown baby. The night when she'd recognized that everything she'd done, all she'd worked for, the love she'd finally found, would be destroyed, stripped from her, leaving her with nothing, the same nothing she'd endured all her life. She knew she wasn't strong enough to go back down that road.

"Emma, honey…"

Emma turned away from her ugly past. She'd never told Michael what she'd nearly done to their child. And she never would. He may have forgiven her for keeping the truth of their daughter's existence for all these years, but *that* he would never forgive.

She forced a smile.

"Are you all right, sweetheart?" Concern carved a line between his sleek black brows. "You've been out of sorts all evening." He came up to her, stroked her cheek with a brush of his fingertip.

She sighed at his familiar touch and clasped his hand to her face, closing her eyes. "I'm fine. A bit tired."

He draped his arm around her shoulder and pulled her close. "Then let's have an early night." He kissed the top of her head.

Suddenly she clung to him, pressing her head to his chest, seeking comfort in the steadying beat of his heart. Michael was her life. Everything she'd done, every decision she'd made, had been for him. His love for her had been the only love she'd ever known. The only kindness she'd ever been given. She'd grown up an outsider, scorned and snickered about in that little backward town of Rudell. She hated it there almost as much as they hated her—almost as much as she hated her mother. But so much had changed since then. Everything except her fear. Her fear of confronting her daughter and confessing not what she had done, but why.

Emma tilted her head up to gaze into the dark pools of his eyes, the edges lined with concern. The jangling of her nerves began to quiet like a church bell that had rung out the hour. Even after all these years, Michael remained incredibly handsome. The same endearing smile that won her heart still had the power to make her stomach seesaw and her pulse pound. His touch continued to stoke the fire within her. Michael was her life. She'd given up everything to live forever in the halo of his love. It was his love that gave her sustenance, flowed through her veins, pumped through her heart.

Emma's entire being suddenly overflowed with emotions so powerful that her eyes filled and glistened. "I love you so very much," she whispered. "So very much."

Michael held her close. "I love you, too, Em." He stepped back, holding her shoulders. He looked into her eyes. "Tell me what's bothering you."

She turned her head away to hide the betrayal. "I'm fine, really." She took his hand. "Let's eat and go to bed."

Throughout the night Emma couldn't dispel the image of her daughter standing in her doorway. Each time she closed her eyes Parris's eager face loomed before her. Her voice echoed in her mind. She'd grown into a beautiful young woman. A beautiful young woman without her. The woman she'd scorned and turned her back on was responsible for raising the woman that Parris had become.

There'd been so many times throughout her life in Europe that she'd doubted her decision, regretted what she'd done. And her guilt would wake her from sleep, guide her through the darkness of the chalet to the kitchen table, put a pen in her hand and pull her fingers across the paper to find out how she was doing, was she well, was she happy, did she ever ask about her? Too many letters were warped by her tears, the ink flowing in black and blue rivers of sorrow. With the new day the ocean's tide of guilt would recede. That is the prayer she whispered throughout the night, that the bright light of morning would blind all those in her path to the sorrow and the fear she held in her heart.

Parris awoke with a start.

She sat up and put her feet on the floor. She walked to the window and peeled back the white draperies. The town was still very much asleep. The few signs of life were the occasional car or abandoned cat or dog scurrying for shelter. In the morning dimness, houselights and the illumination of the streetlamps resembling probing cat eyes appeared to float, disembodied against daybreak.

There was still at least an hour before breakfast would be ready in the main hall. Nervous energy pushed her back and forth across the room. Noon was an eternity from now. She was certain she would leap out of her skin long before then.

Fishing through her suitcase, she pulled out a red pullover sweater and a pair of jeans. She needed some air.

# Chapter Eight

Parris stood beneath the overhang of a wine and spirits store watching the entrance to Voile Bistro on the opposite side of the street, as if the very act of staring would make something magical happen. She tugged the short brown leather jacket a bit tighter around her slender body, willing mind over matter to chase the morning chill away. She wasn't certain what she hoped to accomplish by standing there, perhaps divine a sense of her mother, the woman who'd given her up for a life that she could not live with a child hanging on her hip.

Did she have other children? Did she ever marry? Where and who was her father? The plate glass window of the shop revealed nothing more than what appeared to be a successful business tucked on the other side. Successful enough that Emma was known by name. *Travanti*. Her father's name or the name of the man she'd married? Or the name she'd taken for reasons that only she would know?

Questions tumbled through her mind as she witnessed the sleepy town stretch its limbs and take its first steps into the new day. The heavens were streaked a magnificent purple from the night of heavy rain and already the dew drops, resembling eager beachgoers, were stretched out into thin layers of water waiting to be dried by the sun.

She'd been emboldened when she'd stepped out of Le Moulin du Port and began the half hour walk toward the center of town. The streets were barely lit by the sleepy sun struggling up and over the mountaintops, while trying to snuggle back down into its blanket of clouds.

For the past hour she shared duties with the lamppost, holding up the corner, and she was sure that soon someone would call the authorities to report the loud noises coming from her empty stomach. Feeling more foolish by the moment and increasingly hungry she turned to leave, but slowed her step when a car pulled to a stop in front of the bistro.

Her nerves popped as a woman got out of the car, fumbled with a set of keys and opened the front door. Parris stood rooted in place as the woman turned to close the glass door and their gazes collided.

The woman's eyes widened ever so slightly then settled, in resolve or perhaps resignation. She didn't move as Parris crossed the street and came to stand in front of the door.

*It was the woman from last night.* She was sure of it. Did she work here, as well? Were they friends and business partners? "I wanted to see the owner," she said, speaking slowly so that her words could be made out through the glass that separated them. "Emma."

Emma's heart pounded so ferociously in her chest she struggled to breathe. What was she to do? Turn her away again? Pretend…pretend what? Her temples throbbed as a sliver of perspiration trickled down the center of her spine. Her nostrils flared as she drew in air. Holding on to the doorknob, she was certain, was the only thing keeping her from crumbling to the ground.

"Do you know what time she will be in?"

This was her escape. She could say that Emma was out of town for several weeks. She could tell her…

The door slowly opened and Parris stepped gratefully beneath the threshold. "Thank you." She assessed her with curiosity. "We met last night, didn't we? At Ms. Travanti's house." When she didn't get a response she pressed on. "I was told this was her restaurant. Is that true?"

Emma turned away, drew up her shoulders and exhaled the one word Parris longed to hear. *"Oui."* She heard the breath of relief puff on her back. "Are you a friend of hers?"

"I'm her daughter." She pulled the yellowed letter from her purse. "She wrote this letter to my grandmother many years ago after she'd come here to live."

Emma flinched. She walked to the pastry counter, keeping her back to Parris. "She never spoke of a daughter. Ever. Perhaps you have the wrong person." Slowly she turned around. "How can you be sure?"

"I can't. But I promised my Nana that I would find her. This is the place I have to start."

Emma looked deep into the eyes of her child, seeing the questions, the turmoil and the determination carved on her face. How much had Cora told her? How much of a picture had she painted? Did she include her own role in Emma's defection?

"Would you like some coffee or tea?"

"Coffee would be great. Thank you."

Emma went to the door and locked it, put the CLOSED sign in the glass then returned behind the counter and began perking the coffee. Before long the bistro was filled with the aromas of fresh brewed coffee and warmed croissants. Emma placed a tray of the airy pastries in front of Parris and poured her a mug of coffee.

She sat down opposite Parris at the round table. "So you *say* you are Emma's daughter?"

"Yes."

She lifted the cup to her lips. "What is your name?"

"Parris." She smiled wistfully. "Nana said she named me after the place where my mother had come to live."

"I see." She lowered the cup and embraced it, the warmth softening her bones. "You came from the States. I hear an accent. Southern?"

"I grew up in Rudell, Mississippi." She lowered her head and chuckled. "I'm sure you never heard of it, not many people have." She looked at Emma. "You're not a native of France, either. But you've been here a while."

"You're very observant."

"I just have a keen sense of sound. I guess it comes from listening to music and singing most of my life."

*A singer, like Cora.* "Professional or hobby?"

Parris took a bite of her croissant. "I'm aiming for professional. I've done some shows. I even have a record deal offer."

Emma's fine brows rose. "That's wonderful. Congratulations. You must be good."

Her soft expression lit from inside. "So I'm told."

Emma leaned forward. "Tell me what *you* think."

"Really?"

Emma bobbed her head. "Yes. Tell me."

Parris drew in a breath. "Well, when I sing…nothing else in the world matters." Her eyes danced with emotion, traveling to the special place that was only hers to understand. "I feel transformed and the music, the lyrics, are my lifeblood, what keeps me alive. I become the words and the need to convey their message is more powerful than anything else." She blinked and Emma came back into focus. She smiled sheepishly. "I'm sorry, I get a little carried away sometimes."

"We all need our passions, Parris." Her petite hand slowly curled into a fist. "Something that drives us and gives our life meaning. If not, what is the point of it all?"

"What's your passion?"

"To live the life that I dreamed of as a girl, the life that was denied me. To be accepted and loved without condition. That is my passion. Everyday." She pushed up from her seat and stood. Her chest rose and fell. She pressed her lips tightly together lest she say more than she should.

Parris looked up at this woman standing above her and something inside her shifted out of place, leaving her feeling suddenly unbalanced. She was a stunning woman, who defied a fixed age. Her skin was nearly translucent and clear. Her hair—thick, silky and black with fine streaks of gray—gave her fine features an even more regal appeal. Behind her glasses her deep set eyes seemed to hold hundreds of stories and images that Parris could only imagine. She had the bearing of someone important, not ordinary help, even though her dress was simple; a powder blue oxford shirt, ironed to precision, the sleeves rolled to expose long pale arms and a pair of simple navy dress slacks that gracefully fell from her hips and kissed the tops of her ankle boots, with a hint of something very subtle and expensive that wafted around her when she moved.

"I really must get started preparing for the lunch customers."

"Oh, yes. I'm sorry to have taken up so much of your time." She draped her purse on her shoulder and stood. "Thank you for breakfast. How much do I owe you?"

Emma waved off the question.

"You didn't tell me when Emma would be coming."

"I'm certain that you are wasting your time, but I'll be sure to mention to her that you were here," she said, sidestepping the question. "If she decides to come in."

"But you were at her house last night. Won't you see her there?"

Emma lifted her chin. "She comes and goes as she pleases." Emma walked toward the door and opened it.

Parris stood in the doorway. Her gaze rested on Emma. "Thank you for your time."

Emma nodded.

Parris turned then stopped. She faced Emma. "Can you give her this number?" She reached in her bag and took out a card that she'd taken from the front desk of the bed-and-breakfast. "This is where I'm staying." She handed Emma the card then walked out.

Emma stood in the frame of the glass door and watched as her daughter became silhouetted against the brilliance of the morning sun and Emma prayed that the light would blind her to the truth.

Parris returned to Le Moulin. Marie was in the front room rearranging the flowers on the table.

"Oh, you're out early. I missed you at breakfast. You went sightseeing?"

"Something like that."

Marie stopped what she was doing. She brushed her hands on her apron. "France is no place for sadness."

"Is it that obvious?" She reached for a bright red apple from the bowl on the table.

"Very plain to see. May I ask why you are so sad?"

"Long story."

Marie raised and lowered her right shoulder. "All I have to do today is whatever I choose. And I make no excuse. I've earned it," she said with a grand swing of her arm, the loose sheer sleeve of her dressing gown flapping like a wing. "Come with me to the garden. I have more flowers to disengage."

"Disengage?" she said, laughter rimming her voice.

"It sounds civilized, no?"

Parris smirked. "Sure."

"Come."

Parris followed Marie through the ground floor to the backyard. They exited into a wonderland. The ground exploded in a patchwork of vivid color.

"This is incredible," Parris said, awestruck. "I don't think I've ever seen anything like this."

"It is my pride and joy. And very soothing. I could spend hours cooing to my beautiful friends, turning the soil, planting new life." She knelt down near a bed of brilliant orange roses. "Sometimes in life we have to find the things that take us away from what troubles us so that we can reclaim our joy." She glanced up at Parris, who stood with her arms folded beneath her breasts. "Don't you agree?"

Parris shrugged slightly. "I suppose so."

"If you could do one thing right now to make yourself feel better what would it be?"

There was only one thing. "Find my mother."

Marie's eyes widened for a split second. "I see. And that is why you are here, to find your missing mother?"

"She's not what you would call 'missing,' not in the technical sense." She paused to clarify her thoughts. "She left, many years ago, and came to France to live." She looked boldly at Marie as if doing so would somehow wrench from her the information she desperately sought.

Marie remained silent as she gingerly turned the soil around her blooms and added fertilizer from the pocket of her apron.

"Maybe you know her."

Marie shrugged. "Perhaps."

"Her name is Emma. Emma Travanti. She owns the bistro in the square and she lives in the valley. I went to her house last night when I arrived. The driver told me about the bistro. I went there this morning."

"And…"

"She wasn't there. I spoke to a woman who works there. The same woman who works at my mother's house."

"Wasn't she able to tell you about your mother?"

"No." She lowered her head a fraction and looked off into the distance then back at Marie. "Do you know her?"

"I'm sorry to say that I don't. France is a big place. Are you sure it is the right person?"

"All I know is what my grandmother told me, that she'd come here years ago…right after I was born." She tightened her arms around her waist. "And she never came back." She said the words almost in stunned surprise, as if the reality of it were sinking in. She drew in a breath. "I made a promise to my grandmother that I would find my mother. And when I find her she *will* tell me the truth. She'll tell me why." She nodded her head as she spoke to reaffirm her commitment to herself and to Cora.

Marie watched the shadows of emotions move across her face and heard the underlying pain skimming the words. It took a lot for a mother to leave her child, extraordinary reasons. During her growing-up years, she'd lay in bed at night and pray that when she awoke her mother would be gone. Her prayers were never answered. She endured her mother for sixteen horrendous years until she left home, never to return. She couldn't imagine being on a quest to find Lily no matter how extraordinary the circumstance.

"What will you do if you can't find her? If you can't fulfill your promise?"

"Go on with my life…somehow." She frowned slightly. "But I know that once I leave here, no matter what happens, my life will never be the same again. It hasn't been since my grandmother told me that my mother wasn't dead after all."

Marie snapped her head in confusion. "I thought you said that she left and came here after you were born."

"She did. But for reasons that only she and my grandmother know, she wanted me to grow up believing that she was dead."

Marie stretched out her hand, which Parris took, and helped pull Marie to her feet.

*"Merci."* She brushed off her hands on her apron. "One thing I have learned, *chérie,* is that we must be careful what we wish for." She patted Parris gently on the back as they returned inside. "Sometimes the very thing we believe we need and want is the last thing we should have. Those wants bring their own set of consequences. *Oui?"*

Parris's gaze ran over Marie's face, searching for something beneath the surface, an answer that eluded her. But she saw nothing. "I'm sure that they do, but that's a risk I'm willing to take."

Marie studied her for a moment then smiled broadly. "A woman of determination. I like that." They entered the main hall of the bed-and-breakfast. "Did you eat? Although we don't offer lunch to our guests," she said in a conspiratorial whisper, "I'm sure Marc can prepare something for you."

"I actually am a bit hungry," she said, albeit reluctantly.

Marie clapped her hands with a single pop. "Wonderful."

"Are you sure it won't be a problem?"

Marie craned her long neck back and let out a throaty laugh. "Marc will do whatever I ask if he knows what's good for him. Besides, we are lovers and he adores pleasing me."

"Oh…"

Marie lowered her voice and hooked her arm through Parris's. "It is the very thing that got me ousted from the theater…so many years ago. He was the theater owner's husband." She smiled wistfully. "Vivienne made quite a scene when she found us." She sighed. "I can't blame her for her outrage. But Dominic was beautiful. Too beautiful for a man. Every woman wanted him. I suppose by the time she gets rid of or ruins women's lives over her cad of a husband there won't be a single woman of note left in all of France!" She laughed uproariously at the notion.

Parris didn't know if she should laugh at the outrageousness of it all or be totally appalled. She opted for laughter. "What did you do when she…walked in on you?"

"Screamed, of course!"

They were both doubled over with laughter when Marc walked into the kitchen, carrying in a basket of laundry.

"Nothing more refreshing than seeing two beautiful women laughing." His blue-black eyes swept from one to the other.

*This was Marc?* He was young enough to be Marie's son. An exquisite specimen of a man, a cross between the bad boy arrogance of a Colin Farrell, and the swarthy good looks of a young Antonio Banderas.

"Marc, this is our newest arrival. Her name is Parris. Parris, this is Marc."

Parris extended her hand, which he took and brought to his lips, planting a warm kiss on the top of her knuckles. "My pleasure. If there is anything that you need during your stay…" He allowed his sentence to drift off before he finally released her from his grasp.

Marie waved her hand like a wand. "Marc is very dramatic."

He smiled at his benefactor, displaying perfect teeth and a deep dimple in his left cheek, which is always appealing during youth, but almost ridiculous when one ages, Marie thought absently. Those who rely solely on looks rather than talent or some manner of skill were eventually doomed to obsolescence. She was sure that was to be Marc's fate, but until then she would make the supreme sacrifice of "looking after him."

"Parris and I would love a light lunch."

"Right away." He gave Parris a slight nod of his head and walked out.

"Wonderful chef. It's how we met actually. He was working in some little restaurant in Paris near the Louvre. He'd prepared the most exquisite escargot and I insisted that my waiter introduce me to the chef." She flipped her hand. "The rest, as they say, is history." She led the way to her room that was much like Parris's, only larger and bolder in color. "It's a bit chilly today but still nice enough to eat on the terrace. The sun will soon warm things up." She opened the terrace doors and stepped out, checking the table and chairs. She made a face. "I'll have to get Marc to dry these off." She turned to Parris. "Do you have a lover?"

Parris blinked several times. "Excuse me?"

"Do you have a lover? Someone to care about you or at least pretend to? A beautiful girl like you should have someone."

"I—"

"Oh, don't be embarrassed." She waved her hand. "Sex is wonderful. We all do it, you know. And since we do, isn't it best to do it with someone worthwhile?" She stared at Parris with wide-eyed innocence.

Parris felt laughter bubble in her stomach and she couldn't keep the grin off her face. Marie was a real character. Before long she found herself telling Marie of how she and Nick met, the obstacles that they'd faced with Tara and Frank, the illness and subsequent loss of her grandmother, losing her job and her apartment, and then her and Nick finally crossing the invisible line that had divided them.

"Was it worth the wait?" Marie asked with a sparkle in her eyes.

"Yes, it was." The revelation singed her cheeks.

*"Magnifique!"*

There was a light tapping at the door.

*"Entrez."*

Marc opened the door and rolled in a skirted cart with silver serving trays on top.

*"Amoureux,* I wanted to eat outdoors but the table and chairs are still damp. We totally forgot to turn them down last night," she said and winked at him.

"That we did."

Parris watched the exchange with fascination, the way Marie had not a care in the world about calling him "sweetheart" in front of her or inferring that they'd spent the night together, and Marc had no problem being her obvious boy toy and reciprocating with little touches and extra stares while he set up the table for lunch. He opened the leaves of the cart, turning it into a table that could comfortably seat four.

"I fixed your favorite," he said, turning over the bowls and ladling in a delicious-smelling soup.

"Ahh." Briefly Marie closed her eyes in rapture. "Tomato basil." She focused on Parris. "You must try it. Superb." She gazed up at Marc. "It is one of his many specialties."

Marc then placed a tiny saucer in front of them and topped it with a perfect little Quiche Lorraine. "For the main course I prepared perfectly shaved roast beef sautéed with broccoli, onions, roasted potatoes and mushrooms, tossed in a creamy cheddar cheese sauce with green beans almondine," he said with a flourish.

Marie clapped as if she'd witnessed the closing act of a stage play.

Marc bowed. *"Bon appétit."*

"I told you he was dramatic," she said over her laughter. "Please enjoy."

They spent the hour talking about the sights Parris should be sure to see and Marie's one trip to the States before Marie shifted the conversation back to Parris's mother.

"What is it that you really want to find out from your mother?" she asked, daintily wiping her mouth with the linen napkin.

Parris put down her fork and pushed her plate aside. "I want her to tell me why she left and why she wanted me to go through life believing she was dead. I want her to explain to me how she convinced my grandmother to hold on to that lie all these years."

Marie looked her in the eyes. "Why does it matter? Did you have such a horrible life that her absence would make a difference somehow?"

Parris drew in a breath. "I need to know. For myself. I need to fill this void, this feeling that I was somehow unworthy of my own mother's love. Do you have any idea what that's like?" She pushed back from her seat and stood.

"Please, sit. Let me tell you a story of a mother's love."

With reluctance, Parris sat back down.

"For sixteen years I lived under the tyranny of my mother. A woman who thought nothing of hurting me in any way she saw fit. I was a slave to her whims, her moods, her disappointments." She glanced away. "She said she beat me, humiliated me, locked me in rooms, gave me to men to pay off her debts all to make me strong." She laughed but there was no humor in the discordant sound and Parris cringed as it grated against her. "I left and never looked back." She swung her gaze to Parris. "Your mother may have done the very best thing for you by giving you to your grandmother. Perhaps she knew the kind of mother you would need and that she would never be."

Parris's bottom lip trembled. That picture didn't mesh with the images that her grandmother had conjured up over the years, at least the few times that she even spoke of her mother. But Nana had lied, too, and she took her reasons to her grave. If she didn't find Emma she may never know the truth, and that unknowing would forever haunt her.

"Even if everything you say is true, I still need to hear the words from her."

"You are certainly a stubborn young woman. I hope it serves you well." She lifted her fork. "Your food is getting cold."

## Chapter Nine

A plate crashed to the floor in the spotless kitchen. Emma simply stared at the broken pieces of china at her feet.

"I'll get that, Ms. Travanti," her assistant, Nicole, offered. "Are you all right? You are so not yourself today." She reached for a broom behind the storage cabinet.

Emma rubbed her brow, wishing the simple act would rub away the tangle of thoughts running through her head. "A little tired. I think I'll go home. You and George will be fine. Philippe knows what the menu is for today." She took off her apron and hung it on the hook.

Nicole looked at her curiously. Emma never left the store early once she came in. It was her heart and soul. Every minute detail, from the décor to the daily menu, was her doing. Most business owners were mere figureheads, running their operations from a distant office. Not Emma Travanti. She prided herself on being a hands-on owner and it showed in the loyal customers—whom she knew by name—and a business that stayed in the black. And it wasn't as if she needed the work. Quite the contrary. Her husband ran one of the most successful wineries in the valley. She did this because she loved it, and it showed.

Emma reached for her coat then turned to Nicole. "I may be out for a few days." She swallowed. "If anyone should come looking for me…I'm out of town."

"Of…course. Are you sure you're all right?"

She pressed Nicole's shoulder. "Yes, just please do as I ask."

Nicole nodded as she watched her employer leave. She looked around. This was her chance to prove to Emma that she could be trusted to run the bistro. And she would.

All along the route home she kept looking in her rearview mirror, expecting at any moment to see Parris on the road. What was she going to do? She couldn't run forever. God, what if Michael found out that Parris was here and had come looking for her? They had to get away until she could sort things out. Until she could find a way to tell her husband that their daughter had finally arrived.

For nearly thirty years she'd held that ugly secret from her husband. Lied to him about who she was and their child that she'd "lost during childbirth" while he was stationed abroad. But when her mother's letter arrived several weeks earlier she had no choice. She'd taken a chance telling him the truth… what she had done. She'd deprived him of his only child. And it was his unwavering love for her, his compassion as a man, that had allowed him to forgive her.

Yet there were nights when she lay next to him that she wondered how deep his forgiveness truly went. There were times when she would catch him looking at her as if he didn't know who she was before the light of familiarity would reach his eyes. It was those moments that played with her consciousness, when her guilt would outweigh reason. Michael had been her life for more than three decades. She may have given birth to Parris, but she did not know her or what bringing her into her life would mean. And she wasn't sure if she was willing to risk it, even now.

She put the key in the door to her villa and stepped inside. Her housekeeper, Vivian, came running to the front from the kitchen.

"Madame! Are you ill? You are never home at this hour."

"I'm fine, Vivian. I decided to take some time off. Is Michael here?"

"He went to the winery. He said he would return by dinnertime."

Emma nodded. "Thank you." She started for the stairs. "Vivian, I think I'll surprise my husband with a little trip. Would you be so kind as to get our luggage out from the spare room?"

"Of course. Right away."

Emma hurried upstairs. She needed to make some calls and quickly. If she could keep Michael out of town for a few days, a week at most, she was sure that Parris would get tired of her search and go back home. She sat on the side of the bed and opened her nightstand drawer. Taking out her address book she flipped through the pages for the number of the spa in Paris that she and Michael loved, the Evian Royal Resort in the mountains of France. Parris would never find them there. And perhaps she could get her husband to look at her with that old familiarity in his eyes.

Her gaze landed on the number. She reached for the phone and dialed before she changed her mind. After listening to the array of services and agreeing to almost everything, she booked them into the Evian Royal Resort for a week with all of the amenities. It would cost a small fortune, but her peace of mind would be worth it.

Satisfied, she hung up the phone just as Vivian appeared in her doorway with the luggage on a rolling cart.

"Where would you like these?"

"You can bring them inside. Put them in the corner for me, please."

"Will you be leaving soon?" Vivian asked as she took the bags off the cart and placed them in the corner. She glanced at Emma over her shoulder.

"Yes," she said, her answer muffled by the rows of sweaters, suits, slacks and blouses as she rifled through her closet and tossed random clothes on the bed.

"How long will you be gone?"

"At least a week. Maybe more." She turned to Vivian. "I will need you to keep an eye on the house." She bobbed her head, ticking off a mental list. "And check in at the bistro."

"Of course." Vivian watched while Emma went from the closet to the drawers and back again. She'd worked for the Travanti family for nearly ten years. Every day and every year had been a pleasure. Mme. Emma was always even-tempered and calm, full of laughter. She'd never seen her angry or out of sorts even when the ceiling leaked during a terrible storm and nearly destroyed one of the upper rooms where she kept her artwork. Or the time when the roast burned and there was a house full of guests to feed. She didn't become agitated or flustered when Monsieur Michael came down with double pneumonia. She was steady, strong and calm, demanding the best care from his doctors and seeing to his every need. But this Mme. Emma, Vivian didn't recognize. Short, agitated, nervous. She couldn't begin to imagine what could have so disturbed her.

"Should I prepare dinner, then?"

Emma snapped her head in Vivian's direction. She frowned for a moment. "Yes…yes, please. Michael will be hungry. Then we can leave."

"Yes, madame." Vivian left and closed the door quietly behind her.

Emma stared at the disaster that was now her bed, a reflection of what her life had suddenly become. Restlessly she ran her fingers through her hair, dislodging the knot at the nape of her neck. Her hair fell in a soft tumble across her shoulders. She closed her eyes and massaged the stiff muscles in the back of her neck. What was she doing? This wasn't the answer. She pulled out the chair from beneath her dressing table and slowly sat down. But she didn't have a better solution. At least not now. A few days away would help her to clear her head, decide what was best…for all of them.

Emma drew in a long, steadying breath and turned to view her reflection in the beveled mirror. Everything was going to be fine. It would work out. It always did.


Parris did a quick calculation in her head to figure out what time it was in the States. France was six hours ahead. It was almost seven o'clock. Granddad should be up and about. Hopefully she could catch him before he did his afternoon house calls. She stretched across the bed for the phone and connected with the international operator. After several rings the comforting voice of her granddad came on the line.

"Granddad, it's Parris!"

His deep chuckle warmed her like nothing else. "Of course, it's you. Who else calls me Granddad? How are you?"

"I'm fine. Still struggling with jet lag."

"What time is it over there?"

"Almost seven at night."

"Humph, humph, humph. Well, tell me how things are."

She sat up against the stack of pillows and told him about her arrival at Le Moulin, her visit to Emma's house and the bistro.

"Hmm. This woman that you met, she was at both places—the house and the whatchamacallit?"

"Bistro?"

"Yes, bistro."

"She was at both places," she said slowly, not giving voice to the innuendo that floated across the phone lines.

"What did she look like?"

"Look like?"

"Yes."

"Well...she was a bit shorter than me, very pretty, dark hair, green eyes."

David's chest tightened. "And she told you that Emma wasn't at home and then at the restaurant that she had no idea when she would be coming in?"

"Yes." Parris's pulse picked up speed. "Granddad, what are you getting at?"

He hadn't seen Emma in years, not since she was a teenager. But he remembered her beauty. Her porcelain skin, inky black hair and those stunning green eyes, the eyes she'd given to her own daughter. More importantly he remembered her rage and her anger at Cora. A hatred that was palpable, that lived and breathed in the house like a third tenant. Did she still harbor such resentment that she would look her own daughter in the eye and lie to her about who she was? Was Emma's heart that hardened, even after all of this time?

"Granddad?"

He snapped out of his musings. "Perhaps you've done all you can. Maybe you should just come on home."

She leaned into the phone. "What are you not telling me?"

"Sometimes people go away because they don't want to be found, sweetheart."

"I promised Nana."

"I know your grandmother would understand. Let it be."

"Let it be?" Her voice pitched. "You're telling me to forget it after I've come this far? You were the one who insisted that I 'fill the hole' inside me. You!" Her breath pumped in short bursts.

"Maybe I was wrong. Maybe Cora was wrong, too."

"What really happened all those years ago?"

David felt the walls closing in around him with nowhere for him to go. "Your mother, well, maybe you should just let her be."

"You *never* refer to my mother as your daughter, too." She said the words in a whispered sense of sudden wonder. "Why, Granddad? You were married to Nana."

"I told your grandmother to leave things be," he said, his voice weighted down with the enormity of the lie they'd all engaged in for decades.

Parris held her breath. "Tell me. I need to know the truth. Ple—"

"I didn't father your mother."

A jolt of incredulity physically rocked her. "What…are you saying?" She gripped the phone.

"Your grandmother went off to Chicago. When she came back we got married. It was the happiest day in my life. And when we found out we had a baby coming, I was the proudest man in Rudell."

The veins in her temples filled and pounded. She didn't want to hear it. Didn't want to hear what a part of her heart had suspected for years. But if no one said it, if no one said the words, it would never be true.

"Until the baby came."

The pain in his voice cut through the phone lines, echoed like a shout across a canyon, deep and penetrating.

Her thoughts raced. It made awful sense now. The piece of the puzzle that had eluded her fell into place.

When she hung up from her grandfather she was no longer the same person. She'd been inexorably changed. The space inside her that needed to be filled with the essence of who she was, where she'd come from, had been flooded with a poison that now spewed from her in a torrent of tears and physical rage.

"Noooo!"

She tore through the room like an unleashed storm. Everything within her reach became a victim. She'd come to find her mother. Find out why she'd left her only to discover that the person whom she'd loved and idolized all of her life, the man who became the standard by which she judged all men, was not of her flesh and blood. And the woman who was her mother was the offspring of some unknown man. All along her Nana knew. She'd lied to Granddad. She'd lied to her. Who were these people who'd shaped her life? Her stomach heaved. She ran to the bathroom, sinking to her knees, and Marie's words haunted her. *Be careful what you wish for.*

The ringing phone stirred her from her huddled position on the center of the floor. Through bleary, swollen eyes she looked around at the destruction she'd wrought. Clothes were upended from her suitcase. The bed pillows joined the toiletries on the dresser that had been swept to the floor. The curtains that hung on the French doors were wrenched from their rods. She pushed up on her hands and knees, stood and made her way to the phone on wooden legs.

"Hello." Her voice sounded ragged to her ears.

"Parris. It's Nick. Your grandfather called me."

The instant she heard his voice the nightmare of the past hour came flooding back and she broke down again, rambling in fits and starts about what she'd learned.

Nick was barely able to piece it all together but what he was able to understand was that Parris was broken and he wasn't there to pick up the pieces.

Her sobs slowly simmered to soft whimpers. The sound tore at his heart. "Come home. Tomorrow. Get on a plane and come home or I'm coming to get you. One or the other. Your choice."

She sniffed. "I can't even…think straight." She wiped her eyes with the sleeve of her blouse.

"Don't think. Just do it. Pack your bags and go to the airport in the morning. I'll look up your flight information on the Internet and rebook you for tomorrow afternoon."

She looked around the room. Just the thought of having to fix the mess she'd made and pack her bags was too much to deal with.

"Listen to me, you're coming home. Tomorrow. We'll work it all out when you get here. I promise."

Her throat tightened. "All right."

"I'm going to call you back in an hour with the information for tomorrow."

"Okay."

"I love you. It's going to work out. Everything will be fine."
She couldn't imagine how that would be possible—ever.

The soothing steam from her bath began to work its magic. The lavender-scented oil calmed her to a point where the violent pounding in her head had been reduced to a dull hammerlike thump. She rested her head against the lip of the tub and closed her eyes.

Tomorrow she would be home or at least back to someplace familiar. And over time she would put all of this behind her. She would forget that her mother was not dead. She would push from her thoughts the realization that her grandmother harbored the secret of her real existence for years and took the truth with her to her grave. She would stop thinking about the fact that her grandfather wasn't her grandfather at all, but some nameless, faceless person. When she tucked all of those ugly things away in some deep corner of her mind, it wouldn't matter that even she was no longer who she'd believed herself to be. And if that were true, then how could she possibly risk being in the life of someone else when hers had only been an illusion, one that she may never see clearly?

The water cooled, the scent dissolved, and Parris, with great reluctance, pulled herself up from the comforting embrace and stepped out.

A soft tap on her door made her draw her belt tighter around her robe. She ran her hands through her damp hair, pulling it up and away from her face as she approached.

"Yes?"

"It's Marie. May I come in?"

Parris took a quick look around. It had taken her nearly an hour, but her room finally resembled the one she'd rented. Her clothing was packed. All that was left to do what settle her bill and go home.

She turned the knob and stepped back out of the threshold.

"I didn't know if you'd planned to go into town for dinner or if you'd like Marc to fix you something." Her eyes scanned the room as she spoke and settled on the suitcase. She focused on Parris. "Leaving?"

"Yes." Parris closed the door behind Marie. "In the morning. I was going to come down to tell you after my bath." She folded her arms.

"Oh. I see. Well," she said on a long breath, "I will be sure your bill is ready." She paused, angled her head to the side as she took in Parris's still slightly swollen eyes. "Did you find her?"

Parris turned away and walked to the center of the room then to the French doors. "No." She raised her chin a notch. "And it's just as well. This search has brought me nothing but..."

"More questions."

Parris turned around. Marie's brow arched with her question, her mouth soft with compassion.

Parris nodded. "Questions I may never know the answers to."

"Which may be just as well. Too often we hunt around and around, dig and dig only to discover that it is a very dirty business. What is past, *chérie,* is done," she said with a wave of her arm. "Nothing can change what has already happened. Not even knowing." Her eyes widened with her conclusion.

Parris almost smiled. "I'm sure you're right. It simply doesn't feel that way right now."

"And it may never feel that way. But—" she shot her finger toward Parris "—you can either let it consume you or you can be like the phoenix and rise from the ashes!" she said, her voice flooded with bravado and theatrical passion.

Parris bit back a smirk. "I'm really going to miss you."

"And I you, *chérie*. But as they say in the dressing room of life, the show must go on. *Oui?*"

"*Oui.*" For the first time in several hours she actually felt a little better. Yes, she would certainly miss Marie's optimistic enthusiasm and cavalier attitude about life.

Marc was tapping on Parris's door promptly at nine the following morning. Nick had rebooked her on a flight leaving at one that afternoon, but with the sudden surge in terror attacks around the globe, airports were on higher alert than usual and unprecedented delays due to security added to the time needed to board.

"I came to take your bags."

"I can manage."

"Ahh, but why should you?" He winked and Parris saw once again why Marie was so taken with him. Marc exuded that European sexiness that was as much a part of who he was as his name.

"You know what, you are absolutely right."

"But of course!"

Parris stepped aside to let him in. He took her two small bags and before she knew it she was sharing a hug and words of wisdom from Marie.

"Tomorrow is not promised," she whispered in Parris's ear before they separated at the door. "Enjoy your today." She pressed a piece of paper into her hand with her number. "Stay in touch."

"I will. I promise."

Marie kissed both of her cheeks and waved as she got into Amin's cab en route to the airport.

"I'm so happy that you kept my number. How was your stay?" Amin asked as he headed toward the highway.

"I didn't actually find what I'd come looking for." She watched the town slowly dissolve in the rear window and the open landscape of rolling hills and valleys take its place.

"I am sorry to hear that."

Parris leaned on the armrest and braced her chin on her palm, reliving the past few days. She didn't think she'd ever be able to put into words the depth of her sadness. The enormity of the sham that was her family. Family is the foundation. The rock. The fabric of individuals and society. Her frown deepened. What was hers? A mere figment.

It would take her time to reconcile it all. Some of it she would never understand, but she knew that the most difficult part would be to forgive. That pained her most of all.

The cab came to a stop at the intersection before entering the roadway to the airport.

Parris sat straight up then leaned forward, gripping the back of his seat. "Amin, can you turn around? Quickly?"

"Turn around? Go back to Le Moulin?"

"No, back to the villa. The house you took me to the night I arrived."

Amin stole a glance at her over his shoulder, the staunch determination that set her delicate expression left no room for doubt of her intention. He was certain that if he said no, she would jump out of the cab and find her way without him. He bobbed his head. At the next opportunity he turned around and headed for the Loire Valley.

Parris chewed on the nail of her thumb, staring at the images of what could be, reality disappearing into the background. She didn't know what she was going to do, what she would say. All she knew for certain was that she could not return home without stamping out the final smoldering ash of her make-believe life. She checked her watch and prayed that there would be enough time.

"I really don't know why you didn't at least talk with me about this first before you made these plans," Michael grumbled as he put on his shirt, looking at his wife in the reflection of the mirror. "Why the big hurry to take a sudden trip?"

She came up behind him and slid her arms around his waist, pressing her head against his back. "I wanted us to be spontaneous for a change. No weeks of planning and deciding, just go on the spur of the moment." She came around to stand in front of him, then perched on the edge of the dressing table. "Besides—" she reached up and began to button his shirt "—we could use the time alone to be pampered." Her expression danced with mischief.

Michael physically relaxed. The straight line of his mouth softened. "I suppose you're right." He stroked her cheek. "It may be just the thing we need."

She leaned up and kissed him lightly on the lips. "I know it is."

He turned away in search of what she didn't know and she drew in a silent breath of relief. The night before they'd gone round and round in circles about the trip, the money being spent, the suddenness, the reasons why. The questions and his surliness went on and on. She'd almost broken down and given in when he finally relented, albeit with great reluctance, sleeping with his back to her. But she'd won as she always had.

"I'm going to take the bags out to the car. We should get

on the road before the traffic gets too heavy." He walked out, shrugging into his jacket.

Emma glanced down. Her hands were shaking. She balled them into fists. Soon this would be over. This ugly turn in her life would be done. She would come up with a plan and she would execute it.

Michael brought out the two large suitcases, turned on the car to warm it up and put one bag then the other in the trunk of the car. Their hand luggage could go in the backseat, he decided as he closed the truck and came face-to-face with his past. It was Emma. Younger. The same but different. He involuntarily staggered back a step.

"Hello. I'm sorry if I startled you. I was wondering if Emma Travanti was here. My name is Parris. I came by a few days ago, but I was told she wasn't here."

A tumbling sensation began in the pit of his gut and spun upward to his head. *Parris.*

They both turned to the sound of the house door being opened. "Michael, I—" Emma gasped at the sight of her daughter standing on her doorstep. Her gaze tore between the stunned expression of her husband and the dawning light of understanding that shimmered in her daughter's eyes.

Michael gripped the trunk. "Emma?" The word, a ragged indictment.

Parris's accusing gaze stripped Emma down to the root of her selfish evil. She stood naked and accused before them.

Emma's hand rose to her chest. A million explanations raced through her brain but no words came from her opened mouth.

Parris turned to the man before her who'd visibly aged in a matter of moments. She spoke only to him. "My grandmother,

Cora, told me that my mother, Emma, was not dead as I'd been told all my life." She blinked back the tears that flamed her eyes. "She wanted me to find her. I promised her that I would. On her deathbed I promised her." She saw the lines of agony carving a path across Emma's perfect face. A part of her relished it. Enjoyed the pain that paled her skin even further. "I wish I could say that I'd fulfilled my grandmother's request." She raised her chin a notch. "Sorry to have bothered you." She turned and hurried back to the cab that sat at the end of the driveway, her heart breaking into a million pieces. Tears blinded her as she stumbled down the road, half-walking, half-running.

Her pulse pounded so violently in her ears that she didn't hear Michael call out to her or the limping footsteps that tried to catch her before she got in the cab and demanded that they leave. Pounding on the backseat. Now. Now. Drive!

Michael banged on the trunk of the cab as it sped away, kicking up dirt and gravel. For several moments he stood there, frozen as he had been only moments ago, and watched the car become smaller and smaller. He turned to see Emma standing in the doorway. Then as quickly as his bad leg could take him he reached his car, tugged the door open. Emma grabbed his arm. He shoved her roughly away and got in. His hands shook as he tried to insert the key.

"Michael!" Emma yanked on the door handle.

Vicious, cold eyes turned on her. "Get away from me," he roared through the window and took off.

Emma crumbled to the ground, her agony echoing in the stillness of the morning.

Michael drove faster than the law allowed in the hope of gaining sight of the cab along the winding roads that led out of the valley. He could hardly think. The sick sensation in the pit of his stomach threatened to overwhelm him. The images played again and again in his mind's eye. It felt like an eternity but it was only a matter of minutes. He'd been stunned, frozen in place as he listened to his daughter's lilting voice, saw the very image of her mother outlined on her face. He should have done something, said something, claimed her. But he hadn't been able to process what was happening, as if it was happening to someone else and he was merely a spectator.

He'd foolishly allowed his unbridled love for Emma to make room for forgiveness for what she had done. They were young. She was afraid. But her deceit had damaged them. He knew that. He wanted to believe that their love was strong enough to sustain them. But this. He shook his head in grief and stepped down harder on the gas.

When Emma received the letter from her mother telling her that she'd finally told Parris the truth and that she would one day come to find her, Michael never in his wildest imagination would have believed that yet again, after forgiving her for the unforgivable, she would have been willing to continue the lie. He saw the fear in Emma's eyes. And the kernel of painful acceptance in Parris's. They'd met before. Right there at his home.

My God, what kind of woman had he married? He had to find his daughter.

# Chapter Ten

Amin's concern for his passenger grew with each passing moment. The shuddering sobs that she tried to hide behind her clenched fist pierced at his heart. He had no idea what happened between those white people that she'd gone to see, but it had devastated her. He continued to steal glances at her through the rearview mirror. She looked suddenly small and vulnerable and desperately in need of someone to take care of her, at least for now.

"Is there someone I can call for you?"

She sniffed and shook her head. "No. Thank you," she mumbled. Her voice was hoarse. "I just want to get on the plane and go home." She released a long shaky breath and turned her face to the passenger window.

They approached the last exit before the entrance to the

airport. "We will be there shortly." It was nearly eleven. "You should have plenty of time to make your flight."

She nodded numbly as the daymare of the previous hour replayed behind her swollen lids. Emma had known all along who she was, from the moment she appeared at her house, during the time she sat opposite her at the table in the bistro. She knew. She looked her in the eyes and knew that she was her daughter. Yet, she did nothing but continue the farce that had been her entire life. And that man. Was he her husband? Was he part of the ruse, as well? The knot in her throat grew, threatening to cut off her breathing. She pressed the button on the armrest, let down the window and gulped in the exhaust-filled air as the airport loomed ahead.

Amin pulled up behind the line of parking cars, jumped out, took Parris's bag from the trunk and set it on the curb. He opened her door and helped her out.

The sadness of her eyes twisted his heart. "If you ever return, look me up. You have yet to meet my daughter." He squeezed her shoulders.

"I will." Parris pressed her lips into a tight smile, and tried to blink away the tears that threatened to spill. "If you're ever in New York, you be sure to come see me. Hopefully, I'll have a singing job soon." She sniffed and tried to look hopeful.

"I will do that."

She reached for her bag. "Thanks for everything, Amin." She bent a bit and pecked him lightly on his rough cheek. "Take care." She turned and merged with the passengers flooding the airport terminal.

Michael had long ago lost sight of the cab and was now driving aimlessly through the streets of southeast Paris. He drove by rote, stopping and going as need be. His mind was in turmoil and his spirit in disarray. Whatever semblance of a life he thought he and Emma still had was finished. For more than three decades he'd lived with a woman that he didn't know, one he'd only imagined. That realization sickened him. And she'd allowed the fantasy to be nurtured. She fed it and watched it grow, entangling him like the vines that crawled along the walls of their home, until he was unable and perhaps unwilling to extricate himself.

*Parris.* She had no idea who he was. Perhaps she didn't even know of his existence. There was no telling what Emma had convinced her mother of so long ago. He pounded his fist against the steering wheel. The shock of the pain shot up his arm, jolting him. He squeezed his eyes shut for an instant until it subsided. A car horn blared behind him. He glanced up at the green light, flexed his fingers and moved across the intersection.

All the years they'd lost. They would never be recovered. Never. And he didn't know how he could live with that, how he could live with Emma.

Emma paced the gleaming wood floors, swinging between near hysteria and resolve. Tears clouded her vision. Pain squeezed her heart. At every sound she dashed to the window, praying that it was Michael and hoping that it wasn't. How could she face him? What could she possibly say to explain the horror of what she'd done? And what of Parris? When she'd looked into her eyes and saw the recognition turn to revelation then disgust, she knew there was nothing that she could do. As the old folks in Rudell would have said, the chickens have come home to roost.

She grabbed a vase from the table and threw it across the floor. It exploded against the fireplace into brilliant crystal pieces. Her life. Broken pieces. Her life as she knew it was over. If there had been a chance to salvage her marriage that, too, was gone. All she could do now was wait for her sentencing. After all, she'd been tried and convicted. No one cared why she'd done what she did, why she lived a life of lies, what had compelled her to do the unthinkable—give up her child and pretend to be dead all these years. She swallowed over the tightness in her throat. No one would understand the torture she'd lived with every day of her life, the torment that had permanent residence in her soul from the stain that she'd been born with and been forced to endure.

Did anyone give her a choice? Did anyone care about a little girl who was hated, mistreated, looked down upon and laughed at? A girl who grew up with not a friend in the world, not even her mother, a woman who could barely look at her.

Who knew what that was like, what that did to the soul? She withdrew to the window and sunk down into the chair. To wait.

"Can I get you something to drink?" the flight attendant asked, stirring Parris from the turn of her thoughts.

She glanced up. "No, thank you."

The flight attendant pushed the cart up the aisle.

So many emotions flooded her that she was actually numb, as if she were on some kind of overload and the anger, hurt, confusion, rage, sadness and acceptance all merged together into a huge ball of nothingness that settled in the pit of her stomach and spread outward like anesthesia. She curled a bit tighter in her seat, gathered the thin blanket around her shoulders. This was worse than losing her grandmother. This was an inexplicable loss, one that she struggled to wrap her mind around. A mother who not only played dead for decades, but once resurrected and face-to-face with her own mortality also chose to disavow its existence…still. She had a choice to claim what was lost between them or live as she'd always lived. Again, Emma chose her own life over that of her child.

Parris looked out of the window, the sky midnight black, bottomless. She closed her eyes and prayed for a bottomless, dreamless sleep.

After the unbelievably long walk from the plane through the winding corridors of customs at Kennedy airport, Parris handed over her passport for inspection.

"Welcome home," the customs agent said, returning her passport with a smile.

*Home.* She actually appreciated the sound of it. During the flight, between sleeping in stops and starts, she'd arrived at a place in her consciousness that France was another world, a life that she was not, and would never be, a part of. She would take the good from it; meeting Marie and Amin. The rest… She'd spent all of her life to date without her mother in it, and she would live the rest of it the same way. Her grandmother's dying wish had been fulfilled. She was no longer obligated to anyone other than herself. She would pursue her career and, most important, her relationship with Nick.

Thoughts of him, the idea that they could be a "we," made it all bearable in a scary way. She hoisted her tote bag over her shoulder and pulled her carry-on behind her along the bumpy carpeted floors following the signs to Baggage Claim and Ground Transportation. As soon as she pushed through the glass doors she saw Nick and her insides seesawed. She felt the smile begin deep in her center, wiggle its way upward and spread across her mouth. Her heart thumped.

Nick walked right up on her, his gaze fixed, took her bag from her shoulder and lowered it to the ground, unwrapped her fingers from the handle of her rollerboard, hooked his arm around her waist, pulled her so close that air couldn't get between them. And he kissed her. Long, deep and slow, and he didn't give a damn who was looking. It felt too good and he'd waited too long to feel her in his arms and have her mouth meshed with his.

Murmurs of longing shifted between the air they shared.

"God, I missed you," he said against her mouth.

Parris held him tighter, feeling for the first time in days that she was finally on solid ground. "I missed you," she sighed.

He took a reluctant step back and stared down into her eyes. A string of emotions passed across them resembling a line of traffic, every make and model on display.

"Let's get you home."

A shadow of a smile tugged the corners of her mouth. "Home. I like the sound of that."

He kissed her forehead. "Let's go."

The car ride from the airport to Nick's Harlem apartment went by in a flash, perhaps because her eyes drifted closed from the moment she was strapped in, to the time Nick gently shook her shoulder.

She blinked, trying to orient herself. "Here already?" She glanced around, surprised to see that they were in front of his building.

"Jet lag will get you every time. One minute I was telling you all about the club, then I glanced back and you were out like a light."

She grinned sheepishly. "I could have sworn I heard every word."

"Hmm, riiight." He turned off the car and hopped out, came around to her side and opened her door. "Here, go on up." He handed her the keys. "I'll get your bags."

She covered her mouth and yawned. "Okay." She took the keys, got out and felt every muscle groan in protest as she went inside and up the stairs. When she opened the door to the apartment a genuine wave of relief, or maybe contentment, floated through her. The knots that were wrapped around her stomach began to loosen and the sinking sensation, the feeling of emptiness, didn't feel quite as empty.

The door closed behind her. "You didn't get very far," Nick teased upon finding her still in the foyer.

She turned suddenly, her expression set as she approached him. "I don't know what I would have done without you."

"That's something you don't ever have to worry about." He stroked her cheek. "I promise you."

She stepped into his open embrace and rested her head against his chest.

"I hope you don't mind that I have no plans to continue to treat you like a guest."

She tilted her head back to look at him, her brow creased.

"The guest room is for guests. My bedroom is for me and my lady."

Her green eyes sparkled. "Would I be presumptuous if I took it to mean that *I'm* your lady?"

"Not at all," he said, spacing each word for emphasis. He pecked her on the lips and walked past her with the bags to deposit them in his room.

Nothing further needed to be said. She followed him to *their* room.

Nick had no intention of pressing her for details. He'd pretty much pieced it all together during that painful conversation they'd had while she was in France. Bottom line, her mother disowned her, refused to acknowledge her existence and was bold enough to look her in her face and have a conversation with her. Every time he thought about it his temples pounded. He wanted to hurt that woman, the way she'd hurt Parris. He wanted her to feel the pain and humiliation that Parris experienced, only worse. He'd never tell Parris just how much what happened to her affected him, the ugly thoughts that ran through his mind, ways to make her mother pay. That dark side of him, that part of his life, he worked really hard to keep in the past, tucked away and out of sight. When it had reared its ugly head, it had taken Sammy to make him realize that doing something stupid would be just that—something stupid.

"Those days are behind us, man," Sammy had said. "We've come a long way from the street life. We were the lucky ones. Most of the brothers we came up with and ran with are either dead or in jail. We had something to fall back on, our music, our skills. It saved our asses. And being your boy all these years, there's no way I could stand by and watch you do something that you'll regret. And you know I can't let you roll alone, which means I'd have to get my hands dirty, too."

Nick was hunched over his drink. His red eyes stared into the melted ice. He'd been talking about taking a flight to France and paying a visit to this Emma or sending someone from the old days to do it for him. Someone who'd do just about anything for a price.

"What do you hope to accomplish, man? You hurt this woman—or worse—and then what? You sure as hell can't tell Parris. So this isn't about fixing this for her or making her feel better. This is about you. If you want to do something for

Parris, if you want to help her, then just be there for her, man. Simple as that."

He was glad he'd listened to his old friend, he thought as he cuddled next to Parris, listening to the soothing rhythm of her even breathing. His blood had been boiling and all he could think about was hurting the one who'd hurt Parris. He pressed his face into the downy softness of her hair and silently vowed to keep her safe and happy, no matter what.

## Chapter Eleven

Leslie awoke with a monster headache. She'd been getting them more frequently of late and Celeste made her promise to see a doctor, which she never got around to doing. Slowly she sat up, closed her eyes as the pain slowly washed through her, before settling down to a dull throb. She pushed up from her full-sized bed, which was too small and too old for her plus-sized frame. Yet another thing on her agenda—get a bigger bed. When she stood, the room shifted slightly left then right. She gripped the headboard to keep from falling. Her heart thumped. Her head thumped harder.

That was a first, she thought as the out of body moment slowly passed. Gingerly she walked down the short hallway to the bathroom before going in to check on her mother. As she stared at her reflection in the mirror she silently prayed that it would be a good day for her mother. She had an important meeting with Nick Hunter, Sammy Blackstone and Parris McKay at what would soon be Rhythms, the hottest new nightspot in Harlem. This job could turn her whole business around and maybe her mundane life as well. She turned on the faucet and splashed warm water on her face before applying her daily facial wash. Her baby-smooth complexion was her strongest physical attribute and she worked diligently to ensure that it stayed blemish free.

The faint sound of a ringing bell floated above the rush of water as she rubbed the granulated cream into her cheeks. Slowly she lifted her head, keeping her eyes shut to keep the water out, and angled her head slightly to the right in the direction of the sound. There it was again. Her heavy chest sagged. Mother was awake. She could barely speak, couldn't get around without major assistance, but the one thing she could do was ring that damned bell.

"Coming!" she yelled, tossing her head back to throw her voice. Water and the specially formulated soap slid down into her eyes. The sting was red-pepper hot and in concert with the string of expletives that burst from her lips as she hopped from bare foot to bare foot, tossing cold water on her face while trying to squeeze the pain out of her eye.

Momentarily blinded in one eye, she pressed a cold cloth to it as she hurried to tend to her mother.

"Mornin'. Sorry, I was in the bathroom."

Her mother's brows drew together and her mouth tried to form words.

"Got some soap in my eye when I was washing my face," Leslie explained as she approached the bed. "Need to get up?"

Theresa bobbed her head, the faintest sound which could have been "yes" was barely audible.

Leslie lowered the railing on her mother's hospital bed, something the hospital insisted that she purchase to ensure that Theresa didn't take a tumble. At her age, the doctor had warned, a broken hip was more deadly than a stroke.

Of course, her mother's medical plan didn't cover a hospital bed, so Leslie had to dip in to her meager business account to buy it. And pretty soon the coverage for the home health attendant was going to be cut off as well.

The doctor insisted that Theresa should have been doing much better by now. Her brain cells were normal and there was no major neurological damage. At this point, Gracie, the physical therapist, was beginning to believe that Theresa's inability to speak and move around on her own was more in her head than in her body, which she'd quietly expressed to Leslie on more than one occasion.

"Your mother wants *your* attention, not mine," she'd said one evening last week on her way out.

"What do you mean? I'm not a therapist."

"No, but you're her daughter."

Leslie thought about the remark as she practically lifted her mother out of the bed, both of them grunting and grimacing as Theresa was finally steady enough to grip the handles of her walker and shuffle to the bathroom.

Beads of sweat dotted Leslie's forehead and slid down her temples as she plopped down on the narrow bed, feeling it sink beneath her, in sharp contrast to her near weightless mother. She inhaled slow and deep and wondered how much longer she could do this. It was a cruel trick from the Almighty that after years of animosity, verbal standoffs and hostility, the two of them would be forced to live with each other. And her mother, who'd never mothered her, was reduced to having to depend on the one person who held her in contempt. They may have to love one another for no reason beyond the ties of blood that bound them, but they despised who they were as people. Neither of them lived under the illusion that there was a relationship between them.

Leslie listened to the muffled flush of the toilet, followed by running water in the sink. She checked the bedside clock. It was almost nine. Her appointment was at one. She needed to fix breakfast, straighten her mother's room, help her eat and get dressed and hopefully Gracie would arrive in time so that she could make her one o'clock meeting.

Bracing her palms on the side of the bed she pushed up and stood, pausing momentarily to make sure she didn't experience another episode. She walked over to the bathroom and tapped lightly on the door. "You okay?"

Theresa grunted her response, which Leslie took for a yes. "I'm going to fix breakfast." She started to tell her that she would be going out as soon as Gracie arrived, but thought better of it. Recently, each time Leslie made plans to go out, or had an appointment that would take her out of the house, Theresa would become totally unmanageable. She wouldn't eat, refused to participate in her physical therapy, wouldn't help at all in getting herself in and out of bed or off the recliner, preferring to transform herself into dead weight. Leslie felt chained to the house, chained to her mother, and she resented it and her more every day.

Today she didn't give a damn what tricks her mother pulled. She wasn't going to blow this appointment. It was too important. Securing this job and doing it well could finally get her the recognition she'd been struggling to attain in the design business. She'd done a variety of small jobs; friends' home office spaces, the lounge at Downbeat, a couple of start-up businesses, but nothing on the scale of a nightclub. Getting this job meant freedom. It was the least her mother could do for her.

Gracie arrived by noon, which gave Leslie a good half hour to get herself ready, although she wouldn't have a minute left to spare. The moment Gracie arrived, Theresa's eyes brightened like a light in a dark room. Leslie's feelings for Gracie hovered on the fence. On one side she desperately needed her to make living with her mother bearable. On the other she resented the give-and-take between her mother and Gracie. Theresa saved her weak smiles, eagerness and mini-milestones of physical improvement all for Gracie. All she got were grunts, and looks of scorn or disappointment—she no longer knew the difference. Her mother had such a low level of tolerance that nightly Leslie questioned why she bothered.

As she put on her wool coat, which was getting too small, she knew why she bothered. There was a tiny part of her—the little girl in her—that was still looking for her mother's love and acceptance. And maybe if she ever attained it, maybe if her mother could ever love her enough, she would tell her what she needed and deserved to know about who she was.

Leslie buttoned her too-tight coat, threw a wool scarf around her neck and heard the shredding sound of the inside lining of her coat opening up like a chasm. Muttering a curse she turned over her shoulder. "I should only be gone a couple of hours. But I'd really appreciate it if you could stay until I get back, just in case I'm running late."

Gracie waved her hand and took a seat next to Theresa, who sat in the recliner with a food tray in front of her. "We'll be fine." She patted Theresa's hand. "We have exercises to do today." She winked at Theresa, who smacked her hand.

"'Bye, Ma."

Theresa didn't bother to look at her daughter, focusing instead on Judge Judy.

Gracie looked at her over Theresa's head and mouthed, *Go on, we'll be fine. Do good.*

Leslie's chest pinched. If it weren't for Gracie giving her those words of encouragement and, of course, Celeste, she didn't know what she would do. She pressed her lips tightly together, turned and walked out.

Nick still found it hard to believe that he and Parris were sharing the same space and that the obstacles that they'd faced from the moment they'd met more than a year earlier were no more. Their relationship was an open door and they'd begun to take those tentative steps to the other side.

While he'd lain next to her last night, feeling her warmth, the pillow softness of her skin, every inch an invitation to become enveloped by it, listening to the steadiness of her breathing, he wondered what it was about Parris McKay that made him want to be a better man. She'd had that effect on him from the beginning when she questioned and challenged him to examine his reasons for dealing with Percy and his questionable money, his strong-arm tactics as well as his intimate relationship with Tara, Percy's daughter. Her presence in his life compelled him to look beyond his mirrored reflection and examine who he was, and, more importantly, who he wanted to be. Walking on the dark side of life had been who Nick was. It was in his blood since he was a teen, hustling on the streets of New York City. It was second nature to fall under the mystique of Percy and all that he represented. And it gave him the chance to do what he loved—play his music. But it all came at a price—his soul—and it nearly cost him Parris. There was an innate decency about her that made him believe there was still goodness in the world. It wasn't that she was preachy or holier than thou. It was more about her living by a code of values and seeing the best in people until they showed her otherwise, which was why it infuriated him so that anyone would dare to hurt her as her mother had done.

He walked up behind her as she stood at the sink and curved his arms around her waist. He pushed her hair away and kissed the back of her neck. His body stiffened when she leaned back into his embrace. He moaned deep in his throat.

"Did I tell you how glad I am that you're here?"

Parris turned in his arms. "Tell me again."

"I'm glad you're here. Very glad." His gaze moved languidly across her face.

She rested her head on his chest.

"Everything's going to be okay. I don't want you to worry. I know we haven't really talked about what happened and we don't have to. But I want you to know that I'm here for you if you decide you want to talk about it."

She nodded her head. "I know. Right now, I want to put it behind me. Maybe at some point when it doesn't ache so bad…" She leaned back a bit and looked up at him. "What I do want to talk about is the club, the plans." She moved over to the table and leaned against it. Nick stepped between her slightly parted thighs.

"I set up a meeting with Leslie Evans for one o'clock over at the club. I'm hoping you're up to coming with me. I'm sure she'll be glad to see you again. Not sure how bad the jet lag had hit you."

Parris grinned. "Not bad, but I'm sure it will. I still want to come. I'd like to keep tabs on the other woman who's going to be vying for your attention and approval," she teased, tracing the shell of his ear.

Nick pressed closer. "There's only one woman whose approval I'm interested in and she has all of my attention." He sucked on his bottom lip as he caressed the curve of her hip.

"Is that right?" She draped her arms around his neck and linked her fingers before easing his head toward hers.

The warmth of his lips sent a sudden and unexpected current ripping through her that physically shook her. Nick pulled her closer. The pulse of his erection pressed alarmingly hard and stiff against her pelvis. She rose up on her toes to angle him right in her center and they moaned at the perfect fit.

Parris reached for the hem of his shirt and tugged it out of his waistband. Nimble fingers unfastened his jeans. He gave one pull on the belt of her robe and it opened as if the magic word had been uttered. His jaw clenched when his gaze traveled down her half-naked body. Slender and curvy all at once. Honey-brown skin that was as sweet to the tongue as it was tempting to the eye. He inhaled her, filling his veins with the soft scent of her.

With one hand he pulled a chair out from beneath the table, switched positions until he lowered himself onto the seat and Parris onto his lap. His thumbs grazed her nipples and she shuddered.

"All the time I want you," he confessed, nibbling her neck.

Her body heated to his touch. "You have me...all the time." She pressed her lips against his and for the moment nothing else mattered.

★ ★ ★

Sammy was parked in front of the soon-to-be nightclub when Nick and Parris pulled up behind him. They met at the front door.

"Hey, lady," Sammy greeted, kissing Parris lightly on the cheek. "Welcome home."

"Thanks. Good to see you."

Sammy shook Nick's hand as he lifted his shoulders toward his neck to ward off a blast of chilly air. "Guess we can wait inside out of the cold. Is, uh, Celeste joining us?"

Nick and Parris shared a short, knowing look. "Not that I know of," Nick said, hiding his smirk while he worked the locks on the gate. The metal rattled against the frigid air, echoing like shotgun fire. He pulled open the gate and unlocked the door. They stepped into the chilly dimness.

"I can't wait to get this place up and running," Nick said, walking around as if for the first time.

"It's going to be *the* spot," Sammy announced with conviction.

"Especially with our very own star," Nick said, turning his smile on Parris.

"Speaking of star, what are you doing about that contract offer?"

Parris blew out a breath. "I know I've got to take care of that, and soon, before they take the offer back. If they haven't already. There's just been so much going on."

Sammy nodded in agreement. "Hey, if they want you, they'll wait."

"And if not, then it wasn't for me."

"For real. You have more talent in one note than half of these folks perpetrating themselves as musical artists." He made a hissing sound. "Please."

Parris chuckled. "Thanks for the vote of confidence."

Sammy winked.

They all turned at the sound of knocking.

"There she is," Nick said, walking over to open the door. "Hey, Leslie. Good to see you. Come on in."

"Whoa, it's cold out there," she said, shaking her shoulders against the biting chill as she stepped inside.

He stood aside to let her pass. "Sammy, Parris, you remember Leslie—the wonder woman who's going to turn this dump into a showplace."

"Well, if she could transform Downbeat's lounge, anything is possible," Sammy quipped before bussing Leslie's cheek. "Good to see you."

"Thanks, Sammy." She turned her smile on Parris. "Girl, how have you been? I sure miss hearing that voice of yours on Friday nights."

Parris laughed and stretched out her arms for a hug. The two women embraced. "I miss it, too, but hopefully not for long," she said, turning a warm eye on the partners.

"It's all up to this lady right here," Nick said, indicating Leslie. "Once she works her magic we'll be good to go."

"No pressure," Leslie teased, unbuttoning her coat, but she turned down Sammy's offer to take it, remembering what she knew was an unsightly rip in the lining. "Celeste was right. This will take work, but it's definitely doable." She turned her focus on Nick, feeling confident on familiar ground. "Tell me what you have in mind." She pulled a notebook and pen from her large purse.

"Let's sit over here." Sammy pulled out some chairs at the shaky table by the window to give them the most light.

Leslie took copious notes as Nick outlined his plan for the space then he showed her around.

"I can get some preliminary sketches to you by the end of the week. I'll also check with my suppliers for fabrics and furnishings and get some estimates. I'd like to take some pictures if you don't mind."

"Do your thing," Nick said.

She took a digital camera from her purse, walked to the back of the space and started shooting.

"Hope the place doesn't scare her off," Sammy commented to Nick.

Nick chuckled. "If I remember correctly she doesn't scare easy. Remember the afternoon she got into a shouting match with Percy over the change in wall coverings for the dining area?"

"Oh, man, do I." Sammy chuckled and shook his head.

"I missed that one," Parris said. "What happened? She actually got into it with Percy?"

"Well, you know how Percy is about wanting what he wants when he wants it," Sammy began. He went on to explain about some kind of mix-up with the fabric and that Percy went completely ballistic and turned his fury on Leslie. She'd let him rant and rail, tossing out some ugly comments about her career, before she simply stepped up to him, slapped him in the chest with the contract, the swatches and his signature, and said that if he broke the contract she'd spend the rest of her life and every dime she had to sue him until the name out front read *Leslie's Place*. She planted her hands on those wide hips of hers and dared him. Percy was so stunned that all of a sudden he burst out laughing, doubling over until he had to sit down. When he finally pulled himself together, he pointed his cigar at her and said, "I like you. You got more balls than some of these men around here."

"Leslie became kind of a legend around the club after that," Nick added. "Of course the story has grown to epic proportions since it happened." He and Sammy chuckled at the memory.

The scenario seemed implausible to Parris as she shook her head in awe. Rumor had it that more than one person had abruptly disappeared after rubbing Percy the wrong way, which was why she was so happy that Nick was finally out from under Percy's dark cloud. As she watched Leslie move into the kitchen area she realized she had a newfound respect for her. In the few times that she'd seen her and spent time with her at Downbeat, she viewed Leslie as a nice, talented, perhaps withdrawn young woman who was trying to make a go at what she loved. But in fact, this was a woman who had a fire deep in her soul, someone who wasn't going to compromise her ethics or be bullied by someone who appeared to have control. She liked that—a woman who dictated her own destiny and would not allow other people or circumstances to do it for her. Maybe that was the glue that connected Leslie and Celeste, an underlying need to be their own woman, at whatever the cost. And each of them had their own way of achieving that end.

Leslie returned and finished up photographing the front of the space, the bar and stage area, and the entryway. She turned to the waiting trio. "That should do it." She dropped the camera into her purse and handed Nick her card. "If you think of anything or have any questions before I get back to you, please give me a call."

"I will."

Leslie released a breath and stuck out her hand. "Thanks for the opportunity. You won't be disappointed. Good to see you again, Parris, Sammy."

"You, too," they said in unison.

Nick walked her to the door. "We'll talk at the end of the week."

"Sounds good."

"Oh, Leslie," Parris called out.

Leslie peered around Nick's shoulder.

"If you talk with Celeste, tell her I'm back and I'll give her a call soon."

"I sure will. 'Bye, everyone."

Nick closed the door behind her.

"So, you and Celeste are friends?" Sammy said under his breath before Nick returned.

Parris angled her head to one side with a smirk on her face. "More like acquaintances. Why?"

"Nothing. Nothing. Just asking is all."

"Hmm. Are you sure that's all it is?"

"Can't a brother ask a question without something being read into it?" he asked, scowling.

Parris was not moved by the fake frown. "Methinks thou dost protest too much," she said with a twitch of her eyebrow and walked toward Nick before Sammy could respond.

"You two fighting again?" Nick asked as he draped his arm around Parris's shoulder. They'd been known to have infamous debates about music and musicians. Their combined knowledge could fill a library and always fascinated anyone who was privy to one of their legendary battles.

Sammy stared her down and she returned the gesture. Sammy was the first to relent. "Let's go."

Nick looked at Parris, who shrugged. "Let's."

The trio stood outside in the bitter cold while Nick secured the gate and the locks on the door. He turned to Sammy. "See you at the jam session tonight."

"Absolutely. Bring your A game."

Nick chuckled. "No doubt. We both better."

They slapped palms before clasping hands.

"Make sure he's on time," he said to Parris with a wink.

"I will." She lightly kissed his cheek and whispered, "It's okay, you know."

His gaze darkened. The corner of his mouth curved ever so slightly.

Parris slid her arm through the crook in Nick's and they hurried off to the car.

Michael sat still as stone in the overstuffed chair near the window. A cold ceaseless rain fell for the second day in a row, painting the city and the small town a dull gray, shrouding it in fog. The world beyond his window looked surreal, a reflection of his life. One day everything was the way he'd always imagined it would be—married to the love of his life, with a secure future in the vineyards, traveling and living well. Yet in a matter of days, what they'd built together for the past thirty years began to crumble. His heavy staccato sigh was from one who'd sobbed for hours and all that was left was the unimaginable emptiness that echoed in the soul. He braced his chin on his palm as he watched the water continue to fall. A streak of lightning stabbed the heavy clouds and surely struck his heart.

The muscles of his throat tightened as the images beyond the window began to blur and his anguish spilled in a single path down his cheek. No one in his family knew what he'd only recently discovered about Emma's true heritage. The initial shock rendered him unable to process the winding, twisted story of Emma's life and the child of theirs that she'd given up in order to have a life with him.

He'd been moved by her sorrow, imagining what life must have been like for her. The fear that she lived with and the burden of the secret she'd carried. His words had forgiven her for her deceit, even promising that he understood and would stand by her, love her as he always had and be there with her when *their* daughter came, as Cora's dying letter to her daughter had intimated.

But in the weeks that passed since that life-altering day he'd had the time and the space and the presence of mind to really think about the enormity of the sham that his life and his marriage had been for the past thirty years. He was in love with a woman he did not know. He'd forgiven her for a sin that surely must be unforgivable. What kind of man did that make him? *A fool.* A fool, blinded by love and beauty and promises of a forever happiness with a woman who made him feel tall as a mountain. A woman who became the very air he breathed, the blood that flowed through his veins, his only reason for opening his eyes with each new day.

His weary gaze rose to the sounds of movement above his head. A stranger in his home. A woman he did not know. Some stranger who would turn her own daughter away, their daughter, to keep her secret. His chest seemed to split with the pain, and its wretched ache burned like hellfire.

With great effort he turned in her direction. Emma. *His Emma.* He was dying inside as he watched her carry her bags to the door. Her usually pale face was splotched red, her green eyes rimmed in crimson. The lips that he'd kissed even in his dreams were pressed into a tight line, but not tight enough to keep her cheeks and chin from quivering. The knot in her throat worked up and down.

Water floated in her eyes. She blinked rapidly before finally finding her voice, which was weak and thready. "The car is here." Her nostrils flared.

Michael couldn't speak. There was nothing left to say. It was over. They were done.

The car horn blew, startling them both. She picked up her bag. "I'm sorry," she whispered before turning away and hurrying out the door.

Michael listened to the opening and closing of the trunk. The car door slamming shut. The engine revving. The cobblestones tickling the tires. He listened until there was no sound.

## Chapter Twelve

Thank God for caller ID, Celeste thought as she popped three ice cubes in a glass and splashed them with Diet Coke. It was her mother again. If her count was right this was call number fifteen in the past two days. She watched the lights on the phone flash with each annoying ring. Finally the ringing stopped. Moments later the number in the message box showed sixteen.

Humph, she was off by one. Celeste swung away from her perch by the sink and sauntered back into her bedroom. She'd listened to the ranting messages that her mother had left, lambasting her about her inappropriate behavior the night of the party. How dare she walk out? How dare she make her look bad? Didn't she have any sense of protocol?

So rather than deal with her mother's outrage and belittling, she chose to ignore her, refusing to pick up the phone, refusing to return her calls. If Corrine could have a temper tantrum so could she. As for Clinton, he seemed satisfied with her explanation of a headache. He'd been, as she suspected, too involved with meeting the right people to notice her absence. What she needed was some space from that life and all that it involved. She was planning to meet Leslie for a rare girls' night out. The times they were able to do girlfriend things had diminished exponentially since Leslie's mom had the stroke and was moved into Leslie's apartment. What a life-altering bitch of an event that was, she thought. She'd been pretty sure that Leslie was going to come completely unglued. It was no secret that the rope of tension between Leslie and Theresa was hanging as tight as a noose, and neither of them was above kicking the chair out from under the other.

She shrugged out of her robe and tossed it across the foot of the bed. It was sad really, she mused as she flipped through her rack of sweaters in her closet. Leslie's entire existence revolved around her animosity toward her mother for keeping the identity of her father away from her. Year after year, like a disease, it ate away at her spontaneous laughter, her sense of adventure, the warm and funny person that she once was. Now, she went through the motions, and the only thing that gave her any pleasure was her work.

Guilt is a terrible thing, Celeste concluded as she pulled on a pair of black leather pants. That was the root of it all. Sure, Leslie tried to convince her that it was the way things had always been between her and her mother. But the truth was, the seed of what bloomed deep inside Leslie was guilt. Although all the doctors, nurses and Indian chiefs told her that it wasn't her fault, she didn't believe them.

She'd let her frustration, anger and insecurity mushroom

into a final showdown between her and Theresa, and the next thing she knew she was calling an ambulance with her mother having suffered a major stroke. That was more than a year ago.

Celeste selected a teal cashmere sweater with a deep V in the front. It was one of her favorites. Unfortunately, she thought as she leaned closer to the mirror and applied her lip gloss, she was the last one to offer mother/daughter advice. Personally, she couldn't stand her own mother.

She dropped the tube of lipstick in her purse, stuck her feet into her ankle boots, snatched up her coat and was out for the night.


Tracey's was located in lower Manhattan on West 9th Street and Broadway. It was a favorite hangout for Celeste because it was off the beaten path of the stuffy, elitist restaurants and clubs that Clinton took her to. Here the music was loud, the food was fattening and the crowd was real.

Celeste stowed her car in the local parking lot and walked the half block to the club. Even for a cold winter night, the smokers of the club were huddled out front taking those few precious puffs. Celeste eased by the group and pulled open the heavy wood-and-brass door and was greeted with a blast of heat-filled, fried-chicken-and-shrimp air and a cacophony of voices and laughter. The dimly lit club was packed from wall to wall. She hoped that Leslie was able to get a table somewhere. She peered over heads and around bodies as she wove her way through the tight room until she reached the bar. She turned sideways, slipped in between two thick bodies and waved down the bartender.

"Whaddayahavin'?" he shouted.

"Apple martini."

"Comingrightup."

Celeste turned halfway around to continue scoping out the crowd in search of Leslie. She hoped that her friend hadn't been waylaid at the last minute by drama from her mother—which Theresa Evans was notorious for doing. More than a time too many, Celeste had entered Leslie's name for sainthood. Because she knew if she had to take care of Corrine Shaw day in and day out, she would jump out of her parents' penthouse window and slit her wrists on the way down.

Her drink arrived and she took the first toe-curling sip. Tracey's may not be much for ambiance but they made the best apple martinis in the city. She paid for her drink, tucked her purse beneath her arm and wiggled her way to the other side to get a better look at the door.

She'd been to Tracey's dozens of times during the week and on the weekends, but she never remembered it being so crowded. The dance floor was full of gyrating bodies. The bar was lined from end to end, two rows deep. Every table was full and now it was standing room only for the die-hard Tracey's fans.

"Whew, they must be giving something away in here tonight," Leslie said, coming up behind Celeste.

Celeste turned, and nearly had her drink knocked out of her hand by a young couple trying to get by.

Celeste rolled her eyes at the duo that didn't bother with apologies. She licked the sweet brew off her hand. "Hey. I didn't see you come in."

"I got here about a half hour ago, got our table then stood in line for the ladies room," she said with a short laugh. "You know how that can be."

"Hmm, don't I. Please, let's sit. My cute boots are beginning to pinch."

Leslie led her around the dance floor to the other side, where they had a ringside view of the stage.

"Wow, you lucked out with this table." Celeste took off her coat and draped it over the back of her seat.

"I called this afternoon and made reservations."

Celeste smirked. If Leslie was nothing else she was organized and efficient. She, on the other hand, was accustomed to walking into a place and getting the best table on name recognition alone. When she went out with Clinton, he made the reservations. It never even occurred to her that a place like Tracey's would take reservations. Live and learn.

The stage lights shifted and the owner, Tracey, stepped up to the microphone. Tracey was a big girl in size, but not in height. She stood just over five feet, but weighed in at well over one hundred and fifty pounds. She had a voice that would make the hair on your arms stand up, enriched with the soul of Aretha, the angst of Billie, the riffs of Ella and the passion of Shirley Caesar. Her bold, multicolored swing dresses were her personal fashion statement. She had no problem letting people know she was in the room. Tonight her colors were crimson, burnt orange and sunshine yellow that twisted and curled around each other on a diaphanous dress that kissed her midcalf.

"Good evening, ladies and gentlemen," she said in a voice that sounded as if it was wrapped in the finest silk. "We have a treat for you tonight. So sit back, order plenty of drinks and enjoy the sounds of Turning Point."

The lights dimmed and there was movement on the stage as the entertainment took their places. Then the slow, soul-stirring whine of a sax bit into the air. The spotlight silhouetted the lone musician at the microphone, and Celeste and Leslie both yelped in delight, "That's Nick!" The piano tinkled in the dimness before being joined by the deep rhythm of the bass and a tease of brushes against the tight skin of the drum.

Heat started from the balls of Celeste's feet and rose slowly upward until the warmth lit a fire in her chest. She couldn't tear her eyes away from the piano player, as he held his head at an angle, eyes closed in an almost orgasmic joy and his long, slender fingers made intimate love to the keys. Sammy Blackstone. She'd had no idea when she'd see him again and certainly not here. Breathing was suddenly hard to do. She reached for her martini.

"This is a treat," Leslie said, sitting back and bobbing her head to the beat.

Celeste couldn't take her eyes off of Sammy. Seeing him in this environment opened her imagination to him in a new dimension.

"That's Sammy Blackstone on the piano," Leslie informed her. She turned to look at Celeste. "Are you okay?" She tapped her arm when she didn't respond.

Celeste halfway looked at her. "Huh?"

"I was asking if you were okay. You looked a little dazed."

Celeste suddenly grabbed Leslie's arm. "Come with me to the ladies room."

"Now?" Leslie whined in protest.

Celeste pressed her polished lips together. "Fine. But the instant they stop playing, let's go," she said, barely opening her mouth.

"What is wrong?"

Celeste waved off the question and Leslie reluctantly returned her attention to the band. Maybe things hadn't gone so well with Nick after all. Maybe the financing fell through. Maybe Celeste found a better buyer. Maybe Nick changed his mind. The questions were louder than the music. She grabbed Celeste by the wrist and off to the ladies room they went.

Leslie checked the stalls, found them all empty, then pressed her back against the door and folded her arms beneath her heavy breasts. "Okay, let's hear it. What the hell is going on?"

Celeste flushed, tucked her honey-blond hair behind her ears and paced in a circle as she spoke. "I met him the other day. And something went off inside me. I never felt that way before about a man. I can't stop thinking about it. About him. I know he doesn't feel the same way. At least I don't think he does. But I can't stop fantasizing about him." She looked at her friend with pleading eyes, begging her to understand.

"What in the world are you talking about? Who are you talking about?" Her incredibly smooth features were bunched together into hills and valleys of confusion.

Celeste took a breath and finally stood still. "Sammy."

Leslie shook her head as if a fly had teased her nose. "Say what? Sammy? Blackstone?" With each word her voice rose in pitch. She squinted at Celeste to see her better. "Huh?"

Celeste lifted her chin. "Yes. Sammy Blackstone."

"Get outta here." She began chuckling until she saw how annoyed Celeste was becoming. She cleared her throat. "Well, I'll be damned. For real?"

"Never mind," she spouted in disgust. "I shouldn't have said anything." She tried to push past Leslie to get out but that was futile.

"Hey, I'm sorry." She clasped Celeste by the shoulder, her expression contrite. "Seriously. I'm sorry. It was just a shock."

Celeste rolled her eyes.

"So...tell me what happened."

Celeste took a step back from the door and went to lean against the sink, careful of any wet spots. She began telling

Leslie about the day she met Sammy at the club, how she felt when he touched her, the look he'd given her. "I know it sounds twelfth grade but I don't know how else to explain it. The night I went to my mother's gathering, all I could think about is what would happen had I brought Sammy instead of Clinton."

"Cee, I don't want to bust your bubble or anything, but do you think that maybe your attraction to him is the same thing as what you do with the rest of your life—do things to piss your parents off?"

"Doing things and feeling things are different, Leslie. I may be mixed up in the head sometimes, but I'm not stupid." She cut her eyes in Leslie's direction, the beginnings of a Cheshire cat smile on her lips. "But could you just see their faces?"

Leslie held up her hand. "I can't even imagine." She heaved a sigh. "So, what are you going to do? You plan on letting him know you're here?"

"I don't know. What do you think?"

"I think if you feel something you should deal with it...on all levels." Her tone was filled with the enormity of taking on an interracial relationship. Had it been any other white girl, it probably wouldn't be a problem, but the Shaws were one of those "blue-blood families," who prided themselves on their whiteness, their ancestry, their money. Corrine just may have a heart attack.

"What if what I saw in his eyes was just my imagination?"

Leslie had never, in all the time she'd known Celeste, seen her look so uncertain, so vulnerable. She was always the one with the answers, the quips. This was a revelation. "I guess you'll never know unless you take that chance."

They held each other's gaze and Celeste understood that

Leslie would be there for her if she fell flat on her face. She drew in a breath. "Okay."

"Okay, what?"

"Okay, I'm going to see what happens. If I get the chance to talk to him…I will."

"Then let's go before you change your mind and we miss all the music." She flashed her a big smile and they walked out.

By the time they returned to their table, the quartet was finishing up a number. Sammy saw Celeste and he nearly missed a note. *What was she doing here, of all places?* He tried to concentrate and keep up with Nick's changes even as his line of sight and concentration was on Celeste.

Sam was a guy straight from the streets. He prided himself in his blackness, on being a black man in America even though it was still the hardest job on the planet. He loved black women, the sassiness of them, the beauty of their skin, hair, the darkness of their eyes. But something happened when he met Celeste Shaw and he hadn't been able to shake it. The whole idea of him and a white girl went against every grain of who he was, but he couldn't stop thinking about her and the possibility of a "them."

Mercifully, the set came to an end. Nick lowered his sax and spoke into the mic over the rousing applause of the audience.

"Thank you. Thank you! We're going to take a short break and we'll be back with a special surprise."

The band moved off the stage and music from the DJ filled the room. The crowd returned to their loud conversations while some took to the small dance floor.

"I need another drink," Celeste said, getting up. "You want anything?"

"No. I'm good." Leslie held up her half-filled glass of Diet Coke.

Celeste moved through the tightly wound bodies until she got to the bar. "Apple martini," she shouted to the bartender.

"Definitely a ladies drink," a voice from behind her said.

Her heart banged against her chest. She glanced over her shoulder and up into his eyes. Her throat went completely dry and she wished she had her drink before she strangled.

The bartender put her drink in front of her.

"I'll take care of it," he said, placing his hand on top of hers when she went for her purse.

A charge raced up her arm. "Thanks," she managed to say. She grabbed her drink and took a sip.

"This is the last place I expected to see you," Sammy said.

"Why?" she countered, immediately on the defensive.

He held up his hands. "Whoa, take it easy. I'm just saying this place is kind of off the beaten path, that's all."

She relaxed her tight shoulders. "Leslie and I have been coming here off and on for about a year."

His right brow rose and fell.

Silence hung between them, louder than the noise and music.

"So, how have you been? Close any more deals?"

She took a sip of her drink and tried to relax. "No. The market is really bad right now. Everyone is really cautious."

"Same thing I told Nick. Times are tight. But he insisted that the time was what you made it." He shrugged. "I gotta agree. You make your own magic in this world." His gaze swept over her. "What do you think about that?"

Her brain was on scramble. The crush of bodies had pushed them within a breath of each other and the warm scent of his cologne short-circuited her common sense. "Hmm, magic is what two people make it."

A slow, easy smile moved across his mouth and sparkled in

his eyes. "Yeah," he affirmed, saying the word like a musical note. He glanced over his shoulder then back at her. "Gotta run. You and Leslie plannin' on being around for a while?"

"Sure."

He nodded. "Good. I'll see you after the set." It wasn't a question, and before she could pull herself together he was up onstage taking his place behind the piano.

Somehow she had the presence of mind to return to her table. Her hands were shaking and her back was damp. She wrapped her fingers around her glass.

"I saw him when he came over to you," Leslie said in a conspiratorial whisper. "What did he say? What did you say?"

Celeste blinked, looked at Leslie and said, "I have no idea."

The band launched into a series of original pieces that were a mix of jazz and R&B soul that had the crowd on their feet. Then the spotlights dimmed on the band and focused on a lone image.

The slender figure held the stem of the microphone, stroking it like a lover as the sultry and haunting strains of Billie Holiday's "Strange Fruit" rose through the charged air, bringing a shuddering hum of quiet on the audience. Parris covered the piece with her own unique play on the words and melody, riffing above and below the notes, making it totally her own, before smoothly segueing into an original composition, "When I First Saw You," that had the audience bobbing their heads and popping their fingers. Then she did a totally soul-stirring rendition of Kem's "I Get Lifted" that had the audience banging tables and hollering for more.

"She is awesome," Celeste shouted over the din.

"Told you. And she isn't even warmed up good. I've listened to her some nights when she was at Downbeat and her voice would make your soul ache." She continued rocking her foot and bobbing her head to the music.

Parris was in another space, taken on a ride by the music, the emotion held her in its grip as she allowed the words to become an extension of herself. She closed her eyes, let the words flow, and all was right with the world. The disappointments, the losses, the lies, none of it mattered. Not when she sang, not when she rode the crest of Nick's sax notes. It was like making love in front of an audience, intimate and public, erotic and raw, needing and wanting it so much you had to share the power of what you felt and it didn't matter that anyone saw you naked and vulnerable. That was music to her and had been since she was a little girl singing in the church choir in Rudell, Mississippi, in the shower, local clubs, in her dreams. This was when she truly came alive.

The roar of the crowd's applause vibrated within her center. The lights blinded her to the faces in front of her, but she knew they were there, feeling her, feeling the rhythm.

Nick stepped next to her as the houselights came up. "Parris McKay. Give it up!" he shouted into the mic.

Parris stole an ecstatic glance at him then took a bow of her head. "Thank you, thank you," she said to the audience. She waved and walked off, leaving the crowd on their feet.

Tracey ambled back out onstage. "Let's have another round of applause for our guests tonight, Turning Point featuring Parris McKay! Give it up! Please enjoy the rest of your evening here at yours truly's, Tracey's," she hollered over the clapping and foot stomping, then sauntered off stage.

"Don't look now," Leslie said into the mouth of her Diet Coke, "but here they come."

Some of Celeste's drink dribbled down her chin and she quickly reached for a napkin.

"Sam told me you two were here," Nick said, walking up on them and holding Parris's hand with Sam close behind.

"Hey," Parris greeted with a broad smile as she looked from Celeste to Leslie.

"You were fabulous, Parris," Celeste said in awe.

"Thank you." She smiled demurely.

"What about me?" Sam asked, stepping into the conversation but his stare and question were directed at Celeste.

"You weren't half-bad," she teased.

He pressed his large hand to his heart. "I'm wounded."

They all laughed.

"Mind if we join you, ladies?" Nick asked.

"Sure. Grab an extra chair," Leslie said.

Sam snatched an empty chair from the next table and pulled it next to Celeste. Nick and Parris took the two vacant seats at the table.

"What are you ladies drinking?" Nick asked.

"Diet Coke," Leslie answered.

"Apple martini, right?" Sam said to Celeste.

Her throat was suddenly bone-dry again. She nodded her head in response.

"What about you, babe?" Nick asked Parris.

"I think I'll take an apple martini, too."

Nick stood. "Be right back."

"I had no idea you all would be here tonight," Leslie said. "It was definitely a pleasant surprise. I hadn't heard you sing since Downbeat."

"Nick pulled me in at the last minute. These two kept talking about a jam session tonight. When we got here the truth came out," she said, laughing.

"How was your trip?" Celeste asked, turning to Parris.

"Not what I expected," she said, the light dying from her eyes. "But, as they say, it is what it is."

Celeste thought about Parris's confession to her about her mother and her decision to seek the truth. It was clear she didn't really want to talk about it, at least not now. She touched Parris's arm lightly in understanding consolation. Parris mouthed her thanks.

Nick returned, balancing their drinks like the experienced waiter he once was, and set them down on the table. He took his seat and then raised his glass. "A toast—to good music, good friends and good times ahead."

They all touched glasses.

"Speaking of good times, are we still on schedule?" Nick asked Celeste.

"I'm hoping to wrap everything up this week, for sure. Then it's all yours."

"And I'll have the first set of drawings and quotes for you in a couple of days," Leslie added.

Sam raised his glass of Hennessy. "Let the good times roll."

The DJ switched the tempo to a Luther Vandross classic, "A House Is Not a Home."

Sam leaned toward Celeste's ear. "May I?"

She turned and they were practically nose-to-nose. She could see her reflection in his eyes. She'd swear the entire club went dead quiet waiting for her answer. "Uh, sure."

Sam stood and helped her out of her seat then led her onto the dance floor with his hand at the dip in her back. It felt like a heating pad, Celeste thought as she found a space and turned into his hard body. He looked down at her and lightly wrapped his arms around her waist. They found their rhythm and moved to the sway and pull of the music, the plaintive cry of Luther begging his baby to be home when he got there, like a magnet, drew them together. For an instant, Celeste's muscles tensed when she found herself flush against the bold, defining lines of Sam's long, hard body. Her heart skipped and stumbled in her chest, shortening her breath. He stroked her back as if letting her know it was okay and she could feel the strumming in his throat and chest as he hummed along with the melody. She closed her eyes and allowed her body to unwrap itself from the knot it was in. She rested her head against his chest and was relieved to discover that for all his outward cool, his heart was racing as fast as hers.

Leslie sat at the table alone, nursing her Diet Coke after insisting that it was fine for Nick and Parris to leave her at the table to dance to their favorite song. As she watched the couples that were snuggled up on the dance floor and scattered throughout the club, she took an unfiltered look at her loveless life. A condition she'd been in for longer than she cared to admit. The last man whom she'd been involved with eventually became fed up with her array of insecurities, her own doubts about his feelings for her and her overall dismal view of men in general. That was nearly three years ago. She'd had a date or two since then but it never went beyond the first outing. And then her mother got sick.

She finished off the last of her soda. A woman's laughter rang out behind her. She turned and saw the thrill of happiness splashed across the woman's face as she leaned into the man who held all of her attention.

Leslie couldn't ever remember that kind of laughter, that unabashed joy, and had no clue what it felt like. For so long all she felt inside was a gaping hole that was filled with anger and resentment, a hole that she tried to fill with food when she reached her teens in an attempt to rid herself of the bitter taste always in the back of her mouth. The one bright spot was long gone, having left its indelible mark years ago. When she was a little girl and her mother worked the overnight shift, her mother's brother—Frank—would come to keep an eye on her. So many times she'd ask her uncle Frank where her dad was. Did he know him? What did he look like? Why won't Mom tell me who he is? He'd never answer her directly but would find other ways to soothe her childhood curiosity.

Uncle Frank was so handsome and he always smelled good. He would stroke her ponytails and help her into her pajamas, taking his time as he put the nightgown over her head, and tell her how beautiful she was. Sometimes when she would cry, he would climb in bed next to her and put his hand between her thighs, or rest his head on her budding breasts until she fell asleep. Once when she was about ten he sat on the edge of the tub while she took her bath, talking to her in the deep lulling voice that she loved, while he helped wash between her legs. She remembered the shuddering sensation and the way her eyes almost rolled to the back of her head when he touched her there.

Then one day, Uncle Frank didn't come back. Leslie blamed her mother. She never saw him again, only in the faces of the men she met throughout her life. His face and the imagined image of her father.

It wasn't until years later that she understood what had gone on between her and her beloved uncle. She never told anyone, not even Celeste. But she always wondered if her mother had known.

A sob lodged in her throat, rose then stuck in the roof of

her mouth, and in a room teeming with people and laughter, she felt utterly alone.

When the two couples returned to the table, Leslie begged off with a "monster headache," and bid them all good-night.

As she lay in bed that night, she imagined Uncle Frank's smiling face, the scent of his cologne, and wondered why he never told her about her father, either.

# Chapter Thirteen

The cab drew to a stop in front of Emma's destination. Throughout the winding ride from the place that had been her home for more than two decades, Emma barely moved, hardly blinked as the landscape—and what semblance of her life remained—became smaller and more distant.

The only image she could conjure in her mind's eye was Michael as he'd watched her leave. As she'd walked toward the waiting car, she'd prayed that she would hear his voice calling after her, his footsteps on her heels. And she would turn, and he would be there, tall and still incredibly handsome, with a glimmer of hope in his sea-blue eyes, and he would tell her to come inside out of the rain and they would work it out. Somehow they would work it out.

He didn't. And the cab pulled away and she watched the house until she couldn't see it anymore and she knew that her life was over. She had no one to blame but herself and the choice she'd made all those many years ago. A choice that haunted her mother, Cora, then her daughter, Parris, and destroyed the one person who'd ever made her happy. Michael. Yet, her choice had been made for her before her tainted birth.

"Madame? Madame?"

Emma turned in confusion to see the driver peering at her from the opened passenger door.

"This is the address, madame. We are here."

Her chest constricted. Here. "Yes, thank you," she mumbled and reached for her carry bag and purse on the seat next to her.

The driver extended his hand and helped her out.

She dug in her wallet and handed him his payment. Her bags were on the curb. Her knees weakened.

"Madame!" He grabbed her arm to steady her. "Are you all right? Should I call someone?"

Emma drew in gulps of air as her head began to clear. Rain splattered her face. "There's no one to call," she said almost to herself. "Thank you," she added absently. She walked the few steps to the front door and the driver came behind her and placed her bags at her feet then hurried back to his cab.

For several moments she stood on the porch listening to the sound of the rain hitting the roof, bouncing off the sidewalk and sluicing in between the cobblestone paths. She was still standing there when the door suddenly swung open and a young woman jumped back and gasped in surprise.

"Oh! I'm so sorry. I did not hear the bell." She held a bag of trash in her hand. "Come in, *s'il vous plaît*." She dropped the trash in the can. "Can I help you with those?"

Emma numbly glanced at her bags. "Yes," she whispered.

The young woman grabbed up the bags and hurried inside. "I do apologize for having you stand out in the rain. I was in back." She led the way in with a suitcase in each hand and set them down beside the front desk.

"Now," she said on a breath, a smile blooming on her peaches-and-cream face.

Her shoulder-length hair was the color of a summer sunset, brilliant red with flecks of gold. She would always have to shield her delicate skin from the sun to keep the inherent freckles at bay, Emma distractedly thought.

"How can I help you? Do you have a reservation?"

"No. I'm sorry, I don't."

"Well, you are in luck," she continued in the same cheery tone. "We have three vacancies. Do you know how long you will be staying with us?"

She couldn't think. She didn't know. A day. A week. Forever. "Ahh, perhaps a few days." She gripped the edge of the counter.

The young woman opened the register to the current date and turned it to face Emma. "If you would sign in for me, please." She handed Emma a pen. "We still do things the old-fashioned way," she said by way of explaining the handwritten register.

Emma took the pen, printed and then wrote her signature.

The young woman turned the book around and read the name. "Emma Travanti."

Emma could do no more than nod.

"Welcome, Madame Travanti. My name is Franchesca. I'm here for the weekend. Should you need anything do not hesitate to call on the room phone. Would you prefer a view of the mountains or the pool?"

"Whichever is fine," she said in a threadbare voice.

Franchesca looked at her curiously. "Are you ill, madame? You are very pale."

"I...just need to rest. It's been a long day," she said, forcing energy into her voice.

Franchesca hesitated. The last thing she was prepared to handle was a sick guest. "Will you be paying by credit card or cash?"

"Cash."

Franchesca told her the first night must be paid in full and she would receive a bill daily until her departure. "We believe that our guests are all trustworthy. But just in case they aren't, I will need to hold your passport, credit card or driver's license until you check out." She smiled sweetly.

Emma opened her purse and handed over her passport.

"I'll put this in the safe and then I will show you to your room."

Emma had stopped listening to Franchesca's chatter as they walked up to the second floor and she was taken to her room. She'd tuned out the chirpy monologue about the room's attributes, meal times and the history of the inn. All she wanted was her husband back and she knew that was an impossibility. Anything short of that was just going through the motions.

Finally, Franchesca closed the door behind her, and Emma found herself alone. She went to the window and drew back the drapes. The sun, which had barely made an appearance all day, had begun its final descent. The overcast sky was ringed in a smoky gray with hints of orange as if something in the foggy distance was on fire. The unrelenting rain made everything look as if it were being viewed through a prism.

She stood there, the ache so deep her chest heaved under the weight of the pain bringing her to her knees. Curled inside herself the sob bloomed in a mushroom cloud spewing out the anguish that roiled within her. Deep, wrenching cries shook her slender frame like a rag doll thrown into a storm. She cried for her loss. She cried for the lie she had lived. She cried for the love of a mother who she never allowed herself to know. She cried for her husband. And she cried for the child she'd abandoned for a life of happiness that was now a thing of the past. She cried until she was spent and weak. Huddled in the corner in a strange room, exhaustion finally rescued her. Her fitful sleep became filled with images of time gone by and everything she had done since that fateful day at the river had led her to this moment...

*She'd been angry with her mother, Cora, and had stormed out of the house, seeking refuge at her favorite place, the flat rock just beyond the riverbank. Why did she always feel this way, so angry and so lonely? she'd thought. And there was no one to share her thoughts, answer her questions about herself, tell her how to be happy.*

*One day she would just get away from this place, she vowed, as she stared out across the gentle ripple of the water. She'd get away and make a new life and forget all about Rudell and the people in it.*

*The sound of a car coming down the uneven road drew her attention. She craned her long, milky neck to see who was coming. The car drew closer and came to a stop. A white man, dressed in a good-looking blue suit with a black fedora cocked over his eyes, stepped out of the car. Instantly she was on guard as a rush of fear scurried along her limbs. White folks didn't come to these parts, and when they did it usually meant trouble. She sat perfectly still.*

*"Excuse me, ma'am." He politely tipped his hat.*

*She blinked in confusion. Ma'am. "Ye-yes sir."*

*"I was hoping you might direct me toward the highway. I was on my way to Biloxi for the night and got turned around somehow." He laughed lightly.*

*Slowly Emma stood. "If you stay on this road, you'll see a fork. Stay to the left and you'll find the highway."*

*He smiled gratefully. "Thank you, miss. Last place I want to be is lost in these woods after dark." He looked around nervously and chuckled. He gazed at her for a moment, angled his head to the side. "Pretty thing like you needs to be getting home, too. You know how these Negroes are, see a pretty, white woman—" He let his voice drift off, but his meaning was clear. "Hate to see anything happen to you. I'd be happy to give you a lift into town."*

*Emma tried to make sense of what this white man was saying to her. White woman. Pretty, white woman. She couldn't respond.*

*He stepped closer and took off his hat; his sandy brown hair glistened in the waning light. He was almost tall, slender in a rangy sort of way, and young—no older than her, she'd guessed.*

*"Miss, are you all right?"*

*Emma snapped to attention. Her mouth trembled into a smile. "Yes. Fine, sir." She bobbed her head.*

*"Name's Hamilton. Elliot Hamilton."*

*"Emma. Ma-McKay." Her heart sounded like thunder.*

*"Pleasure, Miss McKay." He stuck out his hand, which she tentatively shook. "The offer is still open."*

*"Offer?"*

*"For the ride—into town. Are you sure you're all right, miss? You look flushed."*

*Emma touched her cheek. "No, I'm fine. Just the heat." She looked straight at him, just to see if she could. No slap came, no flurry of curses, just a curious smile. "Thank you for the offer. But I'll be fine. I—I'm waiting…on a friend."*

*Elliot looked around then checked his gold watch. "I'd wait with you just to be certain you stay safe until your friend arrives, but I really need to be moving on."*

Her chest heaved in and out. "It's fine. Really. Thank you."

He put his hat back on and slid his fingers along the brim. "You be careful out here."

Emma nodded.

He turned then stopped. "I guess you hear this all the time, but… you sure do have the prettiest green eyes I've ever seen."

Emma felt her face heat. She arched her chin just a bit but wanted to hide her face, so unaccustomed was she to compliments. "Thank you…Mr. Hamilton."

He tipped his hat. "My pleasure." He returned to his car and drove off.

Emma watched the car until it disappeared in a cloud of dust. Her knees began to wobble and her entire body trembled. She reached behind her for the rock and lowered herself down.

Her thoughts tumbled over each other like a cascade of rocks kicked from the top of a hillside. She raised a shaky hand to her face, ran it over the smooth skin. She touched her hair, stuck her hands out in front of her and stared at them. She gazed down the road where the white man had gone. And for the first time in her eighteen years of life, she felt the inklings of hope.

She'd returned home, ignoring Cora's offer of dinner on the table. Instead she ran up to her room, stood in front of the mirror and slowly took off her clothes. Inch by inch she examined her body in the reflection with new eyes; the smooth pink-and-white skin, firm breasts with round, pink nipples, tight, flat stomach and narrow waist, the patch of hair that was as silky as the hair on her head, tapering down to long legs and thin ankles. Her excitement mounted. A slow smile crept across her face and brightened her eyes. With a toss of her head she stared boldly back at herself. "Yes. Yes. Yes," she uttered in a tremulous whisper.

That evening on the rock of the Left Hand River, a door opened for her. A chance was there for the taking. And standing in front of her bedroom mirror she made a decision that altered the lives of everyone she knew, past, present and future. Once she set out on that path there was no turning back. She couldn't. She didn't want to.

Living the life of a white woman, in New York City, away from the scorn-filled eyes of the Rudell townfolk, had finally brought her some measure of happiness. It brought her respect, recognition. Not the nasty stares of her youth, the snickers behind her back when she walked the streets of Rudell, a mother that couldn't look her in the eye, a life of loneliness and heartache. Living a lie had brought her Michael…

*He'd walked into her then place of employment, Meridian Real Estate, like a hero from a movie. When she'd looked up and saw him standing in the doorway something inside of her stirred. A sudden rush of heat flowed through her veins, and her heart beat a little faster. Michael Travanti, her future, stood in front of her dressed in full army uniform. He'd swept his cap from his head, uncovering inky black hair that glistened beneath the overhead lights. Even the standard buzz cut looked appealing on him. He was of medium height, not much taller than her, but his ramrod-straight regal bearing gave him the appearance of a towering knight—strong and invincible. His uniform coat spread snuggly across his shoulders, the sharp creases in his slacks, even and severe, fell just above highly polished black boots. One couldn't help but admire the angular structure of Michael's patrician face. Perhaps not considered classically handsome by many, there was a warmth and pleasantness about his Roman nose, rugged, square jaw, prominent cheeks, wide mouth and warm olive complexion. What set him apart, for her, were his striking Mediterranean blue eyes that seemed to take in everything around him.*

"May I help you?" she finally said.

"I hope so."

*He'd been commissioned to the army office in New York, he'd said, and was in search of an apartment, which Emma was happy to help him find.*

*And so it began, the start of a romance that surprised them both with its power, its durability, its joys.*

*Michael met Emma after work each evening and took her to picture shows, dinner or maybe just a walk along the brightly lit avenues. He bought her flowers, boxes of chocolates, embroidered handkerchiefs with her initials. He was the gardener tending to a field that had been left fallow. His tenderness, laughter and easy way of giving showered down upon the parched wasteland of Emma's soul, spreading its nurturing waters until she bloomed day by day. His touch clipped the thorns from her heart that kept people at bay. His smile was the sunshine that strengthened her belief that she was worthy.*

*Until she met Michael, she'd always felt that what she deserved were things: new clothes, shoes, a seat on the bus, a good job, a window seat at a restaurant, to walk down any street and not be scorned for who her mother was and the color of her own skin in the wrong place. Those were the things she thought she deserved because they replaced the one thing she knew she'd never have or wasn't worthy of receiving, the love of her mother....*

A roar of thunder shook the heavens and jolted Emma from the depths of her torturous sleep. The entire building vibrated and the sky illuminated with a searing bolt of lightning. Emma's tear-filled eyes looked heavenward, seeing only darkness, a reflection of what she felt inside. She had no more tears to shed. Her throat was raw, her limbs stiff from sitting curled in the corner, rocking, thinking, remembering. She couldn't live like this. She couldn't endure the depths of this nothingness. How? How?

Slowly, painfully, she rose to her knees, gripped the walls for support, and stood. She looked around, momentarily confused by her surroundings. How did she come to be here? She shook her head, tried to make the fleeting pieces fall into place and make sense. Her throat clenched. It wasn't a dream.

She looked down at her clothes, her blouse that clung to her from tears and sweat, the slacks that were bunched, damp and wrinkled and her wet shoes that she'd never taken off her feet. One by one she peeled the items away from her body and tossed them in a pile in the center of the floor. Like an automaton she collected her toiletry pouch from her suitcase, walked to the bathroom and turned on the tub, following her nightly ritual as if doing the familiar would somehow restore her life to normalcy.

She stood over the tub, watching the water slowly rise. Had she not been interrupted that night, had the call not come, oh, how different her life would be. She looked into the rising water and the images of what she'd almost done mocked her from the depths….

*She'd taken Michael to the airport. He'd been called back to duty. Although he'd insisted that she stay home with her being so close to delivering their first baby, she insisted just as strongly that she wanted to see him off. As she'd stood in front of the window at the airport watching his plane roar down the runway, she was overcome with dread. She'd convinced Michael not to send for his mother; he was now gone and she had no real friends. She was truly alone. And as that day wore on, the fleeting pains that had begun earlier that morning, that she told her husband nothing about, returned in short bursts, but became more intense each time. By nightfall she was pacing the floor in agony, sweat beading on her forehead. At times the pains nearly bent her in half.*

*She remembered thinking that it was too soon, too soon, and during a momentary reprieve from the searing pains she almost made her way to the door when another onslaught of torment slammed into her, bringing her to her knees. The only thing that kept her from falling to the floor was her grip on the knob as a flow of blood and water ran down her thighs. Tears of agony rolled down her cheeks. Her body shook as she curled into a fetal position on the cool wood floor. She realized she'd never make it to the hospital. She tried to think how far away was the phone. In the bedroom. She squeezed her eyes shut as an unbelievable urge to bear down overwhelmed her. Something inside seemed to rip and she screamed in agony as the building pressure widened her.... She would have to do this alone....*

*Hours later, weak with exhaustion, she looked down at the tiny little girl she'd wrapped in a clean sheet. When she stared at the perfect features, the wisps of curly dark hair and miniature fingers, she realized with complete desolation that everything she'd worked for, sacrificed for, was over. Forever. Her little brown baby. Her Negro child. Her heart squeezed in her chest. Her greatest nightmare had come true. But when she nursed her infant daughter during the hours after her birth Emma began to feel something she didn't want to feel—a connection, a surge of warmth and tenderness. And as her baby nursed, Emma touched the wiry curls, ran her fingertips along the cottony skin. She suddenly felt full, her heart seeming to swell with a joy she'd never before experienced. This was her and Michael's daughter, what they had created out of their love. "I don't want to love you," she'd said. "I can't. Don't make me."*

*She wouldn't let herself feel, wouldn't let herself fall in love with the child she had borne of love. She was sleeping so peacefully, her small face, so much like her own, created a tender picture. For a moment doubt froze Emma, made her second-guess herself.*

*Maybe she could leave, she'd thought, disappear with her baby and build a new life in another place. Her gaze slowly rose and her reflection in the dresser mirror stared back at her, the face of a white woman. She lifted the baby to her breasts, pushing out a breath of resolve. She took the baby to the bathroom and turned on the tub.*

*While the water slowly rose, Emma unwrapped the baby, the cord still protruding from her navel, the lifeline that connected them. She wouldn't think about that. Couldn't allow herself the luxury of being distracted by sentiment. She knelt down by the side of the tub and lowered the baby toward the water. And then her daughter's eyes squinted open, and jade-green eyes, just like hers, gazed back at her. Emma's heart rocked in her chest as the baby's tiny fingers grasped a loose curl of hair and held it. Her stomach seesawed. The baby whimpered....*

Marie and Marc sailed through the front door, dripping wet and giggling like school children. They shook off their wet coats and hung them by the door.

"We're home!" Marie sang out.

Franchesca appeared from the sitting room with an armful of clean towels. "Welcome back. From the looks of you a good time was had, I would say."

Marie grinned up at Marc. "And you, my dear child, would be right."

She sauntered into the reception area, took a trained look around her precious space and concluded that all was well. "How have things been in my absence?"

"Fine, madame. One guest checked out this morning and one checked in a few hours ago."

Marie clapped her hands in delight. "See, life is a balancing act. *Oui?*" She came behind the desk and pulled out the registry. Of course, when Franchesca was not looking she would check the finance sheet and the inventory. She was a sweet girl, but one could never be too careful with the help. She flipped open the registry to the current date and scrolled down the short list of names. She frowned at the name. *Travanti.* She peered closer at the printed name. *Emma.*

"What is it, sweetheart?" Marc asked, seeing the look of distress on her face.

Her gaze flicked up to meet his inquiring one. She was about to say nothing when a bead of water plopped down on the page in front of her. Her head jerked back. The trio looked up and an artery of water crept across the ceiling.

"Oh, my goodness," Franchesca cried out.

"I'll go up," Marc said, clearly annoyed. "I'm sure there will be a mess to clean."

Marie felt a sudden swell of heat in her center and her pulse picked up speed. She glanced down at the register. The letter *E* was being washed away on an inky river. That last conversation with Parris raced through her head. *She was here.*

Marie flew from behind the desk and hurried toward the stairs, leaving Marc and Franchesca in her wake. The room was directly above the reception area, the second door on the right. She pounded on the door. "Madame Travanti, open the door." She pounded again.

Marc and Franchesca had just reached the top of the landing. Marie turned and said, "Get me a key! Hurry." Franchesca raced back downstairs to retrieve the key. Marc came up behind Marie.

"It's all right. The guest probably feel asleep and left the water running," he said, trying to soothe her and ease the absolute look of panic from her wide-eyed face.

Marie ignored him and pounded again. "Madame, open the door!"

Franchesca returned with the key and handed it to Marie, who quickly opened the door. The trio practically tumbled into the room and was greeted by a trail of water that led to the bathroom. The bedroom was empty. Marie hurried to the bathroom and halted to a stop at the door, expecting the worst and finding it. For an instant she lost her breath as she focused on the body in the tub, blood streaming from her wrists, her skin as pale as a sheet of paper.

Franchesca screamed and didn't stop.

"Quiet!" Marie demanded, her eyes filled with fear and fury. "Be quiet before you alarm the guests."

Franchesca pushed her fist to her mouth but was unable to tear her eyes away from the sight before her.

Marc and Marie pushed into the bathroom. He checked the pulse in her neck, trying to feel for some form of life. Marie turned off the water.

"Well?" she asked anxiously.

He shook his head. "I can't tell. We need to get her out of this tub."

Marie turned to Franchesca, who was still as a statue. She needed to get the panicked girl out of the room. "Go and get me those towels. Bring me some sheets and some scissors." Franchesca stood frozen as Marc carried the wet, cold body of Emma out of the tub and to the bed. "Now!" Marie yelled. Franchesca jerked to attention and hurried out.

Marie wrapped the icy cold body in blankets while Marc dumped the pillow out of its case and began tearing it. He handed several strips to Marie. In unison they bound her wrists where the ugly, ragged cuts still oozed, not needing instruction as if they'd always worked together saving the life of a perfect stranger.

"Who is she?" Marc asked, tying off the strip.

"The mother of that young woman who was here. Parris."

Marc gave Marie a quick glance and then looked at the body on the bed. "Are you sure?"

*"Oui."* She reached over to check for a pulse. The faintest beat tapped against her fingertips. "She's alive," she whispered. "Barely."

"She needs a doctor. I'm going to call the ambulance." He got up to reach for the phone. Marie grabbed his arm.

"No. No hospitals."

"What are you saying? She could die here. Is that what you want?"

"Listen to me. We can't take her to a hospital. This is an attempted suicide. They will commit her."

"That is what she needs."

"No," Marie said, "it is not what she needs." She looked at the alabaster face, the chest that barely rose and fell. "She needs forgiveness."

"Marie—"

"*Chérie,* I promise, I will explain it all to you. Trust me."

Marc looked into Marie's eyes, saw the conviction there that she would do this with or without his help. "All right," he finally conceded.

"Good. We will need to call a doctor. I know someone who is discreet."

Franchesca appeared in the doorway, still pale and panicked, with the requested supplies.

"Come in and close the door," Marie quietly ordered. "We need to talk."

# Chapter Fourteen

Dr. Lamar, an old and trusted friend of Marie's from her entertainment days, finished the last suture on Emma's right wrist. He covered it with a light ointment, gauze and sterile tape, identical to her other wrist.

Marie and Marc held hands and watched in silence. Lamar checked Emma's pulse and shone a light in each of her eyes before putting his instruments away. He angled his body on the bed to face his audience. "She is very lucky. Had the water been warm rather than icy cold, you would have called the coroner." He stood, his belly jutting out in front of him. "Without the proper tests I can't tell if she took any drugs. Did you find any empty bottles?"

"No," Marie answered, although she didn't think to look.

"I can't take the risk of giving her a sedative until we know for sure. But for the time being I'm certain she will sleep for a few hours. I would caution against leaving her alone. When she wakes, she will be disoriented and probably very frightened."

Marie nodded her head.

"Keep her warm and calm. Call me if you need to."

Marie rose and squeezed his plump hands between hers. "Thank you, Jean."

He bobbed his bald head. "For you, anything." He gathered his bag and coat and Marie walked him downstairs and to the front door. He turned to face her as he donned his hat against the still pouring rain. He took a small bottle from his bag and handed it to her. "In the event that she needs something to help her sleep. It's a mild sedative. But keep it with you at all times," he warned. "How much do you know about this woman?"

Marie drew in a breath. "Only what I've been told."

He wagged a stubby finger at her. "I won't say don't get in over your head because you have already done that. Those who attempt to take their lives are very desperate, Marie, very sad, very lonely. Without help, she will try again. Hopefully, she will not be your burden."

"I will keep that in mind," she said, clutching his arm. "Travel safely."

He gave her one parting look then turned and hurried to his car as quickly as his thick legs would take him. Marie waited until the car was out of sight then returned to sit vigil over her guest.

Between the three they took turns watching over Emma throughout the night. She didn't stir until midafternoon the following day. Marie, who was resting in the chair pulled to the side of the bed, heard Emma's moans. She jerked up in the chair, her head pounding and her eyes burning from a series of mini-naps. She leaned over Emma. Her eyes fluttered open, then closed. She moaned again and slowly opened her eyes, tried to focus.

"Don't try to move around," Marie said, stroking Emma's forehead. "You gave us a bit of a scare."

Emma blinked, trying to make out the image in front of her.

"Do you know what happened?"

Emma lifted her right arm, the white bandage illuminated in the afternoon light. She dropped her arm to her side and turned her head away from Marie.

"My name is Marie...Emma. May I call you Emma?"

Emma didn't respond. She only stared at the wall. The pulse in her throat, Marie noticed, thumped at a rapid pace.

Marie sighed, stood up slowly and stretched her stiff limbs. "You've been sleeping for quite a few hours." She spoke softly as she moved around the bed and adjusted the covers. "The doctor said you need your rest. You can stay here until you are well enough to leave." She paused. "Unless there is someone you would like me to call." She saw Emma's hands clench into fists and she gritted her teeth as the pain shot up her arms. "You shouldn't do that," Marie said with practiced calm. "You have stitches."

Emma's narrow lips tightened. She blinked rapidly to stem the tears that welled in her eyes but failed.

Marie gingerly sat down on the side of the bed. "Whatever the trouble, you can get through it. Fate brought you here to us."

"You should have let me die," she said, her voice dry and cracked.

"Perhaps. But I'd rather not have a suicide in my brochure as a tourist attraction."

Emma closed her eyes.

"Nothing is so dreadful as to want to end your life."

"You don't know that. You don't know what I've done."

"Perhaps I know more than you think."

"No one knows," she said in a faraway voice.

Marie watched the tears fall and dry on her cheeks. The resemblance to her daughter Parris slowly took shape, like watching a transformation in a movie. The curve of the face, the sharp nose and sweeping brows, but it was the arresting green eyes—one set in a face of alabaster, the other in brown sugar—that linked them, that and the weight of their private pain. Her heart ached for them both.

She was uncertain of how much she should say, how much this woman was willing and ready to hear. Instead she spoke of inconsequential things: the running of her inn, the string of guests who'd visited over the years, the coming of spring and her days as an entertainer. She spoke in low, soothing tones as one would to a child while telling them a bedtime story. She watched as Emma struggled to stay awake before finally drifting off into another deep sleep.

A light tap on the door drew her attention. It opened slightly and Marc stuck his head in. Marie tiptoed away from the bed.

"She woke for a little while, but just went back to sleep." She pushed her hair away from her face. "I want to bathe and change clothes."

He kissed her forehead. "I missed you in bed last night."

Her cheeks glowed. "But of course," she teased. "As I missed you." She eased past him, making certain that her body connected with his. "I'll be back shortly." She stroked his cheek and went down the hall to her room.

Marc took up his post next to the sleeping patient and wondered how long she would be their burden.

★ ★ ★

It was two days before Emma was willing to get out of bed and sit on the terrace. All during that time, she spoke little, no more than asking for water or a sip of soup. She was like a ghost living in a human body, devoid of energy or essence, merely existing because she'd been forced to. So Marie took it as a good sign that she agreed to get some air. Perhaps she was coming back to the land of the living.

"France is always so beautiful after the rains," Marie was saying as she looked out onto the hillsides. The sky was a crystal blue and the landscape beyond resembled a work of art, with the rich brown and green colors of the mountains, and the outline of the city's brilliant colors. "Don't you agree?" She ladled seafood bisque into Emma's bowl and her own before taking a seat. "I have traveled all around Europe but I don't think I could ever live anywhere else." She raised her soup spoon to her mouth and took a sip. She closed her eyes in delight then looked at Emma. "You must try the soup. It is Marc's special recipe." She watched, mildly satisfied when Emma finally lifted her spoon to her mouth. "Excellent, *oui?*"

"Yes," Emma murmured.

"Where is your home, Emma Travanti?" she asked gently.

Emma glanced for an instant at Marie then said, "I have no home."

Marie tossed her head back and laughed. "We all have a home. Somewhere. It may be a place we will never return but we all have a beginning."

Emma's eyes stared out to the world stretched in front of her, beyond the Loire Valley, beyond the borders of France, across the oceans, deep into the bottom of America along the winding roads, rippling rivers, towering trees, ramshackle homes and voices laced with molasses, thick and sweet.

"Mississippi," she whispered.

Marie's heart thumped. She schooled her expression. "Ah, I have only heard and read about Mississippi. But you must have come here long ago. I don't hear that, uh, how do you say, 'Southern drawl' in your voice." She smiled at Emma, hoping to encourage her to talk. She needed to be absolutely certain before she said too much.

"Thirty years," she said wistfully.

Marie nodded. "That is a long time. You must have come as a young girl."

"I...came with...my husband." Her face tightened as if the words brought her excruciating pain.

"Ah, a husband. I have never been fortunate enough to be caught by one of them." She laughed lightly and was pleased to see the glimmer of a smile on Emma's lips. "But they are good to have I've heard."

Emma turned somber eyes on Marie. "They are. Michael is a wonderful man." Her throat worked up and down. Her nostrils flared. "He doesn't deserve what I've done to him." She shook her head back and forth and her body shuddered. She sniffed hard and reached for the linen napkin on the table. She dabbed at her eyes and nose. "But I didn't know what else to do," she blurted out. "Do you know what it's like never to be loved? Never? Not even by your own mother?" Her voice cracked with pain. "To walk down the streets of the place where you live and be whispered about, mocked? To have your mother be the source of ridicule because of you? All your life!" Her face flushed. She stood and went to the railing of the terrace. Marie flinched, ready to grab her if need be. "And then one day you see a way out." She stared at Marie. Her voice took on a sense of urgency. "A way to live. And you find someone, someone who finally loves you. Gives you what you've been searching your entire life for. Makes you feel whole and worthy. And you realize that you will do anything, anything to keep it." She looked away. Her chest rapidly rose and fell. "And then everything changes. The one thing you dreaded. A baby. A child that could take it all away because she doesn't look like you. She doesn't look like him. She is a black baby. Because you are black. And he doesn't know. And he must never know," she rambled, growing more agitated with each revelation.

In fits and starts Emma told Marie of the night of Parris's birth and her terror. Of taking the infant to the tub with the intention of drowning her, but the phone rang, telling her that her husband had been captured in Germany, but the army was working to get him out. She'd made up her mind at the moment to take the child to her mother, back in Mississippi to be raised. She made her mother swear that she would never tell the child about her, only that she died. She walked away from that house and never came back. Everything would have been fine. Michael would have never known until the letter came from her mother as she lay dying. Her mother needed to cleanse her soul before she left this world, the letter read, so she'd broken her promise, she'd told her daughter the truth— that her mother wasn't dead. She was alive and living in France. She said she'd named her Parris after the place Emma had chosen to live.

Marie's chest tightened. *So it was true.*

Emma slumped down in her seat. "She came to France," she murmured, seemingly spent by her confession. "I saw her for the very first time since she was two days old and I...turned her away." Her eyes wandered. "And then she was there, on my doorstep and...Michael...saw her. And, and I denied her, three times. Like Judas." She covered her mouth to hold back her sob. "He...he told me I had to leave. Our marriage was over." She frowned. "I...had nowhere to go." She looked at Marie with a confused cast to her eyes. "My life had been with Michael. My whole life. When...I got into the taxi, I looked in my purse and found the card for this place." Her bottom lip trembled. "She'd given it to me when she came to my bistro." A tear slid down her face. She looked into Marie's eyes. "I had nowhere else to go." She covered her face with her hands and wept.

Marie rose from her chair, knelt down beside her and gently put her arm around Emma's shuddering shoulders. Fate is such a mischievous bitch, she thought.

By the end of the week, Dr. Lamar had returned, checked Emma's wounds, changed her dressing and advised her to keep them dry for at least another week, to avoid infection.

"How has she been?" he whispered to Marie as she stood with him at the door to the inn.

"She's been talking a bit. Eating a little. I've gotten her to go as far as the terrace." She forced a smile.

He sighed. "Does she have any family that she can call?"

"No."

"Well, my dear, at some point you will have to make a decision. Unless you intend to hire her, she can't stay here forever." His cheeks puffed as he smiled. "Take care of yourself."

Marie waved as he drove off. She gazed upward to the floor

above. He was right. She couldn't stay there forever and she had no clue as to what Emma Travanti's plans were for her future.

The sun was warm to the skin. Birds hopped and chirped from treetop to treetop. The air was crisp and clean. Spring was on the horizon. It was the time of year Marie loved most, when new life began to bloom. She spent hours in her garden, nurturing her plants and vegetables, talking to them like old friends.

"Do you garden?" Marie asked Emma, who sat in a lawn chair off to the side.

"My mother did. We had a patch of land behind the house. She'd always try to show me…"

Marie glanced at her. "It's very relaxing, turning the earth, tending the leaves, watching the buds spring to life." She extended a small shovel. "Come. I'll show you."

Emma hesitated then finally pushed up from her seat and came to kneel down beside Marie. She took the shovel and followed Marie's soft-spoken instructions on digging small holes where she would plant seeds. "Push the shovel in and twist." She watched her student complete the first hole. She clapped in appreciation. "Perfect!" That made Emma smile.

They worked side by side with Marie telling her what each seed was, how long it took to bloom and the care that it needed to survive. "Plants are like people, *oui?* They need the hand of someone to care for them from the first bud of life until they are strong enough to stand on their own. And even then they require nurturing."

"I never had that," Emma said softly. "Oh, my mother gave me *things.* Always things. But never her love. It's all I ever wanted."

"Perhaps that was the only way she knew."

"It made me selfish and resentful," she went on. "I wanted her to pay for not loving me. I would see her coming home from cleaning other people's homes, beaten and tired, and I didn't care. All I knew was that I would never be like her."

"And what of your own daughter?"

Emma's eyes flashed. She lowered her head. "It's too late."

"She is a beautiful young woman…inside. I got to know her while she stayed here. I listened to her, saw her hope and her despair. But for all that your mother may have been, she nurtured your child."

Emma folded in her mouth.

"If you believed that it was heartless and unfair the way you were treated by your mother…yet you have become the very woman that you claim to disdain. You have done to your daughter what was done to you." She rose from her knees. "The circle of life has come full, Emma. You have it within your power to make it right."

"I…can't." She shook her head and looked up at Marie. "I can't."

"As you wish," she said on a heavy sigh. "But just like these flowers that need roots to flourish, so do we." She walked away to leave Emma with her conscience.

Alone in her room, Marie's words continued to mock Emma. Hadn't she been driven by the need to discover where she'd come from? Hadn't that unquenched thirst for knowledge led her in search of her father in New York?

She'd begun to suspect the real roots of her existence when she'd secretly opened a letter addressed to her mother from her friend Margaret in Chicago, where her mother had gone to live shortly before the Great Depression. Margaret had gone on about how she'd run into Mr. Rutherford and he'd asked about her, wanted to know if she was well. She'd written that Mr. Rutherford said that one day Cora had just up and run off from her employment without a word and never came back…

*That night at the dinner table, Emma came right out and asked her mother. "Who's Mr. Rutherford, Mama?" She'd never forget the look of alarm turned to shame then dismissal.*

*"Who's Mr. Rutherford, Mama," she'd repeated, demanding an answer.*

*"He's just a white man I worked fo' when I was up north."*

*"For a long time I've wanted to ask you what brought you back here. Just why did you leave Chicago? Did your leaving have to do with Mr. Rutherford? Answer me, Mama! You owe me this much. You owe me the truth."*

*"I don't owe you nothin', girl. I left there and that's that. I've raised you the best way I could, given you everything you ever wanted, ain't never denied you nothin', and here you is, speakin' to me like you's the mother and I's the child."*

*Emma had refused to let the story rest. "Who's Mr. Rutherford? And what does he have to do with you coming back to Rudell? Why are you getting upset unless there's something you're hiding?"*

*Cora's voice was low, her anger barely contained. "I don't have to hide nothin' from you. How do you know 'bout Mr. Rutherford, anyhow? Who told you 'bout him?"*

*"I just know about him, that's all. Who is he? What did he do to you? Is he why you left Chicago? Mama, answer me," she shouted. And the next instance she would never forget for the rest of her life.*

*Cora suddenly seized her daughter by the arm. "I don't have ta tell you a damn thing, girl. It's none of your business what happened, and that's all I'm ever gon' say 'bout that ag'in in my life."*

Cora kept to her word, until the day she died. She never spoke of her life in Chicago or Mr. Rutherford. But Emma's hunger for the truth would not be denied. She left Rudell, in search of her roots, and she found William Rutherford—her father, the man who raped her mother.

## Chapter Fifteen

Nick was relaxing in the living room, feet up on the coffee table listening to some old jazz standards, when Parris walked in barefoot with a bottle of champagne in one hand, two glasses and a corkscrew in the other.

He got up from the couch, a smile spreading across his face. "And what do we have here?"

"A celebration."

He took the glasses from her hand and set them on the table. "Celebration?"

"Yep." She set down the bottle of champagne. "Would you do the honors?"

"Sure." He took the corkscrew and opened the bottle, delighting them both with the pop and the fizz. He filled their flutes to near overflowing. "So what are we celebrating?"

"To finally signing on the dotted line," she said, raising her glass.

He'd received the last set of papers by certified mail that morning, officially declaring Nick Turner and Sam Blackstone as owners of what would soon be Rhythms.

He touched his glass to hers. "And to great things ahead."

They sipped and sat down.

"I can't believe we're finally on our way," Nick said, taking another swallow of champagne. He released a deep breath. "This is something I've been dreaming about since I was old enough to play in a nightclub." He draped his arm around her shoulder and pulled her close. "I have you to thank."

Her brow creased. "Me? This was your dream. Yours and Sam's. And you never let it go."

"Oh, I did. I let it go when I got involved with Percy. I saw the quick money, the notoriety." His gaze drifted off. "The way I was living, the way I made my money had strings attached that were choking the life out of me. I'd convinced myself that working for a man like Percy justified my ends—I could play my music with my band and pretend that I was actually running a club that could never be mine." He took a deep breath and slowly exhaled. "But then one day I look up and there you were asking about a singing gig." He chuckled at the memory and hugged her a bit tighter. "You had that little Southern thing going on in your voice and I remembered thinking, 'So this is a real live Southern belle.'"

Parris playfully poked him in the side. "I wasn't that bad. Was I?" Her brows rose in earnest.

"Let's just say I knew you weren't from around these parts," he teased, dragging out each syllable, which earned him another poke. "And when I heard you sing that first time—" he shook his head "—humph, my heart crossed the Mason/Dixon line for good." He adjusted his body in the seat to face her. His eyes creased as he spoke. "I'd never met anyone like you before. The women who'd been in and out of my life were hard and fast, like the life I lived. All of them looking for the next best thing, which was all I needed—something temporary. You…you were different. You were slow and easy. Made me want to turn down the volume of my life and listen to the melody." His finger stroked her forehead. "Made me want to choose between what was easy and what I honestly wanted for myself."

Parris abruptly got up and went to the window, leaned against the frame. She set her glass on the sill. "Not bad for a little 'ol country girl," she said, trying to make light of his heavy confession.

"What's wrong? What did I say?"

Parris glanced over her shoulder and forced a smile, before looking away. "Nothing." She took a sip of her champagne and lowered her head.

"So, why the sudden change in temperature? It got very chilly, very quickly." He leaned forward, resting his arms on his thighs, watching her, waiting. She thought he didn't hear her the times she cried in the bathroom, trying to drown out the sounds with running water, or the hours she spent at night staring at the wall until frenzied lovemaking and total exhaustion claimed her. But he did. He heard and saw it all. It was like watching a shadow. You knew it was there, that it was a replica of something real, yet you couldn't touch it. But he'd promised her and himself that he wouldn't push her, wouldn't probe, and if and when she was ready to talk about what happened in France, she would. He wasn't the enemy. She needed to know that.

Parris gazed off at the Manhattan skyline, its majesty still marred and forever altered by the gaping hole of rage. What could she say? She was none of the things he imagined her to be. She was no savior, no wise woman who saw into the future and could tell him the best road to travel. She was in search of her own life, one that was splitting at the seams.

Meeting her mother and realizing that Emma knew who she was all along, yet refused to acknowledge her, did something to Parris's spirit, her sense of worth, that she didn't think she would ever recover from. There were no words to explain the wretched emotion of realizing that in the light of the eyes of the woman who gave you life, you had no value. How do you find the words to explain that? And to live with the knowledge that her grandmother, the woman whom she'd idolized and patterned her life after, had been complicit in the lies and deceit, the charade that was her life. She just didn't know how or when she would ever be able to reconcile that and reclaim at least a glimmer of who she thought she once was.

Since her return from Europe, she'd merely gone through the motions of getting from morning to night. She participated in all the excitement surrounding the club. She'd eaten, bathed, laughed, slept and made love to Nick as if her life depended on it—and maybe it did. She needed to fill every waking hour until her eyes shut with finality and her body had nothing left to give.

That is the battle she struggled with. And it was hers alone.

Nick came to stand beside her. He plucked the glass from her hand. "Look at me."

Reluctantly she did.

"I know it hasn't been long since you've been back and the past few months have taken their toll—your job, losing your grandmother...your trip." He clasped her shoulders. "You're not alone. You think you are. But you aren't. I don't want you to just hear the words. I want you to believe them."

Of course, she was alone, she thought, even as she leaned against his strength and murmured that she believed him. She would always be alone in that space that could never be filled, like the yawning emptiness where towering buildings once stood. She would always be standing on the path—alone— looking her mother in the eye when realization descended.

"Dance with me," he said against her ear. Nat Cole's "Un- forgettable" played softly in the background. He took her hand.

As they swayed to the music, wrapped in the strength and security of Nick's warm embrace, she almost believed.

After a long conversation with her friend and former co- worker, Gina—who was calling from her weekend retreat in the Poconos—Parris hung up the phone with a half smile on her face. Of course, Gina had a few choice expletives to describe Emma that even made Parris wince. And she was pretty sure Gina made up most of them. Once again they promised to get together, and Parris assured Gina that she would always have the best seat in the house at Rhythms.

Nick was in the front room practicing a new number. He'd been at it for several hours and had mentioned that the guys would probably be coming over later to run through the numbers and she was more than welcome to sit in.

Any other time the invitation would have been welcome. But after talking with Gina—woman stuff, girl stuff, family stuff— she realized how much she missed connecting with other women. How there was an inherent gene of understanding between women that defied explanation. When one girlfriend said to another "I know what you mean," they actually did.

She got up from the side of the bed and straightened the covers, fluffed the pillows then walked to the window. The sky was overcast and the weatherman predicted perhaps a dusting of snow—ensuring that March went out like a lion. Since she'd moved from the South to New York, she hadn't cultivated a lot of "girlfriends," mostly acquaintances, but none other than Gina, whom she actually confided in, shared things with. She hadn't made that kind of connection with anyone else.

A midnight blue Jag eased to a stop at the red light on the corner of her street. And it brought Celeste Shaw to mind, pulling up in her Jag in the middle of the 'hood. Parris smiled at the memory. Although they'd only really talked that one time during lunch, they'd clicked and found themselves opening up that secret compartment that they kept off-limits to most people. She'd promised Celeste that she would call when she returned from France and even sent a message with Leslie to that effect when she ran into her at Tracey's, and had yet to call.

Parris drew in a breath, looked around. *Why not?* She went to the closet and took her purse down from the top shelf. After flipping through the array of business cards, she found the one Celeste had given her. She went for the phone and dialed the number before she changed her mind.

Celeste stepped out of the steaming shower and wrapped herself in her pink terry cloth robe. She used the sleeve to wipe the mist from the mirror then opened her robe, baring her damp body to the hazy reflection. She looked the same, she thought, as she tilted her head from side to side, except for the still puffy and swollen eyes from hours of crying. But she wasn't. Not in her head.

She was uncertain if her bold move across the color line was an act of outright rebellion against the establishment beliefs of her parents and those like them, or if it was because what was going on inside her was real…since she'd met Sam.

Since Sam left her apartment, for the first time in two days, she had the chance to think about what had gone on between them. Right or wrong. But she couldn't clear her head. She couldn't come to terms with all of the issues that clashed against each other. Of course, in this day and age mixed couples were part of the cultural norm, an everyday occurrence that didn't cause a blip on the radar, at least not in a city like New York.

But she wasn't your average, everyday New Yorker. She was from one of the wealthiest families in the country. Their pedigree dated back to the *Mayflower* and they prided themselves on the family's "pure" lineage from both sides of the ivory ancestral tree. Throughout her entire life she couldn't recall her parents ever having one black friend. Not even a passing acquaintance or a token country club member to at least present the illusion of inclusion. But her parents lived in the rarified air where inclusion and tolerance and acceptance were not discussed, because in their world they didn't have to be. Had it not been for the intermittent influence of her grandfather in her life and her own rebellious streak, she may very well have turned out to be a carbon copy of her mother.

She shivered at the thought and tugged on the belt of her robe and stepped out in her connecting bedroom. Sam left about an hour earlier. Neither of them wanted the time to end, to push them back into the real world. They'd made love so many times in the past few days that she'd lost count. All she could keep clear in her head was that she couldn't bear not having him next to her, on top of her, inside of her, as if his essence was her lifeblood. But he had a session with Nick and she, unknown to Sam, had some soul-searching to do.

Yet from the moment he walked out the door her spirit seemed to give way and the tears wouldn't stop coming. She didn't know why, except that there was a space where Sam was and now he wasn't, and she was experiencing what it would feel like if she gave in and gave him up.

Stupid. It was all so stupid, she thought as she tossed a pair of slacks onto the bed. Stupid, because it was so instant, like some dumb-ass game show. Stupid because this kind of thing didn't happen to her. She didn't allow herself to get caught up in any man.

*Any man*...what about Clinton? They were a couple. Everyone knew it. And although Clinton could never make her feel the way Sam did—never brought her to a climax with the kind of awe-dropping power as Sam, or made her feel all woman with just a look, never made her laugh from the soles of her feet, and never made her feel utter devastation if he left—she'd never cheated on Clinton. It wasn't the kind of woman she was, never had been. *Until now.*

Celeste wiped her eyes with the back of her hand and went to grab a tissue when her cell phone rang. She darted around the bed to grab it, hoping that it was Sam. She banged her knee in the process, damned the dresser to hell and snatched up her phone.

Breathless, she said hello.

"Hey, Celeste... I hope I didn't catch you at a bad time. This is Parris."

She blinked for a moment in confusion. Her mind had been

so focused on it being Sam that it took a minute for her to realize that it wasn't. "Parris?"

"Yes, how are you?"

She plopped down on the side of the bed and forced some cheer into her voice. "Sorry. Banged my knee on the way to the phone. Otherwise, I'm good, how are you?"

"Not bad. A little bored. So I was wondering if you weren't busy, maybe we could…I don't know, go to the place you took me to for lunch, or something. The guys are coming over for a session today and I wanted to give them their 'boys' time." She laughed.

Celeste flinched at the mention of the session. She knew that's where Sam was heading. What she wanted to do was stay home and beat her pillows until she got the answers that she needed. But in thinking about it, she warmed to the idea. She liked Parris and maybe getting out of the house was the medicine she needed, at least for now.

"No. I'm not doing anything that can't wait. Getting out will do me a world of good, but we can always go someplace else if you want."

"How about if we play it by ear?"

"Fine with me. Hey, do you mind if I ask Leslie to join us? If she can get away."

"Sure. That would be great."

"Are you driving?"

"Hmm, not unless Nick loans me his car."

"Don't worry about it. I'll swing by and get you and then we can pick up Leslie if she can make it. It'll make it easier moving around the city in one car." Maybe she would even catch a glimpse of Sam.

"True. You have the address, right?"

Celeste checked the information in her BlackBerry. "Yep. I'm going to call Leslie. I just got out of the shower so give me about an hour and I'll be there."

"I'll be ready."

Parris hung up with a smile on her face and so did Celeste.

Leslie sat bent over her drafting table as she put the finishing touches to the preliminary sketches of the entryway and the front seating area of the club. She was relatively pleased with what she'd come up with so far, but she had yet to hit on the thing that wowed her. And if it didn't wow her, it wouldn't wow her clients. She wanted a signature look that could be repeated throughout the entire space, used on their promotional materials and the menus. Basically she needed to create a brand that was unique to Nick and Sam and the atmosphere they wanted to create within Rhythms. She took a long critical look at her sketch. *Almost there but not quite.*

She leaned back in her chair and rotated her neck. Her eyes caught a glimpse of the clock. It was almost noon. Mother would want lunch in a little while. She was surprised she hadn't been disturbed a dozen times with that bell. She pushed off her stool and walked toward her mother's bedroom when the ringing phone pulled her in the opposite direction. She picked up the one in the living room.

"Hello?"

"Hey, Les, it's Cee."

"Hey." She leaned against the wall. "What's up? I was just going to check on my mother and see if she was ready for lunch."

"Oh."

"You can't be any more disappointed than me," she said, hearing the octave drop in Celeste's voice.

"Not like that," she insisted. "Well, sort of. Parris called a little while ago and wanted to get together. I thought we could do a girls' afternoon."

Leslie sighed heavily. "I wish I could, but today is Gracie's day off. There's no one here to stay with my mother."

"Hmm. Well, how about this, what if I sprung for lunch from somewhere fun and brought it over. Would that be okay?"

Leslie glanced in the direction of her mother's bedroom. "Sure. Let me get her lunch and her up and around for a little while."

"I'll aim for two, is that good?"

"Perfect. See you then." Leslie hung up, and mentally began going through her checklist of what needed to be done before her guests arrived.

Parris had just put on her pullover sweater when her cell phone rang.

"Hi, it's Celeste. There's been a slight change in plans. Since Leslie doesn't have someone to look after her mom today, I thought we could pick up a bunch of great stuff to eat and bring it over there. She said it was fine. Is that all right with you?"

"Uh, sure. No problem with me."

"Good. I'll see you in about a half hour."

"I'll be ready."

"You did what?" Nick sputtered, his eyes wide in genuine shock.

"Would you keep your voice down?" Sam said in a hard whisper. He paced away from Nick, shoved his hands in the pockets of his sweatpants.

Nick shook his head in disbelief. "You don't even know her," he insisted.

Sam turned to Nick, stared him in the eye. "Look, it happened. And I can't say that I regret it."

"Whoa." Nick dropped down onto the love seat. "Coming from you, that's kinda serious."

"What's kinda serious?" Parris asked, popping into the room. "Hey, Sam. What have you gone and done now?" She crossed the room and kissed his cheek then used her thumb to wipe away the lipstick smudge. She glanced from one face to the other. "Everything okay?"

"Yeah, babe. Everything's fine. Just some music stuff. That's all." Then he really zeroed in on her. "You're going out?"

"Oh, yeah, I finally got around to calling Celeste and we're going over to Leslie's for a ladies' brunch."

"You need the car?"

"No. Celeste is going to stop by and pick me up."

Nick and Sam stole a quick glance that Parris didn't miss. "What's going on?" Her question was focused on Sam. He looked away. "Sam…you and…nooo…" Her brows rose.

"Look, it's not what you think."

"What am I thinking?" she taunted, trying not to laugh at his stricken expression.

"Whatever it is, it's not. Okay?" His tone held a definitive note of finality.

"Fine." She shot Nick a look and he shrugged a helpless shoulder. "I'm going to finish getting ready. Is it going to be a problem if she comes upstairs?"

No from Nick, yes from Sam.

"Perfect." She walked out to leave them to their mess.


Celeste pulled up in front of Nick's building, contemplating what she should do. If Sam was already up there, she didn't know how either of them would react. She opted for the coward's way out and called Parris from her cell phone and asked her to come down.

Moments later Parris appeared in the doorway and came down the stairs, her wild spiral curls haloing her face, her slender figure clad in straight-legged jeans, slouch leather boots and a waist-length down jacket, giving her the appearance of a college coed heading off to class. She came toward the car and got in.

"Hi. Thanks for coming to get me."

"Not a problem. Good to see you." She checked her mirrors and waited for Parris to buckle up, then slowly pulled out. "Do you like Thai food?"

"Haven't tried it, but I'm game."

"Great, I took the liberty of ordering. I know this fabulous restaurant on the east side." They drove several blocks and came to a light. "So, uh, did the band get back together again?" she joked, making reference to *The Blues Brothers.*

Parris caught the quip and laughed. "Yes, the last of the quartet arrived just before you did." She took a quick glance at Celeste's sharp profile, wondering if she'd take her query a step further and ask about Sam, but she didn't. "They're all thrilled about getting started on the club."

"Leslie said she has some sketches to show us."

"I can't wait to see what she came up with."

Celeste cast a quick glance in Parris's direction. "She's good," she said sincerely. "And I'm not tooting her horn because she's my friend. She's really as good as I say she is," she added with a smirk.

Parris tossed her hand back and laughed. "I'm sold, I'm sold."

Celeste smiled as they made the turn onto Lexington Avenue.

The Thai restaurant was on Lexington and Fifty-Second Street in the heart of New York affluence. Parris felt suddenly underdressed as she walked among the strollers, casually garbed in their minks, short, long and in-between. Even Celeste flounced down the avenue with her ink-black mink that caressed her ankles as nonchalantly as if it were a tattered denim jacket. Perhaps she'd treat herself one of these days, she mused as Celeste pushed through the revolving door of the restaurant, which brought the still unsigned contract to mind. She'd put her own pursuits on the back burner with all that had transpired in her life recently, and if she didn't get back on track that may be taken away from her as well.

"I placed an order for Shaw," Celeste announced to the hostess at the front desk.

"One moment, please."

Parris took in the sensually lit, posh interior, with its deep wood and bloodred leather furnishings and gold trim. The waiters and waitresses moved between the tables in a hushed silence that underscored the low murmur of voices. She inhaled the tantalizing aromas and hoped it tasted as good as it smelled. She was about to ask Celeste how often she came here when said she would be right back, and suddenly began walking toward a table in the rear. Parris narrowed her gaze and followed Celeste's departure until she came to a stop. The couple was talking with their heads close to each other. She reached out and stroked his cheek. He clasped her hand and held it there. The man's back was turned to Parris but they both looked up simultaneously at Celeste. The woman stared wide-eyed at Celeste, obviously stunned by her appearance. She couldn't hear what was being said, but she could tell by Celeste's usual free-flowing movements that had become stiff and threatening, that it was serious.

The hostess returned with two large bags of food and placed them in front of Parris. "Enjoy," she said. "The bill is taken care of."

"Th-thank you." Her attention was aimed at Celeste, who was coming her way.

Celeste was walking back, head up, fury in her eyes, her face a hot pink. She didn't even stop at the desk but walked straight out the door. Parris came out behind her.

"Celeste, what happened? Are you all right?" She doubled her step to keep up.

Celeste aimed her alarm at the car and it beeped in response. She walked around to the driver's side and got in, tugging her coat around her as she jammed the seat belt in place. She gripped the steering wheel as if her life depended on it.

Parris tentatively reached out a hand to touch her shoulder, not bothering to speak, knowing well enough that people talked when they were ready.

The comforting gesture calmed Celeste in a way that words couldn't. She drew in a long breath and slowly released it. She turned toward Parris. "Let's get the hell out of here so that I don't have to tell this story more than once."

Leslie had spent the past hour and a half tending to her mother, preparing her lunch, helping her to the bathroom, stripping the bed and getting her settled back in it.

"I'm expecting company in a little while, Mama, so I'll be right up front if you need anything." She tried to catch her mother's attention, but Theresa refused to look at her, instead focusing her sights on the afternoon judge show.

Leslie sighed, adjusted the pillows behind Theresa's head, raised the guardrail and walked out, thankful to be free of the oppression that hung in her room like the humidity in summer, sticky and cloying.

As she stood over the sink washing and stacking the lunch dishes she tried to remember a time of laughter and joy shared between her and her mother, but the images and memories of the ill will between them obliterated anything else. She couldn't remember a good feeling, a hug, a smile, an 'I love you.' The lack of affection, like an insidious disease nibbled away at her sense of self, her ability to love herself, leaving her unable to love anyone else. She had no point of reference.

She believed that was the tie that bound her and Celeste. Their common ground. The thing that drew the two most unlikely people together, almost as if their dysfunction was a pheromone that couldn't be resisted. Their unified ambivalence for their mothers, their silent understanding that their mothers molded the women they'd become, fueled their friendship.

Leslie turned off the water and dried her hands on the green-and-white-striped dish towel that perfectly matched the wallpaper that took her nearly two months to locate. Unlike most people, it was not her bedroom that was her haven, it was her kitchen. From end to end, it was magazine perfect, from the matching washer/dryer, garbage disposal, dishwasher, range oven and double-door refrigerator—all in sparkling stainless steel. The granite floor brought to mind the plazas of Europe and its deep murky green with flecks of silver was the perfect complement to the décor. The six-foot island counter was equipped with four jets, a built-in wok, hand-washing sink and cutting board. She'd even had a small flat screen television hooked up so that she could watch her cooking and decorating shows whenever she was in the kitchen, which was often.

She took a slow turn around her beloved space, determined

that it was spotless, then hurried off to her bedroom to get out of her tattered nightgown and put on some clothes. When she thought about it, she was a little excited to have Parris in her home. She may not be a household name now, but she would be one day soon, and Leslie would always be able to say that Parris McKay had eaten brunch at her house. She slid her feet into her open-backed baby blue scuffs just as the doorbell rang.

Leslie stuck her head in her mother's room. The scent of illness, medication and age clung to the air, enveloping the once robust woman on the bed and all who came through the door. For an instant a rush of heartbreaking sadness bloomed within her and lodged in her throat. One day she would be gone, Leslie thought, blinking away the tears that suddenly stung her eyes. The battle would be over and neither side would have won. Then what? She watched the near imperceptible rise and fall of Theresa's chest and sent up a silent prayer of thanks that she was asleep before going down the hallway to answer the door.

"You are kidding me," Leslie said, handing out dishes at the kitchen counter. "He was actually out in public with Allison?" She tossed Parris a look. "That was Clinton's ex before Celeste swept him off his feet...or not, which is apparently the case." To Celeste she asked, "And being all cozy? See, that's why I know you could never be a sista, 'cause if you were, you would have been on the news!"

Parris had to laugh because she knew exactly what Leslie meant.

"I had no intention of messing up my mink coat," Celeste said, tongue in cheek of her defense.

Leslie looked at her and shook her head in feigned sadness.

"I am disappointed. I did not teach you well. You don't wear a mink to a street fight."

They all broke up laughing.

Celeste talked over her chuckles. "I should be hurt. It will be the scandal of the spring. But at least now I don't feel so bad for having—" her voice dropped to a notch above silent "—slept with Sam." Her gaze dived into the depths of her Thai iced tea.

"Excuse me? You did what?"

Parris waited for the punch line.

Celeste cut her eyes from one to the other, then nervously tucked her honey-blond hair behind her ears. "Don't look at me like that."

"You're serious," Leslie said, taking a seat.

Parris thought about the look of want in Sam's eyes the day they were all together, and the conversation that Nick had with her about the vibe he'd felt between Sam and Celeste. Maybe there really was something there. "If you care about him then it shouldn't be a problem. You're both adults."

"You don't know her family," Leslie said.

"And to be truthful I don't know what I feel about him. Part of it was definitely chemistry, another curiosity and a slap in the face to the Shaw tradition," she said, the rancor seeping through her words.

"Look, Sammy is my friend," Parris said. "And he's been like a brother to Nick since they were kids. He has his flaws, but he's a decent guy and he doesn't deserve to be treated like a science project. Hurt because of some white girl's fantasy and twisted version of sticking it to her bourgeois parents."

Celeste's cheeks flushed for a minute as her eyes lit with surprise and a hint of admiration. "I didn't think you had it in you."

Parris tossed her a sharp look of annoyance. "Whatever that's supposed to mean."

Celeste sat up straighter. "You just come across as this reserved, not an ugly thought ever passed through your head type of person."

"You don't know anything about me, who I am, what I've had to deal with. I know what it feels like to be dismissed, not considered a person of value." Images of her mother standing in front of her house flashed in her head. Her stomach fluttered.

"I think we've all had a dose of that," Leslie chimed in.

"Have you ever been scared, Parris? I mean deep down in your gut terrified. Scared to let go of everything that's familiar, even as much as you hate it? Knowing that the decision you make will change your life forever?" Celeste's voice shook. "It's like standing on the edge of a cliff and looking down, and if your parachute doesn't open the landing is going to be really ugly. That's how I feel about Sam."

For a moment they remained silent, each caught up in their own worlds of personal angst.

"I feel like that every day," Leslie said quietly. Her gaze jerked toward the hallway where her mother's room was. "Each morning I wake up with this knot in the pit of my stomach, a sensation of foreboding. My heart races and I go to my mother's room with a sense of hope and dread. Part of me wants it to be over. The other part dreads that it will be. When I see that she's still breathing, those two parts war with each other. Every day. Every day." She drew in a shaky breath.

"My mother and I have never had a mother/daughter relationship. We co-existed together when I was a child and I always felt that she put up with me only because she had to. I wanted her to look at me—" Leslie turned to each of them "—I mean really look at me. Love me, tell me that I was special and important, that I could be anything I wanted to be." She shook her head. "It was almost as if by withholding her love and affection she could somehow punish me for being here." Her lips tightened. Her nostrils flared. "For being a reminder of my father, who she has refused to tell me about. Ever!" She sputtered a nasty laugh. "Not even his name." Her dark brown eyes lit with hurt and anger. "You know what's on my birth certificate under father? Nothing. Blank." Her neck arched and her laughter was filled with scorn.

"I was so hungry for someone to love me, to care about me that—" her brow creased "—that I welcomed Uncle Frank's... touch." In anguished fits and starts she spilled out the memories of her uncle and how she blamed her mother when he stopped coming around, and how she'd tried to find what she'd lost in food, something that would always be there to comfort her.

"Les, you were a kid, and what he did wasn't right. He molested you," Celeste said, squeezing her hand. "You have to know that."

Leslie sniffed. What he'd done to her changed her forever; the way she felt about herself, relationships, intimacy. For that she would never forgive him. "I blame her for that, too. It would have never happened if she'd been a real mother."

"Does she know what happened? Did you ever say anything to her?" Parris asked.

Leslie shook her head. "No. I've never told anyone what happened."

"Until recently," Parris said quietly, turning to Leslie to share what she'd told Celeste, "I believed my mother was dead."

## Chapter Sixteen

Emma gathered her things and meticulously folded each item before depositing them in her suitcase. In the time that she'd spent with Marie, talking about life and the decisions she'd made, she'd slowly come to accept that she could no longer hide behind the guise she'd created, the imaginary life she'd lived for so long. It had ruined everything she'd struggled to attain, leaving her with nothing but her conscience. She'd tried to take the easy way out and even that had resulted in ruin. She'd attempted to reach Michael several times in the weeks that she'd spent at the inn. He'd refused her calls.

"You're making the right decision," Marie said quietly from her perch on the side chair. "We all must reconcile at some point with our lives."

"I know that now." She closed the suitcase and looked at the woman who'd become her savior, her mentor and her friend in a few short weeks. "Things will never be the same for me, but as my mother tried to do before she died, make things right, it's what I must do as well. For the sake of my daughter. She deserves that much. At least if I am not forgiven in this lifetime—" she glanced at Marie "—perhaps in the next, *oui?*"

Marie smiled. "It is what we all hope for." Slowly she stood. "I am terrible with goodbyes. First your daughter and now you. Fate." She walked over to Emma and held her in a tight embrace. "My doors are always open to you," she said against her cheek. "I wish you well, Emma Travanti." She stepped back, seeing the images of mother and daughter merge and switch places. "Marc will drive you."

Emma sniffed, reluctant to leave the sanctuary that had embraced and healed her, yet she knew that she must. "Thank you," she said, her voice swaying with emotion. "For everything."

Marie bobbed her head once, turned and left Emma with her thoughts and her impending future.

It was nearly eight by the time Parris and Celeste said reluctant goodbyes to Leslie. Save for several of Theresa's bell ringing interruptions, the trio had spent the better part of the afternoon into evening peeling away the layers of their lives, amidst tears, laughter, shame, anger and hope. After Leslie's admission of what happened to her as a child, the dam burst and the waters of all of their sorrows, hopes, dreams and fears rushed out, unchecked and unstoppable. Their confessions weren't prompted by tongue-loosening alcohol or the hourly rate of a therapist, dares or one-upmanship, but rather a sense of solidarity; a knowledge that they were not alone because there was someone who understood for having walked in their shoes.

"I really didn't mean what I said about the white-girl thing," Parris said as they rode along the darkened streets to Nick's place.

"Sure you did," Celeste said on a light note. "And you know what—" she glanced at Parris "—it's fine. Made me think about a few things and what it must look like from the outside. If I were you I would have thought the same thing. Probably would have said something much worse." She laughed. "But," she added, blowing out a breath, "I really think that if given the chance we could have something."

"Despite your family's values?"

She hesitated a moment. "If Sam is willing to wing it with a disowned, poor white chick from the Upper East Side that's really cute, we may be able to work something out."

They chuckled.

"Do you really think your parents would disown you?"

"Absolutely."

"What would you do?"

"Guess I'd really have to work this real estate thing."

Parris shook her head in amusement at Celeste's apparent cavalier attitude, which she'd come to learn was merely a front for a young woman who was a real mess underneath, as they all were.

They pulled up in front of Nick's building. Celeste cut the engine.

"You want to come up? Sam may still be there."

"That's what I'm afraid of," she said. "Not quite ready to see him in the real world yet. Besides I'm still supposed to be brokenhearted over Clinton. Remember?"

"What *are* you going to do about that?"

She reached for the safety net of her purse and began rooting around inside. "Nothing to do but move on. The thing between me and Clinton was always more about what everyone else wanted. We're both better off." She shrugged her shoulder. "Once the dust settles I'm sure it will be fine. And the circle of vultures will find some other morsel of gossip to feed off of." She turned in her seat to face Parris. "What about you? Are you ready to let go and move on?"

"I have to, I suppose. I know it's going to take time for the sting to go away, for the images to get so dim I can't make them out. For me to find a way to forgive my grandmother for lying to me for all those years." She drew in a breath and let it go.

"But she tried to make it right—in the end."

Parris nodded. "Yes...she did." She paused a moment as Cora's face floated before her eyes. "I miss her," she said in a faraway voice.

Celeste patted Parris's thigh. "You'll be fine. You have a great guy, a career in front of you, your grandfather who loves you and two new friends who are just as screwed up as you are," she added with a short laugh.

Parris chuckled. "That last part is definitely true." She unfastened her seat belt and opened the door. "Want me to pass a message to Sam if I see him?"

Celeste tipped her head to the side. "I think I'll give him a call. See if he's free tomorrow."

Parris's brows rose. "Sounds like you may be on the road to recovery."

She grinned. "We'll see."

Parris followed the sound of running water when she came into the apartment and found Nick in the kitchen. He glanced over his shoulder.

"Hey, babe. The fellas just left."

She came up behind him and wrapped her arms around his waist, rested her head on his broad back. "Had a good session?"

"Hmm-hmm." He turned off the water, dried his hands on a towel hanging over the sink and turned around. He braced Parris's slender form between his hard thighs. "What about you? How was your ladies only afternoon?" He kissed the tip of her nose.

She looked up at him and saw the light of endless possibility in his gaze if she would only give it a real chance, and to do that she, too, would have to move on. "Eye-opening."

"In a good way, I hope."

She nodded. "I think so. Celeste and Leslie are very complicated women."

"Uh, speaking of Celeste, she say anything about Sam?"

"Anything like what?" she hedged.

"Anything about anything."

She wasn't going to be the first one to give up the goods. "We talked about a lot of things. His name came up once or twice."

He watched her hard-fought expression of innocence with the practiced eye of a musician who knows his audience. And unless he gave the audience what it wanted they'd never give up the applause. "Okay, fine. He told me all about them, that he'd been up at her place for the past two days. I'm still in shock."

"I know," she now confessed.

And like two high schoolers, they tossed pieces of information back and forth until they had a complete picture. The bottom line was, Sam and Celeste seemed to really like each other.

"Do you think it can work?" Parris asked Nick as they plopped down in front of the television.

Nick shrugged. "Hey, anything is possible. Sam seems serious."

"You know her family is stinking rich," Parris said, leaning up against his side with her feet tucked beneath her.

"Really?"

"On both sides of the family."

"Maybe Sam really did luck out," Nick chuckled.

"Well, according to Celeste, if and when her parents ever find out they'd cut her off from the family fortune without blinking an eye."

Nick turned his head toward her and frowned. "You have got to be kidding me. Not because he's black?"

Parris bobbed her head.

"In this day and age?"

"The only line they are crossing is from the east side to the west side. Apparently, the melting pot of society has nothing to do with the Shaws of New York."

"Damn, sounds like a bad reality TV show."

Parris snickered and lightly smacked his thigh. She pointed the remote at the television and surfed for a movie.

They finally settled for one in progress about a young girl who looks white but has a black mother and how she grows up to want the life of the white family in whose house she lives and realizes that she can pass, scorning and disowning her mother, who'd sacrificed everything for her daughter.

As the movie drew to its heartbreaking conclusion, for the very first time, Parris caught a glimpse of the dynamics that may well have existed between her grandmother and her mother.

"My mother looks white."

Nick didn't breathe for a second, not wanting anything to distract her from the words she'd been holding on to since her return.

"My grandfather is not my natural grandfather at all. He's not my mother's father. Some other man is. A white man that gave us our green eyes. She has green eyes, too. Much more striking than mine." She pressed her fist to her mouth. "I should have known. How could I not have known the instant I saw her?" she went on, her tone self-accusatory. "I sat across from her in her restaurant. She talked to me, asked me questions and I didn't know. I felt something but I didn't know what." She drew in a shaky breath, her jaw working back and forth forming the words, reliving the moment. "But when I saw her in front of her house...I knew. And she realized that I did. The whole scene seemed to play out in slow motion, like it was happening to someone else. I felt sick inside. My heart started racing and I thought I was going to faint. I saw panic in her eyes. She didn't want him to know. And he stood there looking stunned and confused. Then he called her name. *Emma.* He looked from me to her. And I knew she'd never admit who I was. Not then, not ever. I would always be her dirty secret. So I ran back to the cab before I was sick all over their perfect lawn."

She wiped her eyes with the back of her hand.

Nick drew her close, let her cry. She'd been back for weeks and this was the first time she'd actually told him what had happened. That one moment that redefined her life.

After some time had passed, he asked her about the man. "Who was he?"

"I don't know." She sniffed. "I got the sense that he may have been her husband or lover. I don't know."

"Could it have been your father?"

Parris sat up, moved out of his protective hold. She vigorously shook her head. "Couldn't be."

"Why not? Did your grandmother ever talk about your father?"

"No." She frowned, trying to recall any mention of her father in the dusty letters that she'd been given or in those final conversations with her grandmother.

"It's possible, Parris. If your mother spent her entire adult life living as a white woman, I'm sure she married a white man—who could very well be your father. In all these years she's never admitted that she was your mother, chances are she never told him about you, either."

"But...but if he is my...father, how could he not know he has a child?"

"I don't know, sweetheart. I just don't know."

Then the jarring thought struck her. "Or maybe he knew, too." She arched her head back and squeezed her eyes shut. "Oh, God...maybe he always knew."

Michael sat in the outer office of Marcel Dominique. He'd debated for several weeks about what course of action he should take. He'd been so emotionally wounded by Emma's treachery that he'd been unable to think clearly. He'd met with his attorney earlier that morning to begin the process of reviewing all of his assets, their joint finances and what deeds they shared. He needed to sever his ties with Emma, and coming to that final decision was more agonizing than the months he spent in a German prisoner-of-war camp.

He couldn't remember when he'd last slept for the full night or what meal he'd eaten. Vivienne was fearful for him and insisted that he see a doctor. He looked ill, she'd said as she tried unsuccessfully to offer him soup, his favorite shrimp salad, steak, tea, or crackers as he sat for hours on end staring out the window. His employees at the vineyard had stopped by to check on him as he hadn't been to work or called in, and they were appalled at his haggard appearance.

It wasn't until today, nearly a month since Emma moved out, that he'd reached for what reserve he had left to begin the ugly business of putting an end to a chapter in his life. He still ached for her. At the oddest times he'd swear he heard her laughter. Her scent still lingered in the rooms that they'd shared so he'd sequestered himself to his study. Anytime he closed his eyes, day or night, her face would emerge, so he fought sleep. Like an amputee, he knew he'd lost a limb yet the sensation of it being there persisted. He still reached for the empty space until he was sure he would go mad. Until today.

After waking once again in the chair by the window, he had his first moment of clarity in weeks and he knew it would be his only salvation. Weak from exhaustion and lack of food, he forced himself to bathe, dress and arrange for the car to take him to his attorney's office. It was a grueling two hours of talking about things he didn't want to discuss, but the very act of reclaiming some semblance of his life helped him to put one foot in front of the other.

So here he waited.

The office door opened. A tall, well-built man with soft brown eyes, dressed in a navy suit, stood in the doorway. "Mr. Travanti, please come in. I am sorry to have you wait." His pencil-thin mustache moved as he spoke. "Some clients never want to end a phone conversation."

Michael stood up slowly and walked to the open door and inside. They shook hands.

"Please, have a seat."

The office was small and tight. Every wall was filled with

books and memorabilia and the very large desk took up much of the available floor space. But rather than a feeling of claustrophobia, Mr. Dominique's office had a lived-in, comfortable feel that put one at ease.

He went behind his desk and sat, folding his long thin fingers together. "Now, how can I help you?"

Michael withdrew a thick envelope from his jacket pocket and placed it on Mr. Dominique's desk. "I need you to find someone and give this to them."

It was smaller than she remembered, if that were possible, Emma thought, when she stepped out of the cab in the center of town. Many other things had changed as well. There were new businesses, the ice cream shop that she remembered on the corner of Huff Street was gone, replaced with an antique shop, and most striking of all was that whites and blacks walked along the same streets, stood out in front of store windows chatting like old friends, and mixed groups of teens shared unified laughter, iPods and the latest celebrity gossip.

This was not the same Rudell that she remembered growing up in, feeling isolated, the town divided by the Left Hand River, one side black and one side white. Divided by race and religion. This was not the same town that harbored the KKK— the night riders—who came under the cloak of darkness and set the house that her grandparents lived in on fire, killing them both to keep them from encouraging the blacks in town to fight for their rights. It was a town with a long, dark, ugly history that had been transformed by new cars, shiny storefronts and government mandates. Or had it? No one knew better than her about the power of illusion.

Emma crossed the busy street and walked to the corner, to

the one hotel in town, as the cab driver was very clear that he could not make a U-turn and that if she'd had her cross streets correct he would have dropped her off right in front of her destination. Rather than debate the customer always being right, she paid her fare, collected her luggage and got out. She inhaled the warm, moist air, the scent of the river in the distance. It had been more than three decades, nearly four, since she'd stood on these streets. The feeling was almost surreal, as if that life could not have happened in this picturesque town.

She pulled open the hotel door and walked the short distance to the front desk.

A young man, no more than twenty, in a starched white shirt and navy blue tie, glanced up. "Good afternoon, ma'am. How can I help you on this nice spring day?"

The words did a slow dance, winding their way to her in that sweet Southern cadence that she thought she'd forgotten. She realized with a pang in her chest how deeply she missed the sound.

"I called earlier. Emma Travanti."

"Sure thing, ma'am. Let me just take a look here." He focused on the computer screen in front of him on the desk. "You're sure right. Here you are." He pressed a button and her registration form spit out of the printer. She almost smiled. Rudell had come a long way. He handed her the form and showed her where to sign. "Will that be cash or credit?"

Fortunately, Michael had not cancelled her credit card, which she'd verified with the bank before she left France, and she had substantial savings of her own from the restaurant and several wise investments. Michael had always encouraged her to manage her own finances. She was glad she'd listened. "Credit." She took out her card and handed it over.

Moments later she was being shown to her room on the second floor of the four-story hotel.

"We do have a small restaurant on premises for the convenience of our guests," the bellhop mentioned as he opened the room door. "The hours of service are located on the nightstand. Unfortunately we don't have room service but there are ice and soda pop machines on the first floor."

"Thank you." She glanced quickly around at her accommodations. Small, but clean and bright. She took her wallet from her purse and handed him five American dollars. His eyes widened.

"Thank you, ma'am. Thank you very much," he said, backing out of the door as if he thought she may realize her mistake any minute and take the money back.

Emma locked the door behind him. She crossed the room to the window, pushed the curtain aside and looked out onto the busy street below. She was back, and the town that once shunned her seemed to welcome her home with open arms. She prayed that the man who helped raise her daughter would feel the same way.

## Chapter Seventeen

It was Saturday and the townspeople of Rudell tumbled onto the streets and roads intent on weekend chores and errands. The population had grown since she was last here and the expanse of land had shrunk to accommodate the new housing and businesses. Many of the plywood farmhouses were gone now, replaced by sturdy-looking two-story brick homes with cement paths instead of dusty dirt roads. Satellite dishes sat at cocked angles on rooftops and the movie theater that had once relegated Negroes to the balcony now featured the latest Will Smith movie. There were more cars now, but it seemed that the people still preferred walking, as she had done. She wanted to see if she remembered.

Emerging from the center of town, Emma followed the path of the Left Hand River to where the houses stopped and the trees bloomed. She came to a dead halt, her heart pounding, when she spotted the rock that she sat on many a day and cried, the rock where she sat that fateful night that altered the direction of her life. She stared at it for a few moments, lifted her chin and continued on her way. She came out into the clearing and much of what she'd remembered was the same. The houses were still separated by trees and land, still not as fancy as the houses in town, and the vibration in the air was that all was still slow and easy and everyone knew everyone's first name and who your people were.

Her throat clenched as she walked and recalled the steamy bone-melting summer afternoons when she would run through the woods, stick her feet in the river and collect eggs from the henhouse. Her mother would make deviled eggs—her favorite snack. She blinked away the tears, secured her purse on her shoulder and kept walking.

And then there it was. Right in front of her, just the way she remembered. Her heart pounded. Heat raced through her body. She stood stock-still at the end of the path that led to the house that had once been her home, her prison. She wanted to go forward but she couldn't move. Images played in front of her. She saw beyond the walls of the framed home into the recesses where she and Cora shared more than twenty years together in a war where the day-to-day casualty was another piece of your soul.

The front door opened and a woman and a young child emerged, turned and waved to the tall, dark and very handsome older man in the doorway. Emma gasped. She wanted to run but she was transfixed by the man in the door. She'd had many ideas of what he may look like, the man who'd loved her mother, the man who raised her daughter.

He was taller than she imagined. His close-cut hair was

totally white and set against skin that was as rich as molasses. The mother waved again. "Thanks, Dr. McKay."

"You take care now."

The mother and child passed Emma at the end of the path. David started to turn back toward the house when he saw her standing there, an apparition. He gripped the frame of the door. His chest heaved for air. He shook his head to clear the vision but it kept coming closer. Haunts didn't walk by day. They came in your sleep and blew in your ear, opened cabinets and turned on faucets, chilled the air or simply sat at your bedside to let you know they were there.

How many nights since he'd lost his Cora had he prayed for one more time to see her face, hold her hand, hear her voice. Finally.

She climbed the one step, looked up at him and said, "I'm Emma."

"Emma?"

She took a step closer. "Cora's daughter."

His posture faltered as he stared at Cora's ghostly image. It was her and not her at the same time. When last he'd glimpsed Emma, it was many years ago. He had no idea until this moment how much she favored her mother. This was his Cora twenty years younger standing before him sure as day.

"I know I should have called," she was saying, her drawl slowly returning, comforted by the lull of the Mississippi breeze. "I was afraid you wouldn't see me." She squeezed her hands into fists to stop the shaking.

A car roared down the road, spitting gravel. David blinked and focused on the woman standing in front of him. "You want to come inside?"

She nodded her head.

"Come on then." He stepped aside to let her pass and shut the door behind them.

Emma grew light-headed the instant she stepped into the front room. She pressed her hand to her chest. It was exactly as she remembered it. She walked through in a dream state as the memories came flooding back, leaving her short of breath.

David walked quietly behind her as she moved from room to room, stopping finally in the kitchen. She pulled out a chair from beneath the old butcher-block table and sat down, remembering all the times she sat across from her mother, hoping and praying that she would look at her, really look at her, and quiet the turmoil that raged in her heart.

"Sweet tea?"

Emma looked up, those green eyes that sent him fleeing all those years ago staring back at him. "Sweet tea?" he asked again.

"Y-yes. Thank you." She put her purse on the chair next to her.

David went to the cabinet over the sink and took out two glasses, got the pitcher of sweet tea from the refrigerator and placed them on the table. He poured hers then his own and sat down. He wrapped his hands around his cool glass and stared into its depths. "You favor your mother."

Emma's gaze snapped up. "Do I?"

"Spitting image." He brought the glass toward his lips but his hands shook so badly he put it back down. "Thought you was her standing out there on the lane." He steadied his hands and took a sip. "Parris came to see you, didn't she?"

Emma's throat knotted. "Yes."

"Hmm." David bobbed his head. "What brings you here after all this time?"

"Things…didn't work right between me and Parris. I need to find her and I knew you'd know how. I have to tell her the things she ought to know. About me, about everything."

David drew in a long breath. "A long time coming," he murmured. "Your leaving, taking on the life of living as a white woman, near killed Cora. And your birth nearly killed me."

Emma gripped the edge of the table as David stood, turning his back to her as he spoke. "We both blamed Cora. All those years, we blamed her for something that weren't her fault." He turned to face her. "I loved your mother from the time we were kids. But she had bigger dreams, bigger than Rudell. So she went off to Chicago. When she come back and agreed to marry me I was the happiest man in the world. She never told me what happened, what he done to her and then here you were, two months early." He swallowed hard. "I brought you into the world right up there on that bed. All I did was take one look at you and I knew you wasn't mine. Couldn't be. 'Bout lost my mind, believing that she… Never gave her a chance to explain. Wouldn't listen. Just packed up my things, walked out and didn't come back for more'n twenty years."

Emma's eyes stung as she witnessed his anguish and regrets, knowing her own. "I know what happened," she managed to say. "I met my father."

David's chest rose and fell in rapid succession. He came to the table, gripped the chair and slowly sat down. "What?"

"I met him…in New York. His name is William Rutherford. Or was, he might be dead by now."

His brow creased into a tight single line. "But…how…how did you know?"

She told him about the letter she'd found addressed to her

mother from her friend in New York, how it talked about this Mr. Rutherford, how he wanted to know if she was all right, why she'd run off from her job with him and never came back.

"I sat right where you're sitting, and I asked about the letter, about Mr. Rutherford, demanded to know why she'd left Chicago, who was he and why did he care?" She swallowed over the tightness in her throat. "She wouldn't tell me." She shook her head slowly. "But I knew. I just knew." She sat up a bit straighter, pressed her palms down on the table. "I kept the article that mama's friend Margaret had tucked inside the letter. It had his picture. It was a few months after I got to New York that there he was again on the front page of the newspaper. He was running for office." She scoffed. "I found out where he lived. I got his phone number and I'd call his house whenever the mood hit me. Most times I'd get a servant on the phone, but one day I got him." She paused as the jarring memory of that day rocked her once again. She tugged in a shallow breath. "I made up my mind I was going to meet him, force him to come face-to-face with what he'd done. I got my chance at the Plaza Hotel, just before Christmas. He was hosting a fund-raiser for his run for office. The lobby was teeming with celebrities, all kinds of movie stars. I found him in one of the banquet halls…."

*She knew it was him as soon as she saw him. He was no longer the grainy, black-and-white image, flat and one-dimensional. He was flesh. Her flesh. He stood there all proud and handsome, laughing with that big smile…and then all of a sudden he turned in Emma's direction. All the air rushed out of her lungs. Brilliant jade-green eyes, her eyes, stared back at her. The resemblance was extraordinary. If there was ever any doubt in her mind, it was gone.*

*"Good evening, Mr. Rutherford."*

*Ever the aristocratic gentleman, Rutherford tilted his head to the right side and regarded her with a dispassionate glance. "You…look oddly familiar. Have we met?"*

*"I'm sure you're thinking of my mother…Cora Harvey, at the time. She cleaned your house, cooked your meals." Her voice rose in both pitch and tenor, emotion warring with reason as the long-awaited confrontation of her dreams unfolded rapidly before her eyes. "Picked up after you and your wife. Do you remember her now?"*

*One of his aides moved swiftly and expertly to Rutherford's side, cupped Emma's elbow and whispered harshly in her ear. "Let's go, miss. We won't have a scene."*

*Emma didn't move, she couldn't. She stared Rutherford directly in the eye, saw his pupils widen in alarm, watched his face turn a dangerous crimson, stopping at the line of his thick salt-and-pepper hair. "I'm Emma." She stepped a bit closer, lowered her voice an octave then leaned toward him with her face just inches from his. "The resemblance is shocking…isn't it…Dad?"*

A tremor of remembrance fluttered along Emma's spine. She blinked, shook her head to dispel the images of that night and settled on David's astonished expression. She glanced away. "After I threatened to go downstairs and address the media with my story he had one of his assistants escort me to his private suite in the hotel. I blackmailed him. I told him I wanted two hundred thousand dollars to keep my mouth shut, to disappear for good. Something I must have heard on a television show. He agreed to meet me and give me what I'd asked for. I went to his apartment on Park Avenue the following day…."

*"You're early."*

*The well-modulated voice came from the recesses of the room. Emma turned toward the sound, momentarily startled.*

*Rutherford appeared like an apparition from behind a door she hadn't noticed upon her arrival. His dark suit elegantly covered his long, still lean body. He purposefully crossed the room in measured strides to stand behind his desk. He pulled open the drawer and extracted a brown envelope, then dropped it with a thud on the desktop.*

*Cautiously Emma moved forward, back straight, head held proudly aloft. She stood directly in front of him. It was then that she noticed his haggard appearance, nothing like the well-groomed, self-assured man of the night before, even clothed in what was obviously an expensive, handsome suit. His eyes were red-rimmed with half-moon shadows underscoring them, and there was a faint outline of stubble coating his angular jaw. The smooth control he'd previously exhibited was replaced by short, almost stilted movements, like a person forced to concentrate on every action.*

*"There's your money. Take it and go. Isn't that what you wanted?"*

*"I want the truth. I want answers."*

*"You want money. You want to ruin my life, my reputation, with your lies and accusations. If that money will make you go away, then so be it."*

*"Ruin your life?" she stammered incredulously. "Your life? Do you have any idea how you've ruined my life?" She stepped closer. "Look at me. Take a good look at me. What do you see? A woman who has spent all of her life not knowing where she belonged, not fitting in, having everyone around her whispering things about her—her mother. Do you know what it feels like to not to know who you are—why you are? Do you know what it feels like to have your own mother look at you with emptiness and shame, the one person in the world who is supposed to love you without question? Look at me, damn you to hell! This is what you've done." She pounded her finger at her chest. "You've ruined my life!"*

*Emma pressed her lips together, drew herself up and took the damning envelope from the desk. Without another word or a backward glance, she walked stiffly toward the door.*

*"I never meant…to hurt your mother. Never."*

*Her steps faltered then settled. Her head rose a notch and her shoulders straightened. For the beat of a heart, she stood there, let his words reach down to that dark tortured place in her soul, and finally there was light. She dropped the envelope at her feet, opened the door and walked out....*

Emma's soft sobs brought David to her side. He pulled his chair next her hers and drew her against his chest, rocking her gently as her cries shook her petite body. He let her cry as his own tears of regret and loss burned his eyes and scorched his cheek.

"She was a wonderful child," he said to Emma much later as they sat together on the porch, dusk gathering around them. "Always had a smile and was the joy of our lives. Voice as beautiful as her grandmother's." He smiled at the memory. "We both wronged Cora, me and you both. I spent the rest of her life trying to make it up to her. You have the same chance with Parris before it's too late." He dug in his pocket and took out a slip of paper. "This is where she's staying in New York, with that young fella that came here for her when Cora passed." He handed it to her.

She took it from him, her gaze thankful. "They were lucky to have you in their life." She stood up slowly.

"I can drive you back to town."

She smiled softly. "I think I'll walk." She leaned down and kissed his cheek. "Thank you." She turned to leave.

"This is always your home, Emma."

She nodded once and began her walk.

As David watched her walk away he prayed that the dark secret that haunted this family for generations would finally see its long overdue end.

# Chapter Eighteen

Leslie finished up in the kitchen and turned out the lights. It had been a long day. Her mother was more cranky than usual, which had totally drained Leslie, emotionally and physically. All she wanted to do was catch the last of the news and crawl into bed. She shuffled out to the living room and turned on the television. Taking her favorite spot on the couch she caught up with the events of the day.

Another dateless Saturday night, she mused as the broadcaster talked about the grand opening of another night spot in Manhattan. At least it was over on the East Side, she thought, as she watched the stars emerge from their cars, pose for the cameras and stroll in under the pop and flash of lights. She nearly leaped out of her chair when she spotted Clinton with Allison glued tightly to his arm walking down the red carpet. They both smiled and waved as if Celeste never existed.

"Well, I'll be damned. He sure didn't waste any time." She wondered if Celeste was watching, and started to reach for the phone to call her, but knowing Celeste she had better things to do on a Saturday night than watch other people have a good time, especially her ex. She pointed the remote at the screen and watched it go black.

Sighing heavily, she heaved herself off the couch, stuck her feet in her slippers and headed for her bedroom. She stopped, as always, at her mother's door for the last bed check.

Her mother's frail body was silhouetted by the night-light that glowed like a halo above Theresa's head. The blanket that covered her slowly rose and fell in time to the soft snores. Leslie stood there for a moment in the quiet, in the dark, thinking of the times when she was a little girl and she'd come to her mother's door eager to tell her about her day, and Theresa would say, *not now Leslie, I'm exhausted. Go to bed, it's late.* And she'd leave brokenhearted with so many things on her mind. Day after day, night after night, until one day she didn't try anymore. And over the years, the stories, the questions, the hurts, the need to know things—girl things, mother/daughter things—congealed into this tight ball that sat in the center of her stomach growing day by day until it erupted that night in her mother's apartment.

Leslie wrapped her arms tightly around her body, her lips squeezed shut as she fought back the cry that battled to escape. It began like any other time she and her mother got together. She'd stopped by that Friday night as she always did—the daughterly thing—to check on Theresa. She was never sure why she made it her Friday night ritual. Theresa never seemed to appreciate it, but Leslie couldn't stop herself, as if she hoped that maybe "this Friday" things would be different.

She'd called ahead as usual to find out if Theresa needed anything. After stopping at the local grocer for the usual fixings for a salad and some Italian bread, Leslie arrived at her mother's apartment on Lenox Avenue. She'd lived in the same apartment for Leslie's entire life. The building was rent-stabilized, and in today's economy, Theresa was barely paying five hundred dollars for a two-bedroom apartment in the heart of Harlem. She would proudly tell anyone who asked that they would have to "sandblast me out of here, 'cause I ain't never leaving."

Leslie smiled to herself, thinking of her mother's favorite line as she stuck her key in the door. The mouthwatering aroma of homemade spaghetti sauce greeted her just like every Friday night at her mother's. It had turned into an unspoken tradition between them.

She found Theresa in the kitchen, stirring the sauce with one hand and sprinkling in the ingredients with the other.

"Just put the stuff on the table," she said without turning around, without a hello. "Then you can butter that bread."

Leslie sighed, shrugged out of her coat and took it to the hallway closet, stopped off in the bathroom to wash her hands then returned to the kitchen.

To the casual observer, mother and daughter working side by side, preparing their traditional Friday night dinner, would evoke the perfect scene of domesticity. It wasn't.

Leslie jammed the knife into the bread, slicing through it. Her breathing for a moment was short and tense until she forced herself to relax as she listened to her mother remind her that she looked like she was gaining more weight and she really needed to make an appointment with her hairdresser for a touch-up.

"I'm never having kids," she suddenly blurted out.

"Probably a good thing."

"Is that how you feel about me, you wish you hadn't?"

Theresa held up her spoon in warning. "Don't start with me tonight, Leslie. I'm not in the mood for another one of your 'woe is me' pity parties."

Leslie gripped the knife, her rage boiling in concert with the pot of sauce. "I always wondered what man could find a woman as cold as you warm enough to sleep with."

It happened so fast she couldn't have reacted in time to ward off the powerful slap that sent her reeling back against the refrigerator.

Theresa's dark eyes bored into Leslie, the muscles of her face twitched as they stood facing each other in a silent war that had gone on for decades and finally the first drop of blood was spilled.

"I despise you," she said from a place so deep and dark inside herself that the voice was unrecognizable. "You've spent your entire life making mine miserable, belittling me, ignoring me. I may as well have grown up alone for all the good you ever were to me! Why did you have me if hate me so much? Whhhyyy?" she screamed. "Do I remind you of him, some horrible time in your life that you'd rather forget so you spend your life punishing me?" She pounded her chest as tears streamed down her face. "Do you know what you have done to me, you selfish, evil bitch!" She lunged toward her, wanting to smash her face in, when suddenly Theresa's eyes widened in alarm. Her mouth opened but there was no sound. Her body stiffened before she collapsed on the kitchen floor.

For several moments Leslie stood there with the knife still in her hand, not able to put together what she was seeing. She stared at the knife. There was no blood. The pot boiled over as thick red sauce ran unchecked down the stove.

"Ma…" She stepped closer. Theresa didn't move. Leslie's heart was beating out of her chest. She dropped to the floor beside her mother. "Ma!" She shook her. Nothing. She pressed her head to her chest. She was still breathing. Leslie leaped up. She needed to call someone. Emergency. Her mind went blank and for a moment she turned in a circle, not remembering where the phone was in a house that she knew like the back of her hand. Finally, her wild gaze landed on the phone. She snapped up the phone on the wall and with shaky fingers she pressed in 911, all the while staring at her mother lying motionless on her kitchen floor.

And all she could think about on the way to the hospital that night, with the shrilling sirens crashing through the night, was that if Theresa died they'd never have their Friday night dinners and she would never have the chance again to get her mother to love her.

"I'm sorry, Ma," she whispered over her tears as she held her mother's thin fingers between her own, pressing her head against the side of the bed, not even remembering walking fully into the bedroom.

Under the protection of dark, in the security of her own home and understanding that retaliation was not possible, she began to talk to her mother, pour out all of the things she'd wanted to say since she was a little girl about her best friend Lynn from sixth grade, when she got her first training bra, how much she hated going to gym because her uniform was too small and all the kids teased her, how she always tried to wait up for her at night just so she could smell her perfume. She told her about Uncle Frank and what he did to her, how his kind of love had damaged her spirit and she blamed herself. "All I've ever wanted was your love, Ma. Just wanted you to look at me and smile sometime, that's all, like maybe you were proud of me and that I wasn't a mistake. 'Cause that's how you always made me feel, Ma, like I'm a mistake. A night you wish you could take back. A night so bad you don't want to remember it or him. So you simply erase him from your mind, from your vocabulary, like he doesn't exist." Her body shook as she cried and talked and cried. "But that makes part of me not exist, either. A part that's been missing all my life. For thirty-two years only half of me has been living."

She wiped the tears away as quickly as they fell. She sighed heavily as she watched the slow rise and fall of her mother's chest. When she glanced toward the window, she was surprised to see that day was breaking over the horizon. She'd sat there all night. She'd cried and talked until there was nothing left to give.

Slowly, painfully, she stood. Her joints were stiff from sitting in the chair for so many hours. She glanced at the bedside clock. It was nearly six-thirty. If she went to bed now, she thought as she adjusted the blanket, she could get in a couple of good hours before her mother awoke and their day began. Leslie eased out of the room, leaving the door cracked.

Theresa opened her eyes and stared up at the ceiling. A single tear trailed down her sunken cheek.

Gracie had agreed to come by for a couple of hours even though it was a Sunday so that Leslie could run a few errands outside of the house. It was going to cost Leslie more than she could reasonably afford at the moment, but she didn't have much of a choice. More and more lately, when she compared her bills to the money that came in, she thought about Celeste's offer to help.

She wasn't sure what it was that kept her turning down her friend's offer of help. She did know that part of it was her own stubborn pride, but more of it was the shackle of guilt. Every day when she helped her mother to the bathroom, to get dressed, to eat, it assuaged the guilt of that night. As much as the doctors told her that the aneurism that had devastated her mother had more than likely been brewing for months, it didn't take away Leslie's belief that it was her fault, and it was her responsibility alone to carry that shackle around.

She'd gotten her mother up, washed and dressed and she was comfortably camped out in the living room in her recliner watching television when Gracie arrived, right on time as usual.

"Thank you so much, Gracie," Leslie said as she put on her coat and grabbed her purse. "I promise I won't be more than a couple of hours. I need to run over to Seventh Avenue to pick up some material that I ordered and stop by the supermarket. We're low on everything."

"Of course." She waved her hand. "Take your time." She settled down next to Theresa. "And how is my favorite patient today?" She patted her hand.

"I'll see you both soon." She opened the door.

"Wait."

The one word was weak and raspy but infinitely clear. Leslie froze with her hand still on the doorknob. Slowly she turned around, her heart pounding.

Gracie was staring at Theresa, and Theresa was looking right at her daughter. Leslie watched the muscles in her throat move up and down. "Please…"

Leslie's purse slipped from her fingers and fell to the floor with a dull thud. "Ma?" She moved slowly toward her until she was kneeling at her side. She took her hand. "Ma?"

"I...I'm so sor-ry."

Leslie squeezed her mother's hand tighter. "It's okay, Ma. It's okay."

Theresa vigorously shook her head. "No," she managed to reply. "Need...to tell you." She waved Gracie away, so she got up and quietly left the room. Theresa turned to Leslie. In fits and starts, some words not making sense, she told Leslie how wrong she had been for so long. That she'd pushed her own insecurities onto Leslie in the hopes that she would be hardened enough not to succumb to the pain that she'd endured from her father.

Leslie held her breath when, for the first time in thirty-two years, her father's name was uttered from Theresa's lips.

"Thomas Manning. Tommy." Theresa's eyes clouded over as she went to a place in her heart that only she could see. "I loved him with...everything in me. I would have done anything for him. I was so happy to find out I was pregnant with you. I couldn't wait to tell him," she said, struggling and reaching for every word. "When I went to his apartment—" she paused "—he was there with someone else. His best friend, Lloyd." Her laugh sounded like a strangled bird. "He took me to the back room and told me he couldn't see me anymore. That he didn't love me, couldn't love any woman."

She frowned and shook her head slowly. "I told him I didn't understand what he was telling me. 'What are you saying?' I asked him. He told me how all his life he'd fought back his urges, tried to live a 'normal' life, but he couldn't do it anymore. He didn't want to hurt me."

Leslie's stomach began to churn. She felt sick.

Theresa focused on her daughter. "I never got to tell him about you. I was so hurt, so stunned, so humiliated. I couldn't tell anyone. Back then it was hard. So I moved away, found a new place to live so I wouldn't have to face anyone. I never looked back." She swallowed. "The only way I could get through my life was to pretend that a part of it didn't exist." She squeezed Leslie's hand. "I thought I was doing the right thing by you. I thought I was." She hung her head and began to weep.

Leslie struggled to gather her racing thoughts. Put the pieces together to what her mother had confessed. All these years, her mother had lived with the doubt of her own womanhood, a secret that had grown and festered through the years, eating them both alive, and like an infant nursing at her mother's breast, Leslie had been nurtured and fed on that fear, doubt and shame.

She wanted to blame her, but she couldn't. How could she, when her mother was just as much a victim of deceit as she had been.

Maybe now, after all these years, after all the hurt and harsh words, they could start at a new place. With trepidation she gently rested her head on her mother's lap, and her heart nearly burst from her chest when she felt the gentle touch that she'd so longed for, stroke her hair.

"I...love...you," Theresa whispered.

"I love you, too, Ma."

Gracie stood in the doorway, took her coat from the hook and quietly slipped out, thinking that as soon as she got home she was going to call her daughter in Philadelphia and remind her how much she mattered.

## Chapter Nineteen

Celeste was busy in her small home office, searching her real estate database for new leads. The company she worked for had just that morning updated their lists. She was hoping to find something that she could sink her teeth into, possibly a multiple dwelling. Those went for top dollar even in the current tight economic times.

The long list of foreclosures went on for several pages. She couldn't imagine having to give up her home. All her life anything she'd ever wanted had been hers for the taking. Her life was one of privilege and as much as she railed against it, she couldn't deny its benefits.

Her grandfather, when she was much younger, had often told her of the dark days of the depression. How one day he was a wealthy man, on the top of the world, a big house with servants, a thriving business in finance, and the next day he had nothing. He and her grandmother struggled for several years before they were back on their feet and able to invest again, he'd said. He'd taken on a job in construction under the New Deal, determined to do whatever was necessary to regain the lifestyle he'd lost, and regain enough footing that he was able to run for and hold political office, where much of his real power eventually came from.

Her grandfather was luckier than most. Far too many couldn't endure the thought of not having, and had taken their lives. It was her grandparents' wealth, combined with that of her father's, that allowed them to live in the rarified world that they did. She supposed she should be grateful.

She continued to scroll until she reached the category she was looking for and began making notes on what looked like good possibilities. She reached for the phone to contact one of the sellers on the list, just as her doorbell rang.

Frowning, she pushed up from her seat, annoyed that the doorman had let someone up unannounced. He'd definitely get short-changed in his Christmas stocking.

She reached the door and peered through the peephole. Corrine Shaw was pacing back and forth in front of her door.

"Shit," she sputtered. Drawing in a breath of resolve, she unlocked the door. "Mother, what a surprise," she said syrupy sweet.

Corrine glared at her and pushed by her as if it was her home rather than her daughter's.

Celeste slammed the door. "Nice coat. Is it new?"

Corrine whirled around to face her, her cheeks flushed with her ever-present outrage. "Would you mind telling me what is going on?"

"What are you talking about?"

"You know perfectly well what I'm talking about." She ripped the newspaper out of her Louis Vuitton purse and shook it in her face. "This is what I'm talking about." She hurled the newspaper on the couch.

Celeste glanced at the front page and Clinton and Allison stared back at her. Her stomach tightened. She knew she'd have to have this unfortunate conversation at some point, she simply didn't think it would be so soon. Her shoulders slumped a little. She walked to the couch and sat down, crossing her legs.

"Well," her mother demanded. "How did you manage to screw this up?"

Celeste's gaze rose to meet her mother's and quickly jerked away. The look of pure fury and contempt stilled the barb she wanted to toss back. It was always like this between them, with Corrine on the attack for some irrational slight or faux pas, and Celeste on the defensive, struggling to find the words to explain whatever misdeed she'd been accused of.

"Do you know how embarrassing this is? I will be the laughingstock of the club. I still get questions and raised eyebrows about this...this real estate thing." As she ranted her pace became more frenetic, picking up more speed with each imagined slight. "And now this! Everyone who is anybody knew about you and Clinton. It was understood that you were to be married. Then to see him on the front page of the newspaper with Allison! My Gawd, what must people be thinking?" Her hand flew to her mouth as if she were really going to burst into tears. "This is all your doing. I know it. It has to be. Clinton understood where his bread was buttered by becoming a part of this family. Bringing together the Shaws and the Averys would have been one of society's biggest coups since Kennedy and Onassis.

"All your life you've done everything you possibly could to

infuriate me, humiliate your family. A disappointment to us all. It's been one thing after another. Enough is enough." She came to a full halt, her finger wagging as she glared at her daughter. "You are going to fix this. You are going to make it right. I will not tolerate another one of your scandals. Do you understand me? Or I swear to you, I will cut you off without a dime. Then see how you can manage to live here—" her arm swept the luxurious space "—or anywhere else for that matter...peddling low-end apartments!"

As she sat there pummeled by her mother's caustic verbal assault her mind tripped backward and forward to all of *these* conversations. For as far back as she could remember, her mother always found whatever Celeste did not up to the Shaw standard, from her ineptitude at ballet, her awkwardness on horseback, to not being at the top of her class or being selected homecoming queen. It didn't matter. Whatever it was it was never good enough or better than so-and-so's child. At least you have money and looks, her mother would generally conclude at the end of her lambasting. And when your looks go you will have the money to fix them.

Celeste wasn't exceptionally smart, or moderately talented. She knew it and had come to accept it. She traveled in a circle of friends that would as soon stab you in the back as share a martini over lunch at Cipriani's. And although she never fit in the world of her parents and their ilk, she knew what she was entitled to; her family's fortune, and with that she could dress herself up, live the high life and pretend to be just as happy as everyone else, because her money allowed her to. Her money and standing in society camouflaged her lack of talent, skills, or brilliance. Without it, she would simply be another pretty face until that, too, was gone.

"You are going to call him and apologize," her mother was saying.

Celeste watched her mother's polished lips move but she'd stopped listening. What would she do? How would she survive? Parris's statement to her of a few weeks ago rose to the surface as she stared at her mother, hypnotically walking back and forth in front of her. *But you benefit from it.*

It was true, she did benefit from it. She'd never had to do anything to earn her way through life. Parris held a job before her grandmother died. She had a voice that could earn her a living. Leslie struggled but she made it work day after day, not only taking care of herself, but also looking after her mother and never asking for help. These were women who never had what she did. And in her parents' eyes they would be "beneath" them and not worthy of their time. But in truth they were the only *real* women she knew.

Suddenly she stood. "Mother, please leave."

Corrine blinked rapidly, her long neck arching back. "What did you say?"

"I said to please leave before I wind up saying something very ugly."

"How dare you? I pay for this place you want to put me out of!"

Celeste folded her arms, looked down at the floor and suddenly wished she had her big deep purse to search through as the words stumbled out of her mouth. "I don't love Clinton. We barely like each other. It was his decision to take up with Allison again, even if I may have pushed him in that direction. If you want to cut me off and out of the family—" she finally lifted her head, her heart was beating so rapidly that her vision clouded for a moment "—then cut me off. I'll find a way to make it, just like everyone else in the real world."

"You have no idea what you're saying. You wouldn't survive a day without your cars and your wardrobe and your expense accounts." Corrine tossed her head back and laughed. "Don't be ridiculous. Now, be a good girl and pick up the phone, call Clinton and invite him over to our place for dinner. We'll—"

"Stop it! Just stop it! Don't you hear what I'm saying? I'm not going to do this anymore. I'm not going to be your puppet on a string. I'm not going to continue to live my life through *your* expectations. I'm thirty-three years old and I don't even know who I am." Her eyes darted back and forth as she paced, and all the years of being assaulted by her mother's caustic tongue came roaring to the surface. "Everything that I've been taught that was important is all superficial, Mother. You gauge your entire life, my life, on our 'position' and who we know, who knows us. I have never felt that I had as much value to you as one of your mink coats. I've *never* been your daughter. Just another possession. Do you have any idea what that's like?"

Corrine's thin nostrils flared. "You've obviously lost your mind."

She knew it would be hard as hell, but if she didn't do this now, in another twenty years she would *be* her mother and she could not allow that to happen.

"No, Mother, I think I've finally found it. You can't run my life anymore. I won't let you. I can't let you. So if you want to disown me because I won't say 'I do' to someone I don't love, then fine. If it makes you feel powerful to take this all away—" she threw her arms up in the air "—then do it." She walked toward the door and opened it. "I never needed a benefactor. I needed a mother."

Corrine drew in a breath, lifted her chin and gathered her coat around her as if she'd suddenly been hit by a cold draft of air. She stalked toward the door and gave her daughter one last look of pure incomprehensibility and walked out without another word.

Slowly Celeste closed the door. The adrenaline still charged through her veins. The exchange of words resounded in the room. She'd never stood up to her mother. She'd always inhaled whatever Corrine set under her nose no matter how much she may have hated the smell of it.

She plopped down on her couch, her legs suddenly feeling wobbly. What if her mother went through with her threat? How would she manage? Where would she live? What about the lease on her car, her credit cards? She pressed her hands to her face. You've really gone and done it now, she thought.

She raised her head and looked slowly around, her heart pounding with the gravity of what she'd mouthed herself into. But then a slow smile crept across her mouth when the appalled look that carved itself onto her mother's face emerged in her head. Now that was worth the price of admission. Corrine Shaw had never been told just where she could put her "upper crust" before and certainly not by her own daughter. Celeste began to laugh and couldn't stop. She was surprised her mother hadn't passed out on the floor. Wiping the tears of laughter from her eyes, she pushed up from the chair, feeling an over-whelming sense of freedom, breathing on her own for the very first time.

She walked toward the phone and dialed Sam's number. If she was going to get kicked to the curb she may as well go out with a bang.

"Hey, I was wondering, if you're not busy tonight, I thought maybe we could see a movie or something," she said the moment he picked up the phone.

He chuckled deep in his throat and it ran through her like a hot toddy. "Sounds good. I'm down. What brought this on?"

"What do you mean?"

"I mean, since we've been seeing each other both you and I know that it's been this unspoken thing that it would be at your place. So, I'm wondering what changed."

She thought about it for less than an instant. "I have," she said softly.

He paused a beat. "So what time do you want me to pick you up?"

# Chapter Twenty

Parris gripped the phone. Her chest rose and fell in jerky motions.

"Took her to the airport..." David was saying. "She didn't say if she was coming straight there, but I went on and gave her Nick's address and phone number."

Her throat was so tight she couldn't swallow. *Her mother was coming to New York?*

"We talked a real long time. She's done some awful things, but so have we all. But she's sorry, really sorry. You ought to listen to her, try to make some kind of peace. I believe I have."

Parris heard the doorbell in the background.

"That's one of my patients." He laughed lightly. "Opened my office in the house. I know Cora is up there fussing." He shook out a breath. "She wants to see you. Tell you the things you need to know. It's up to you if you let her." The bell rang again. "I gotta go. You take care."

Parris sat there so long on the edge of the bed that the dial tone began to hum in her ear. In a daze she fumbled with the phone until she got it back on its base.

"Hey, babe, I'm going to head on over to the club…." Nick tilted his head to look at her. "What's wrong?"

She looked up at him, her focus distant. "That was Granddad. He said…my mother came to Rudell. She was at the house and he gave her this number and address, put her on a plane…and she's coming here."

"When? Today?" He sat down beside her.

Parris slowly shook her head. "I don't know. I don't even know if she'll really have the nerve to show up." The image of Emma standing on her front lawn flashed through her head. Her body stiffened.

"Hey," he said, putting his arm around her shoulder. "Whatever happens we'll deal with it. Okay?" He hugged her tighter. "Okay?"

"Sure…" she said without much conviction. *Emma was coming to New York.*

"Your appointment at Artist Records is in an hour," he said, gently hoping to nudge her back to the present and the immediate issues at hand.

This record deal had been hanging in limbo for months and it took a lot of smooth talking and promises on Nick's part to keep Lenny Epps from just saying to forget the whole thing. He thought they'd gotten over most of the hurdles. The last thing he—or Parris for that matter—was expecting was a phone call like this one.

Sometimes it was hard for him to understand why the issue

with her mother rocked her so deeply. He could barely remember his mother, and what he did remember, he wished that he didn't. Nick wanted Parris to simply say the hell with it and her mother, and move on. She wasn't worth the anger or the hurt or the time Parris spent agonizing over what her mother had done or not done.

But that's not the kind of woman Parris was, he thought as he watched her get up and walk to the closet to pick out her clothes. The corner of his mouth rose and the hardened look in his eye brought on by the mention of her mother slowly softened. Parris reminded him of the earth; caring and nurturing, rich and absorbing, the keeper of the roots. When she felt, she felt deeply and her emotions shaped who she was and guided her. There was nothing superficial about Parris, and that's why he loved her, and whatever the situation was with this woman who was her mother, he would be there for her, if and when she showed up.

They sat side by side in the outer office of the president of Artist Records. The walls were lined with Grammys, American Music Awards, platinum and gold records that dated back to the sixties all the way to last month's sweep at the Kodak Center where sixteen Artist Records performers took home their gold statues. Lenny Epps had been responsible for not only shaping and building careers, but also guiding the direction of the music industry for decades.

The double wood doors to his office swung open and Lenny stepped out. About five foot six, slightly balding with a signature style of jackets and sweater vests, he always reminded Nick of Quincy Jones, just a little rougher around the edges. They stood as Lenny approached.

"Sorry to keep you waiting. Come on in. Let's talk business."

Lenny didn't waste any time. The moment they sat down he dove into his spiel. "I'm looking to begin a new label at the start of the year. And I want to launch it with you. What you do with jazz, combine it with blues and R and B, is exactly what I'm looking for. I can make your sound transcend generations. I'm looking to do an album a year for three years. We'll start touring you the minute the album drops. You'll be on the road eight to ten months a year. If we're both happy at the end of three then we can renegotiate." He looked from one to the other.

Parris folded her hands on her lap and cleared her throat. "I really appreciate you waiting so long to meet with me," she began. "And your offer is a wonderful one. All I've ever wanted to do was sing. It's like a calling, you know." She stole a glance at Nick. She paused. "But I can't take it."

Lenny lurched forward in his seat. "What?"

Nick held his breath.

"It has nothing to do with your offer, Mr. Epps. It has to do with me and what I need to do with my life. I'm at a place where I'm finding out who I am and I can't allow myself to be reshaped by the stylist and the publicist and the record executives, not even my fans. I want to sing because it fills me up inside, not because there's a production deadline. I don't want to wake up every morning and not know where I am." She took a deep breath and slowly stood up. "I'm sorry. Really I am."

With purpose and a sense of inner peace she walked out with Nick at her side, leaving Lenny with his mouth opened in a half smile of amazement.

"I know I should have told you," she said as she stared at the floor numbers as they descended on the elevator. "But I thought if I did you'd try to talk me out of it. Besides I really wasn't sure right up until I sat down in that chair and looked him in the eye. I knew that kind of life really wasn't for me. I know I probably sound totally naive and idealistic, but…" She looked into his eyes, hoping that he would understand.

The doors swooshed open. "Let's just say I'm…stunned. I never saw that one coming." They stepped out and walked to the exit. The cold hands of the wind wrapped around them, drawing them together. "But," he added, exhaling a cloud into the air, "I'm proud of you. It takes a lot to turn down that kind of offer. To realize that your happiness and convictions are more important than anything else." He stopped on the street, turned her to face him and held her by her shoulders. He looked down into those incredible eyes, her hair blowing wildly in the wind. "You are something else," he said in amazement, emphasizing each word. She grinned, relief washing over her face. "Guess those dreams of me kicking back and reaping the benefits of your labor are out the window, huh?"

She reached up and kissed him. "Pretty much."

They laughed all the way back to the car.

For days after the phone call from David, Parris's nerves were thrumming like overly tight guitar strings. She worked hard to try to hide her mounting anxiety, which vacillated from high to low and back again. Nick had enough on his mind with the renovation of the club going full steam ahead. She found herself spending more time with Leslie and Celeste, and that invisible bond that drew them together strengthened as they talked about their lives, hopes and dreams for the future. She was astonished to find out what had transpired between Leslie and her mother, and the change in Leslie was brilliantly obvious. She was calmer. The edge had diminished. She smiled more often and seemed to be working on her wardrobe and her hair. When she spoke of her mother now, the acid was vacant from her tongue. It was a softer, gentler Leslie.

Celeste, too, had begun a shift in her personality and direction. Although she and her mother hadn't passed a word between them since that afternoon at her apartment, with her commission check from the sale of the club, Celeste was looking for someplace that she could reasonably afford on her own, before the inevitable rug was pulled out from under her. She was working full-out at the real estate office, not to mention that she and Sam were an official item.

However, as much as Parris occupied her time with her new friends or the goings-on at the club, that jangling sensation in the pit of her stomach wouldn't go away. She jumped every time the phone rang. When she walked the streets she saw Emma's face in each woman she passed. But after more than three weeks since David's phone call, she was drawing to the inevitable conclusion that Emma wasn't coming. And it was just as well.

Nick shrugged into his jacket. "I'm expecting a delivery at the club this morning," he said in a rush, brushing his lips against hers. "I totally forgot and I'm running late. See you this afternoon."

"I might stop by. If I plan to I'll give you a call," she said to his departing back.

"Sure." He darted out.

She finished cleaning up the kitchen and planned to spend the balance of the morning going over the club's finances and the stack of bills that had been rolling in like a midwest blizzard.

Staying on top of what was going out was essential, especially
since until the club opened there was no revenue. They were
operating on the bank loans and the money that Nick and Sam
had set aside. And the last thing that either of them wanted
was to open the doors of Rhythms in the red.

She took the accordion folder where she kept the bills and
the ledger, and went to work in the living room. Although
Nick's small home office had all of the comforts, it was in one
of the windowless in-between rooms that were common in
these prewar buildings. So there was no natural light. She'd
worked in there for a few hours once before and thought she'd
go out of her mind. She put the folder down on the coffee
table and went to the window to pull back the curtain and open
the blinds. She was about to turn away when a figure across
the street caught her attention. She moved closer to the
window, peering down the three stories. The blood, like
drums, began to beat in her ears, throb through her veins until
her body vibrated. So intent was her stare that the image began
to blur. She blinked rapidly, her heart pounding as she pressed
closer to the glass, her breath against the cold causing patches
of fog to obscure her vision even further. And then she looked
up. Their gazes connected. Parris stumbled backward.

It was her. This time it was not her imagination. It was
Emma standing across the street looking up at her window,
looking up at her. Parris took a tentative step forward, reached
out and slowly pushed the curtain aside, a part of her believing that the woman would be gone as all the others had been,
all the other times, on all the other streets.

But she wasn't.

Oh, God, oh, God, what was she supposed to do? She
glanced again and there Emma stood, seemingly as undecided

as Parris. Then the thought that Emma may decide to simply leave without trying to contact her leaped into her head. She was afraid to take her eyes off of her, sure that if she did, Emma would vanish—this time for good. But neither could she stand eternally at the window.

She spun away, grabbed the keys from the hall table and ran all three flights downstairs. She pulled open the front door and gasped out loud to see Emma standing on the top step, close enough for her to see the light brown flecks in her green eyes.

It felt like an eternity had passed between them, countless images, questions, hurts and fears zigzagged back and forth like lightning during a storm. So quick you couldn't catch it but you witnessed its power, the beauty it could be or the destruction it could render.

Parris gripped the door frame. Her stomach tumbled.

"Hello, Parris."

Finally Parris found her voice. "So…who are you today, the loyal waitress at the bistro or the startled lady of the house?"

"Neither," she said softly, struggling to maintain eye contact with a gaze that held such contempt. "I'm here as your mother, although I know I hardly have the right to call myself that."

"You don't!"

Emma's lips tightened. She nodded in agreement. "I was hoping…that you would give me the opportunity to talk with you…about things." She swallowed, her voice straining. "Us. Your grandmother. Your father. All the things you deserve to know." She waited. Parris didn't move. Didn't speak. "Please," Emma finally said.

Parris stared at this woman who so much resembled her grandmother, and for a moment she nearly forgot the real reason why she was there. *It's up to you if you let her.* Her grandfather David's words echoed in her head. *But it would feel so good to turn her away, Granddad, tell her to go to hell with her explanations so that she would know how bottomless dismissal could feel.*

She stepped aside, holding the door open for Emma to come in and follow her up the stairs. Parris's hands shook as she tried to fit the key into the apartment lock. It took several tries before she was able to get the door opened.

"Come in," she said in a voice so taut she didn't recognize it as her own. She walked ahead into the living room, concentrating on breathing and walking at the same time. "Have a seat."

Emma took off her wool coat, sat down and draped it across her lap. She glanced around. "He's a musician…I understand," she said, lifting her chin toward Nick's sax.

"You said you came here to talk to me. I'm sure it's not about Nick being a musician," she said, each word meant to sting.

Emma's cheeks colored and Parris realized how easy it must have been for her. Looking at Emma no one would ever guess that she had a black mother. She'd sat right across from her in the bistro and she didn't know. She'd only thought that Emma was a beautiful white woman, with lustrous black hair that tumbled in waves to her narrow shoulders, luminous green eyes and skin as pale as porcelain.

Parris took the hard-backed chair next to Nick's sax stand and sat down.

Emma fidgeted with the label on the inside of her coat.

Parris folded and unfolded her hands.

The rubber-band silence stretched as far as it could go until it finally snapped.

Parris jumped. "Something to drink?"

Emma bobbed her head, tried to smile. "Yes. Thank you."

Parris, grateful to find a reason for escape, hurried off to the kitchen. Once there she leaned over the sink, drew in deep lungfuls of air. She turned on the faucet and tapped her face with cold water to cool her burning skin. *This is what you wanted. This is the moment that you've lived for from the instant your grandmother told you she was alive. The truth can be no worse than the images in your mind.* She pulled a paper towel from the roll above the sink and dried her face. Put one foot in front of the other and went to the refrigerator, poured a glass of iced tea and returned to the front room. Emma was still there.

Parris handed her the glass and took her seat.

"Thank you." She took a sip and set the glass down on the table. "Your grandmother was one of the most highly respected young women in Rudell," she began, her voice soft, almost lulling in its cadence. "Your great-grandfather, Joshua Harvey, was not only the spiritual leader, but also the community leader as well. When he and your great-grandmother Pearl were murdered in that fire, the town took your grandmother under its wing. David loved her, but it wasn't enough to keep her from pursuing her dream to sing. She left Rudell and moved to Chicago. She found a job working for a wealthy white family, William and Lizbeth Rutherford. She never made it as a singer, and shortly after the Great Depression hit she returned to Rudell and married David. I was born seven months later."

Parris's heart leaped in her chest.

"The day I was born, David took one look at me and knew I could never be his. He walked out, leaving your grandmother to raise me alone. Everyone believed that she'd tricked the beloved doctor, that she'd gone off and slept with some white man in Chicago and the town that once revered her turned their backs on her and on me. I was trapped between two worlds, neither of which I could belong to, not back then, not in a small-minded town like Rudell.

"I grew up alone, teased, laughed at, talked about and ignored. And each day I resented the woman who'd saddled me with this curse of white skin and green eyes in a black-and-brown world. One day all that changed. That night by the Left Hand River," she said in a faraway voice. She told Parris of the man who thought she was a white woman and the realization that came to her. How from that day on she began sneaking into the white part of town, sitting in their shops, walking their streets, and she knew she'd finally found freedom. She told Parris about finding the letter from Cora's friend Margaret and the mention of William Rutherford, the picture in the newspaper article and how she began to put the pieces together. And one day she left Rudell, got on the bus and headed to New York.

Emma reached for her glass of tea and took a long cool swallow. She gently set the glass down.

"That's where I met your father." She looked Parris in the eye. "His name is Michael Travanti. He was a soldier." She drew in a shallow breath. "He was the first person in my entire life who showed that they cared about me, told me that they loved me, did everything they could to make me happy, make me smile," she said, her voice lifting for the first time with a hint of joy. "I came alive and the feeling was so exquisite, so new and perfect, I knew that I would do whatever I could to hold on to it." She paused, looked away then down at her hands. "Then one day, there was an article in the paper about William Rutherford. He was having a big fund-raiser. And that need to know, to confront my worst nightmare, bloomed inside of me. I got in to see him...and the moment I told him who I was, he knew, and I could see the guilt in his eyes."

She told Parris about her demand for money, and how she dropped it at her feet on her way out of the door.

"I never saw him again after that. He would never openly claim me as his daughter, no matter what I looked like on the outside. He'd raped my mother—a black woman, his house-keeper—when she was barely out of her teens. He could never have anyone know that. And that part of my life I'd closed the door on. It no longer mattered.

"Michael and I married shortly after that and in less than a year I was pregnant...with you. I was terrified. But I convinced myself that I looked white, I'd married a white man and, of course, I would have a child that could pass. But you couldn't."

She told Parris about the night of her birth, the joy and the fear, the knowing that if Michael ever found out he would leave her the same way that David left Cora, and the love that she'd spent her entire life looking and hoping for would be snatched away from her. Gone forever. She couldn't do that. She couldn't go back to living in loneliness.

"So I took you back to Mississippi. I made Mama swear that she would tell you I was dead. That she'd take care of you, because she owed me that much, she owed me some semblance of happiness," she sobbed, as tears filled her eyes and shook her voice. "She owed me."

Thinking back to the dark time in her life she could almost hear her mother's door as she shut it behind her, leaving her two-day-old baby in her mother's care. With each step that she took she wanted to run back and ask her mother to love her, teach her how to love her child. She wanted to feel her baby's soft skin one more time, inhale the newness of her. But she couldn't do that. All she could do was hold on to the memory of what might have been.

Emma wiped her eyes with a handkerchief from her purse. "When you showed up in France...I didn't know what to do." She shook her head sadly. "I'd finally told your father about you when your grandmother's letter came. I couldn't believe he'd forgiven me. But when you actually showed up...I'd lived the lie for so long...I..." She glanced up at Parris to see tears streaming down her face. "I am so sorry. So sorry." She covered her face with her hands and wept, her body shaking, for all the years, all the lies, all the loss, the pain that was caused, the lives that were ruined, all because of one man, one night, decades ago. A night that stripped a young woman of her innocence and set out a course of events that marred generations.

As the story and the images swirled through Parris's mind, she realized the incredible stock of strong women she'd descended from. Each of them during their time were burdened with circumstances that could have broken many others, but they found a way to surmount them. And as much as she may forget that her mother left her, she understood why. She was a young girl who'd finally found acceptance and love and it took a certain kind of strength to let go of your child and place them in the hands of another to raise, hoping that they would give your child the love and the nurturing that they deserved.

When Parris looked up, wiping her face, Emma was putting on her coat. A wave of panic raced through her.

Emma drew herself up and hooked her purse over her wrist. "Thank you for listening," she said, her voice sounding rough and raw from hours of talking. She sniffed, offered a slight smile and turned toward the door. Then she swung back toward Parris, who couldn't seem to move.

"I need to know just one thing," Emma said over the tightness in her throat. "Was she good to you?"

Parris nodded, unable to get the words out, her heart breaking open. "She loved me with all her heart."

Emma's eyes filled. Her lips thinned as she fought back the tears. "G-good. That's good." She turned back toward the door. A hand on her arm stopped her. She looked over her shoulder.

"If...you're not in a hurry, I'd like you to meet someone."

Emma closed her eyes and relief replaced the weight of the years that had burdened her spirit. She looked at her daughter with hope and humility. "I'd like that very much."

# Chapter Twenty-One

"I guess we can nix the annual Mother's Day mourning party this year," Celeste quipped as she unpacked a box of long-stemmed wineglasses.

After her fallout with her mother, rather than wait for the inevitable ugliness, she used her connections at the real estate office and found a one-bedroom condo that she could actually afford.

Leslie sputtered a burst of laughter. "Girl, you are too silly." She picked up a box out of the long corridor. "Where do you want this?"

"I think that can go in the living room."

"This is really a nice space," Parris said, putting the dinner plates in the cabinet. "I suppose you do have some skills after all," she teased. She walked over to where Celeste stood and gently touched her shoulder. "You really okay with this?" she asked softly. She knew it had to be a physical shock to Celeste's system to move from the elite Upper East Side and a penthouse apartment to midtown Manhattan in a one-bedroom condo. It was probably more of a shock to Corrine Shaw, who was nearly apoplectic when Celeste made her unceremonious announcement, according to Celeste's version, which was worthy of a stand-up comedian performance.

Celeste turned, shrugged her shoulder. "It's definitely not what I've been used to, but it's mine. Ya know?"

Parris grinned. "Yeah, I do. So how long will it be before you invite Sam over?"

"As soon as I can get my slow-moving help out of here."

Parris shook her head and continued unpacking. "Moving as fast as I can," she said over her laughter.

Worn-out and hungry, Celeste ordered Chinese from the local restaurant and the trio sat around on the floor eating off paper plates. It was the first time they'd all been together at once in weeks. Although they each knew bits and pieces of the dramas unfolding in their lives they'd yet to share the full stories.

"I'm not too sure I'm going to like hanging around with a broke Celeste," Leslie said over a mouthful of lo mein. "What's the perk in that?"

Parris dribbled her tea down the front of her shirt.

"Very funny, Les. But for your information, I'll never be broke. No matter how long my folks stand on their heads about my lifestyle—as they put it—in two years, when I turn thirty-five, my grandfather's trust fund kicks in. And I can do what the hell I want." She raised her glass and smiled triumphantly.

"Damn, some kids have all the luck," Leslie joked.

"Wow, a trust fund. I never actually knew someone who had one of those," Parris said. She angled her body to face Celeste.

"So what did your grandfather do to be able to leave you a trust?" She spooned shrimp-fried rice into her mouth.

Celeste frowned for a moment in thought. "From what I've been told, he was involved in finances from before the depression. But he was completely wiped out when it hit." She twirled her chopsticks around in the air as she pieced the family history together. "I don't know exactly how he did it, but he worked, saved, started moving around in the right circles, built his company and even ran for office. He was a state senator for New York for a term or two, I can't remember. All I know for sure is that Grandpa Rutherford is filthy, stinking rich and he loves me dearly." She chuckled.

"Wh-what did you say?" Parris stammered, heat burning her chest.

"I said he loves me dearly—"

"No!" she snapped. "Your grandfather, what's his name?"

Celeste frowned, arching her neck, "What is wrong with you? William Rutherford, why?"

Parris stumbled to her feet. Her food rose from her stomach, stinging the back of her throat.

Leslie reached for her. "Parris, you okay?"

Parris tugged in deep breaths to try and settle her raging stomach. She looked at Celeste, really looked at her, beyond the blond hair and white skin to the green eyes they shared, the tiny cleft in their chins and the emotional connection they had from the time they met.

Celeste stood up. "Parris, you're scaring me, what is it?"

"I think…" She blinked rapidly as her mother's voice rang in her head: her meeting with William Rutherford, his apologizing to her for what he'd done to Cora. She focused on Celeste. "Please…tell me what your grandmother's name is?"

Celeste hesitated for a minute, afraid of where this was going. "Lizbeth."

Parris's hand flew to her mouth as she inhaled a sharp breath. She sunk down to her knees on the floor, braced her hands on her thighs.

Leslie's head snapped back and forth between them. "What is going on? Somebody tell me something."

Parris folded her hands tightly in front of her, then reached out to Celeste and took her hands.

"Just before the Great Depression, my grandmother Cora Harvey moved to Chicago, she went to work for a couple, William Rutherford and his wife Lizbeth…"

*Hempstead, Long Island*

"Oh, my goodness, Ms. Celeste. What a surprise. Come in out of the cold."

"Mary, this is…my…this is Parris McKay." She squeezed Parris's hand, in tacit agreement. "Mary's been taking care of my grandfather for as long as I can remember." She put her arm around Mary's shoulder as they walked into the expansive foyer of the two-story mansion.

"And Ms. Lizbeth, too, before she passed, God rest her soul." They walked through several rooms, one of which was a dining hall that could easily hold more than two hundred people.

"This is where we used to have the annual family Christmas party," Celeste was saying to Parris. "It's been a couple of years now."

"Your grandfather is out in the greenhouse. You know how he loves his plants. Go on back there, if you can stand the heat and steam." She waved her hand in dismissal. "I'm going to prepare some lunch. I hope you're both staying." She didn't wait for an answer and hurried back off in the opposite direction.

Parris had remained virtually silent during the entire ride from the city out to Long Island. Celeste tried to make small talk but both of them understood that what lay ahead would confirm what they'd both come to conclude; they were first cousins, their mothers half sisters, and they shared the same grandfather, William Rutherford.

"You ready?" Celeste asked as they approached the greenhouse.

Parris nodded. "As I'll ever be."

Celeste pulled the door open and they were greeted by a gust of warm, moist air and the pungent scent of flowers.

A whirring sound drew their attention toward the end of an aisle of lilies. An old man, with thick white hair and deep wrinkles, buzzed toward them in his electric wheelchair. As he grew closer, a small smile bloomed when he recognized his granddaughter. He began to chuckle even before he came to a full stop in front of them.

"Well, now, what brings you all the way out here? Your mother misbehaving..." He caught a glimpse of Parris and his skin went nearly as white as his hair. His face contorted.

"Grandpa, are you okay?" Celeste bent down to his chair but he didn't take his eyes off of Parris.

"Cora," he whispered in the voice of one who has been witness to an apparition. He stared at her, that dark night of his past came hurtling at him like a speeding train, unstoppable... It all started with the call from his broker, Stuart...

*"Stuart, what do you mean I should have seen this coming? Hell, nobody saw it coming...it has nothing to do with what Hoover did*

*with the farmer and farm relief legislation… Wheat and cotton prices have been erratic for months. You told me to invest in those stocks, they would level out and the market would become stable… No… No… Damn it, man, I mortgaged my home, borrowed from brokers, from banks, sold my liberty bonds. I have nothing left, nothing!"*

He slammed down the phone and began to pace. Then he began to drink, and drink until he felt the powers of the liquor dull his senses, but not his frustration and pain. And then there she was—young sweet innocent Cora who kept his house, fixed the meals and was so grateful for the books he brought home to her. She'd asked him what was wrong, if there was anything she could do to help him, and something inside of him snapped and he slapped her hard across the face, so hard he knocked her to the floor. Her screams, her begging him to stop, her small fists pounding against his chest did nothing to halt his blind rage, his need to regain some semblance of power and control. And when it was over, he never saw her again…until more than two decades later when her spitting image, the result of the one night, walked up to him and announced that she was his daughter—Emma.

As she railed at him for ruining her life, demanding that he look at her, look at what he had done, he felt himself crumble before her tear-filled eyes. His throat worked up and down, the words trapped there for almost two decades, never uttered, had congealed into a knot of remorse that was more devastating than anything he'd ever endured. But to admit that was something he was incapable of doing, standing before this woman who longed to find some part of herself that would somehow validate who she was. To confess to what he had done would make the nightmare of the day a reality, a reality he still couldn't acknowledge. There was no forgiveness or absolution for a depraved deed. And he accepted that. As long as he kept it tucked inside he could somehow face the day and go out into the world with his mask intact. The worst thing, he understood, was to confess to oneself that there was *a corruption, an illness of the soul that enabled you to become every-thing you detested in others.*

*Yet, there she stood. The product of a warped, heinous episode in his life. A young woman who needed more than he could ever hope to give. A young woman he would be proud to call daughter. But he couldn't. They both knew that. So all he could hope to give her was the money that she demanded, to make a small down payment on his redemption, and perhaps things would somehow be right.*

*But as he'd watched his daughter walk away from him, her back straight and her head held high, he knew he must leave her with some measure of comfort, something the money would never be able to do, something from deep in his soul. "I never meant…to hurt your mother. Never."*

The words, no longer a memory, tumbled from his mouth again and again. His thin shoulders shook as Celeste wrapped her arms around him and Parris heard her mother's voice de-livering the message she'd brought Cora from William Ruther-ford, the day Emma brought her newborn baby back to Rudell. *"I never meant…to hurt your mother. Never."*

Behind the closed doors of his study, William asked his granddaughters to sit down. He wheeled over to his safe built behind the lower shelf of the walnut bookcase. After several tries the safe door opened. He dug around inside and pulled out a thick manila envelope, shut the safe and wheeled back over to where they sat.

He looked into Parris's eyes and was grateful that he did not see the contempt that could have easily resided there. "I never thought I'd live long enough to see this day and try to make things right for what happened to your grandmother." He glanced at Celeste. "I know your mother will try to contest it, but it's airtight. It was written right after Emma came to see me and I've had it recertified every year since then." He handed the envelope to Parris. "Please see that she gets this. My lawyers have copies as well so there will be no foolishness." He shook his wizened head then wagged a finger at Parris. "I didn't know Emma had a child, but I know she will do right by you." He tapped the envelope. "It leaves this house, all paid for, to your mother. And she will share in all of my financial assets with her half-sister, Corrine. Corrine won't like it but she'll have to suck it up." He snorted. "Corrine's known about Emma for years," he softly confessed. "Was standing right outside that door listening to me and your grandmother arguing about keeping Emma in my will."

"Grandma knew, too?"

William nodded. "The day that Emma came to our home to get the money that she'd demanded, Lizbeth ran in to her when she was leaving. And she'd been there the night Emma came to the Plaza and announced that she was my daughter." He looked off into the distance. "There'd been whispers for years that I'd had another child, but Lizbeth and I agreed that…it would be too damaging to the family if the truth ever came out. So we put it behind us, moved on." He turned to Parris. "I'm sure you and your mother hold me responsible for a great deal of things. And you would be right. I know this will cannot make up for what happened all those years ago, but maybe it will help." The corner of his mouth flickered. "I wish I would have known her…your mother…and you. My life has been less full because of that."

"Damn, this is waay better than reality television," Leslie was saying as she, Celeste and Parris did a final walk-through of Rhythms, which was scheduled for its grand opening the following night. "Cousins. Humph. I would have paid money to see the look on Corrine's face."

Parris and Celeste snickered. "It wasn't pretty," Celeste said, "but once she realized the will was unbreakable, and my father of all people talked some twentieth century sense into her, we could put the smelling salts away. I'm sure, knowing my mother, she'll find a way to put some kind of exotic spin on it all."

"How's your mother taking it all?" Leslie asked Parris.

"Pretty well, I guess. She's dealing with a broken marriage, a found daughter, a half-sister." She shook her head. "She's gone out to see her father a couple of times. I think it's helped her."

"But what about you, cuz?" Celeste slipped her arm around Parris's waist and dropped her blond head on her shoulder.

Parris drew in a breath. "Taking it one day at a time. It's been a lot of years, a lot of hurt and a lot of bridges crossed. But, it's getting better. I look forward to talking to my mother, hearing about her life, telling her about mine. I know we'll never have that warm and fuzzy relationship, it's too late for that, but we'll have something."

"Speaking of fathers," Leslie said, "have you decided what you're going to do about yours?"

"I tried the number that my mother gave me," Parris said. "It's been disconnected. I sent a letter to the house and it was returned as undeliverable." She lowered her head. "So I don't know…" Her voice trailed off.

"Hey," Leslie said, and hooked her arm through Parris's, while Celeste did the same on the other side, "we're going to be all right." She looked from one to the other. "We've been through it, in ways some folks can only imagine, but we made it. And I know I'm going to be just fine, 'cause I got two rich cousins as my best friends! And as soon as I find a man, too, I know I'll be straight."

They hugged and whooped with laughter.

## Epilogue

They'd all spent the day at the club rehearsing and preparing for the opening. The bar was stocked and the waitstaff was being prepped on the menu. Leslie had been darting in and out all afternoon, checking on all the last-minute details and Celeste had finally gotten Emma a small one-bedroom apartment several blocks away from Parris, and had just dashed in after handing off the keys to Emma. She quickly spotted Sam and they eased away to one of the side rooms.

Parris took it all in with a smile as she watched from the stage, having just finished the last song in the set. She draped a towel around her neck just as Nick came up beside her and kissed her cheek.

"Fantastic as always, baby," he said up against her ear. A shiver of delight ran through her.

Since coming to terms with her mother and their unique

and tumultuous beginnings, she'd slowly begun to accept who she was, or rather *know* who she was. And in doing so, she'd allowed herself to be better at loving herself and loving Nick. She looked forward to waking with him in the mornings and going to bed with him at night. She'd gotten used to being lulled awake by the pull of his morning playing, and simply thinking about it made her smile. The fact that they worked together making music seemed to intensify their passion for each other. When he played, he played for her, and she sang for him and together they made an exquisite sound.

They stepped down off the stage just as a middle-aged man came through the door. He looked around in the dimness. Nick walked over.

"Can I help you?"

The man took his hat from his head. "Yes, I'm looking for Parris McKay," he said with a decided French accent.

Nick looked him over. "May I ask what this is about?"

Parris came up behind him.

"My name is Marcel Dominique. And I have a package that I promised to deliver to Mademoiselle McKay."

"I'm Ms. McKay." She looked at Nick then back at the man.

He went inside his jacket and took out a thin legal-sized envelope, and handed it to her. He put his hat back on his head. "Good day." He turned and walked out.

The envelope wasn't postmarked, nor was it formally addressed. It simply had PARRIS in block letters on the front.

"What in the world…" She walked over to one of the tables and sat down. Nick took a seat. "You think he was a process server or something?" she asked.

"Got me. Have you done anything to warrant being served?" he said, trying to lighten the suddenly tense moment.

She turned the envelope over and unsealed it, pulling out a single sheet of handwritten paper. She read the words aloud.

*Dear Parris,*

*I pray that the skills of Mr. Dominique are as good as his advertisement and he finds you safe and well in New York City. It has been many years since I have been in New York, the city where I met your mother. I will always have fond memories of it.*

*I can never hope to make up for the years that we have lost, that my wife Emma deprived us of. I believed I could never forgive her for what she had done. I could not understand how someone could be so cowardly, so selfish, so evil. It took all these weeks and months, months without her, time apart to realize that I will always love your mother. God help me. I will never agree and never forget what she did to all of us, but I understand. And I believe over time I will find a way to forgive her.*

*The need for love and acceptance is a powerful thing. It, like water, like air, nurtures us. We live and feed off of it and when it is denied, we wither and die—at least inside.*

*I hope to get to see you one day, more than a fleeting glimpse. But if not, I want you to be assured that you will always be taken care of.*

*I am enclosing the number of my attorney and his address. He has all of my papers, which will be delivered to you upon Mr. Dominique's confirmation that he has found you. The papers contain the deed to the villa—yes, the one you came to, the lease to my vineyards to which you will gain full control or sell if you wish, and a share in the bistro.*

*I know that things can never make up for what we all have missed, but these are the things, part of the life that your mother and I built together during a loving three and a half decades. And no one is more deserving of the love we built together than you.*

*I don't know if your mother will seek you out, but if she does tell her that my love for her will never end.*

*I am also enclosing my number and I pray that one day you will find it in your heart to forgive me.*

*Until we meet. Your loving father, Michael.*

The words blurred and danced in front of her eyes. Her body shook with the force of tears. Tears of sorrow, and lost joy, but most of all hope.

Nick wiped her cheeks with the pad of his thumb. She kissed the inside of his palm and pressed it to her face.

"My dad," she warbled in disbelief, over tears and laughter. "My dad." She sniffed and wiped her eyes. "We have so much to celebrate tonight, Nick—the club, us, my mother and now my father."

"I know, baby, I know." He leaned in and kissed her tenderly.

She wished her grandmother could be with her at that moment, to witness that after so many years, after so much hurt and betrayal, the healing had finally begun. She blew out a shaky breath, and stared at the letter again before refolding it and returning it to the envelope. She pushed up from the seat, wiped her face one last time. "I'll be right back."

"Sure." He watched her walk away, amazed at the cycle of life, how paths cross and lives intersect. He was just happy that his path had crossed with Parris's, and hoped that for as long as they had breath they would continue to walk that path together.

Her hands shook and her heart pounded so loudly she barely heard the ringing in her ear.

"Hello?"

For an instant she stopped breathing.

"Hello?"

"May...I speak with...Michael Travanti?"

"This is he? Who is this, please?"

"It's Parris. Your daughter."

★ ★ ★ ★ ★